Walking on Cinders

By

Ben Atkinson

King Edward VII Press

11

First published in 2010 in Great Britain
by King Edward VII Press

Cover illustration by Alex Tudno-Jones

King Edward VII Press
c/o Tall Lime, Sparkhouse Studios
Ropewalk, Lincoln
LN6 7DQ

www.kingedwardviipress.co.uk

Acknowledgements

This book would not have been possible without the help and guidance of friends: Thomas and Chris, my own comrades in arms, Adam Tate for his military knowledge, Heather and Adam W. Alex Tudno-Jones, a designer who I am sure will go onto to achieve great things - thank you Alex! Sue Browning for taking a chance on an unknown author and doing a great critical job. Susie Jinks, Laura Thomson, Paul Hughes, Glen and Jacqui Tillyard and Mark Ellerby for reading early drafts and providing corrections and suggestions for improvement. To Mitch De Faria for always being there for me, and to my family who have provided endless support and encouragement. I'd also like to thank the many other people who in some way contributed to this project. Thank you all!

Follow Ben Atkinson online and keep up to date with everything that's happening:
www.benatkinson.org.uk
www.twitter.com/benatkinson1991

PROLOGUE

London was different. London had changed. The tall skyscrapers and office blocks had disappeared and just beyond the horizon, down towards the docklands, you could see the remnants of the Gherkin, smashed. For the first time in the city's long history, the skyline was clear and the air was clean. If you stood and looked upwards you might see St Paul's Cathedral, Big Ben or the Houses of Parliament dominating the skyline. Behind them was Buckingham Palace, the last remaining stronghold of the British monarchy and a constant target for rebellion.

The city had lost its grandeur and it seemed quieter nowadays. The endless traffic jams had ceased, because there was little fuel left to power such vehicles. Even the Petrol Rule, created by the government some four years previous as way of conserving the depleting stocks of petrol, oil and diesel had to be abolished. Now very few trundled along the once-busy streets. Instead, the roads were filled with cyclists and in some cases, for those who could afford and still believed in them, the new air- powered hover car. There were people walking too, filling the pavements and spilling out into disused taxi lanes.

It was impossible to tell who these people were or what they were doing, but most of them were women, for the majority of men had enlisted into World Service following the outbreak of war. Those few men that remained held powerful roles in government, or in West-End musicals in the few remaining theatres. The war had not treated London kindly. It was three years since it had begun and the future looked rocky.

***

A decade earlier, the cracks had started to show all over the world. The long years of prosperity which had been taken for granted and enjoyed without thought were coming to an end. Nothing lasts forever, and most things had been too good for too long. People had gotten used to living without fear, repression or merciless violence. There were few extremists in this new world, and of those that remained almost all were isolated in the mountains of the Middle East. At this time, wars were localised and had little to no effect on the day-to-day movements of the world.

Advances in technology too had reached their peak, with the computer interface now all powerful in both design and performance. At one time these machines had required human intervention, to push buttons and insert data, but now they were powerful enough to do this alone. This power was minutely controlled through a super- alliance of the largest manufacturers of software and operating systems, all of whom were committed to keeping tabs on the intellectual power of the computer.

The years of prosperity, productivity and new thinking had placed the world on a better footing. This in turn had given scientists, engineers and the leading designers in modern technology a little too much confidence. They were veering close to the edge, bound to make that big mistake. They were not the first, and they would not be the last. But their actions, and the consequences, would affect the entire population of the world. Given time, and through a large global partnership, they realised one of man's more inspiring dreams.

The development of a machine that could travel suspended above the earth had long been dismissed as impossible, and yet peace, a stable economy and a peak in global food production, now meant that the resources were suddenly at hand. The scientists proposed a vehicle which could be suspended a little above the ground through the use of repellent magnets and a new source of electronic power. By specifically positioning the magnets in response to a series of small-scale lab tests with a remote controlled model, those behind the project believed that they could scale up the designs to create suspended motion. This hover car, as it soon became known, would then be crafted from a lightweight carbon fibre material and would use an engine which relied solely on the power of air and water.

Governments and leaders across the world were immediately inspired by the project and could not resist such revolutionary technology. All were in agreement; the design would go down in history as man again conquered the forces of nature. Upon completion of the first hover cars, nations across the developed world placed their orders. They then invested in a great scheme of propaganda and provided monetary incentives, which were aimed at every individual and family. The leaders wanted to replace everything which had gone before. Everyone must own one. Soon they did.

But the world leaders were naive. They had invested in a design which had yet to be proven, and in the first years of hover power, there were a number of problems.

The introduction of new expertise meant that other areas of the design were overlooked. The engineers had chosen older, well-proven machinery, such as manual gear-boxes and a steering wheel more suited to a traditional road-travelling vehicle. These shortcuts had been costly to the finished vehicle, with many hover cars unable to make the tight turns required to manoeuvre around corners. It was this, above all else, that led to many of the accidents reported in those early years.

Suddenly, all over the world, those in charge were paying out for repairs and endowments against anyone who had bought a hover car. In some severe cases the leaders and governments were taken to court over their inability to forward-plan for the rickety nature and short lifespan of the new transport they had purchased. This meant that there was no further capital to offset against the continuing production costs for the many miles of new magnetic road. All over the world, governments were working off borrowed money. It was then that they realised they had made a grave mistake. The years of prosperity were over.

The repercussions of this economic crash spread quickly throughout the modern world. The hover cars were often dangerous, scraping against the ground as the magnetic suspension lapsed, but they were now the only kind of vehicle at most normal people's disposal. It meant they had no choice but to continue making use of their backward design. In the economic slump wages were soon being cut and workers laid off. Governments began hoarding food within their own borders and refused to meet once simple trade quotas. Each country was becoming suspicious of its neighbours and where once there had been friendly, peaceful alliances; there were now hostile negotiations over even the simplest matters.

* * *

Five years prior to war breaking out, democracy across the world descended into chaos, with no one country being able to keep control within its own borders.

At this time a decision was made by the UN to unite the nations together under one rule. This, they said, would return the world to a position of peace and economic prosperity. There had been problems right from the start. On the sixth of May, designated world peace day, the UN had called delegates from all the different countries to Brussels for a meeting, and ultimately a decision regarding the proposition. For seven days the leaders argued amongst themselves, with some taking sides and others trying to play the peacemaker. Many just couldn't understand how such a proposition could engineer peace. They considered the idea ludicrous and branded it impossible and inconsistent, for somewhere at the back of their minds they were scared that such a union might bring about a return of the Iron Curtain, only this time right across the world. The UN had learnt little from history and was slowly losing control. But, as is often the case, towards the end of the conference a new hope appeared on the horizon and the leaders began to see the light.

For the most part, it seemed that each country supported one of two newly emerged parties. They were the Reformed Party and the United Party. These two worldwide organisations had opposing ideals and would provide support for those who swore allegiance to them. If a country decided to adopt either the United or Reformed ideology, they would keep their own form of government in place, with the worldwide organisations then watching over them from above, in absolute control.

The United Party was first established in the western world. Here, alliances were built between members of the European Union, who agreed to support each other in matters of finance and foreign affairs, while decisions were taken in the United States of America and in New Zealand and Australia to join the European powers with whom they had always had strong bonds in the past. Collectively the leaders agreed that peace was well overdue. The United Party supported this view, striving to create a unity that would see the return and establishment of complete peace across the world. But the Party meant much more than this.

Taking into account developments in technology, wealth and the GDP of the modern world, even before the economic crash, they based their ideology on the proven and successful political and social system of capitalism. And why not? For many of the countries targeted to fall under United rule, this system of privately owned labour, goods and resources traded in markets had worked without pitfall for hundreds of years.

They had their enemies too, and for the most part the United Party set themselves against all those who had failed them in the past. This meant that the historical movements of Fascism, Marxism and Communism were considered wrong and through a strong use of propaganda were soon scapegoated.

For the Reformed Party, links and fundamental views were built upon a desire to improve what had gone before. Latin America and those who simply could not face working with the western capitalist powers, including China, Japan, Russia, large parts of Asia and the Middle East, became strongly supportive of the Reformed regime. The leaders knew they could not fail as others had, and in order to prevent this, set about creating a society which took the best points from history. They studied Russia, China and even European powers, in order to create the perfect form of leadership which saw that everyone remained equal. This political organisation set themselves against the horrific terrors of history, which was linked so closely to their desired form of governance. But, however hard they tried they were still unable to shake off this terrible association.

At first the new alliances worked well, drawing funds together which brought the many nations of the world out of an economic darkness. Slowly began the road to recovery, with a return to arable food production and a strange new awareness that things might never be so good again. Most people failed to notice that the sceptics who predicted an Iron Curtain were not wrong. The lines between United and Reformed were no longer blurred, and following the UN ruling, leaders began to strengthen their borders. Hostilities between Europe and the East intensified, especially over the lands that separated Russia from the rest of the continent, and the seas and oceans of the world became ever more dangerous places as the two sides fought over commercial fishing.

For several years the two sides lived relatively independently as superpowers that produced their own goods and became economically stable. But as can be seen in democracy and dictatorship throughout history, there is eventually a need to seek alliances with those around you, either for trade or merely to curb rebellion. Either such alliances are made, or one aims to overthrow the other. The Reformed nations of the world agreed more with the latter, being dissatisfied with the level of raw materials held by United countries before the amalgamation.

The United Isles of Great Britain, were among the first to notice their opponents rearmament. They weren't slow to react and although trade was not immediately suspended, it continued alongside a rapidly progressing arms race and several dissident terrorist attacks on European borders. These hostilities were further fuelled by television debates and news programmes that followed events as they unfolded across the world.

***

To the average person living out their day-to-day life in London in the months that led up to the declaration of war, United governance became just another problematic solution which had not lasted in the long run.

The people of the United Isles of Great Britain had grown used to change. They had lived through the troubled years, when the monarchy had fallen and had been forced to reluctantly hand power over to a newly elected president. They had then dealt patriotically with a change in name and the realisation that a country which was once so independent was now swearing allegiance and taking orders from the whole of Europe and America. The United leaders met twice per year in Brussels and they discussed, always discussed. Things had never been like this before, and many people believed the Reformed countries to be winning the arms race that had enveloped a whole planet. But nobody thought it would happen so quickly, and with such force.

* * *

It was four years since the war had begun, and the fighting was getting more and more intense. The earlier advances in technology were soon undermined and used for evil rather than good, while defences were stronger than ever. It looked as though the war would never end. It was in everyone's living rooms every evening and affected everyone's lives. Nobody could escape it.

1

The morning started, as it always did, with the ringing of an alarm bell that signalled the rising of the dawn chorus and the busy, but troubled commute to work.

Lazily knocking her hand against the top of the alarm clock, a slender young woman rolled over under the covers and wearily opened her eyes. She savoured the sweet few seconds before she realised it was morning and then thought about what was to come. Lying with her head to one side and resting on the pillow, she looked quite beautiful. Her long blonde hair fell effortlessly across the side of her face and her rouged lips still held the make-up from the evening before. To the left of her, lying precariously on the edge of the bedside table, was a name badge that had been thrown down hastily at some late hour of the night. Upon it was the young woman's name and job description.

'Jenny – Waitress'. In many ways, Jenny had conceded to working late each and every night because it provided the perfect cover for her other reckless escapade, the job being run of the mill enough for no one ever to suspect her true calling. But there was one thing against which she had continuously protested and that was shortening her name. She'd never had a problem with Jennifer before, and she craved the respect and knowledge that went along with a name that was so elegant. However, sometimes circumstance led to only one conclusion, the job itself was the most important, even when it came with certain difficulties. Difficulties such as the owner of the café, one Derek Richards, who thought such a catchy new name would seem more attractive to the customers, so the new name, Jenny, had stuck.

Life was good for Jennifer; she had a nice flat, a good circle of friends and an interesting social life, a very interesting social life. For several years now, since the war had started, her various secret indulgences had led to her becoming the new Forces' Sweetheart and she was enjoying every moment of it.

Of course, nobody knew it was really Jennifer behind the glamorous hairstyle and the layers of make-up. Her stage name and the normality of a regular waitressing job made sure of that. If she were to walk down any street in London nobody would recognise her in her normal guise. Sure, she had the same face, but nobody knew her name and so nobody thought for one second that this humble waitress could be the adored Miss Marmalade.

Perhaps it was the secrecy of what she was doing, sneaking out late at night to the city's East End and performing in the underground clubs and pubs for foreign soldiers, or even the secret fame and good fortune that thrilled her so much. Whatever it was, Jennifer was certainly living it up.

But there was the other side of the coin to consider as well. There was nobody to love Jennifer for who she was, and to most her former life ceased to exist completely. More and more often nowadays she found herself troubled by the prospect of being unable to form any lasting relationship for fear of revealing her dual identity. Jennifer lived in a double world and living for herself, fending for herself, was fine in the most part, but when she wanted companionship it was always so hard to find. Of course, Miss Marmalade had many handsome admirers who would run to her side at the click of her fingers, but for Jennifer things were not quite so simple.

It was this that troubled her each and every day. Waking in the morning to the same noise of the alarm, tapping it with the same slight movement of her hand just to stop the ringing in her ears, and then turning over to face the same window just to wonder what the point was in getting up and preparing for work that day. This had become her regular morning routine and eventually she always came to the same conclusion. When she was at the café, she was earning money, and while this incentive was surely as good as any other, she was also confident that the tediously repetitive tasks and mundane chit-chat would take her mind off her own problems, if only for a short time.

Finally coming to terms with the fact that she simply could not lie in bed all day, however much she wanted to, Jennifer pulled back the covers and clambered off the edge of the double mattress. That night she had donned a pale- pink laced nightie and it clung to her shapely body, the colour contrasting with that of her lips, and presenting a picture of innocence. Quickly she decided that the hairbrush and straighteners could wait and instead she padded out of the bedroom and towards her favourite room in the flat.

The kitchen was bathed in the bright light of the early morning. It streamed through the glass in the windows and suffused every crack and crevice in a healthy glow. Being on the top floor of a high-rise complex, there was no need to pull down the blinds at night in fear of being seen, for there was nobody around to look in. Taking this into account, every morning Jennifer paced along the short corridor that led from her bedroom to be met by the early-morning sun.

Standing in the doorway, she looked around the empty kitchen. Her pink nightie fell just below her knees, so that her bare legs were visible beneath and she threw her hands above her head momentarily and yawned wide-mouthed. It was time to find something to eat; she couldn't leave for work on an empty stomach. It seemed to be fate, then, that there was nothing around to eat.

Jennifer turned her head to the left, ran her fingers through her long hair, down her arm and smoothed out the bottom of her nightie. She hadn't realised how busy her schedule had become. Performing as Miss Marmalade most nights of the week and maintaining her waitressing job meant she scarcely had time for anything else. She had simply forgotten to buy food. But there was no way she could go into work without it, not into a restaurant where all day people would be ordering and she would have to serve. She couldn't eat there either, there would not be time and besides the kind of food she served was not exactly the most appetising. No, there were no two ways about it, she would have to call into the rather costly department store on her way.

Feeling pleased that she had now made at least one decision, Jennifer moved on to the next. Clothes, she needed something to wear. As she ran back along the hallway, her nightie flared behind her and she giggled to herself as she reached the bedroom again and fell flat against the covers. Here was a glimpse of Jennifer's cheeky, fundamentally playful side which she only ever revealed when she was hamming up Miss Marmalade for the soldiers, for her alter-ego wasn't vulnerable, and even if Jennifer did want to show this side of her personality to the real world, she knew she was not quite ready yet.

She did not like the idea of becoming Miss Marmalade full-time, she couldn't handle it. By keeping her two lives separate she was distancing herself from the prospect and for now, would just have to put up with living in her small flat high above the city streets.

To the left of the bed was a solid pine wardrobe and to the right a full-length mirror and dressing table. Prising herself away from the mattress and turning the handle on the wardrobe, Jennifer peered inside and rummaged around for the dull greys of her waitressing uniform. It didn't take her long to change, quickly wiggling out of her nightie, ready to submit to that far more presentable persona, and that meant turning to the dreaded straighteners once more. Although she hated to admit it, on several occasions Jennifer had singed her hair when using the things which was embarrassing to say the least. Momentarily she glanced down at the alarm clock and realised how much time she really didn't have, before reaching for her hairbrush and kicking the straighteners halfway across the floor in her rush.

She was finally ready, and on her way out of the bedroom she slipped her feet into the stiletto heels she loved so much, adjusted her lipstick from the night before with a quick pout in the mirror, and then she was gone. Racing up the hallway, still a little uneven on her feet, Jennifer grabbed the door keys and headed for the balcony.

The door clicked shut behind her and she twisted the key in the lock. Pulling the handle down, just to check, Jennifer began the long descent to the city streets below.

If you stood at the corner of Elm Street and looked up, you would be able to see a snake-like metal curve of steps twisting its way down the side of the dingy high-rise block of flats. If you stood at the top of this spiral, you would see the most amazing view across the open skyline of London. By now, however, Jennifer was halfway down the steps and so could not see much of anything, apart from the boarded-up windows of the decrepit factory opposite.

You couldn't describe the area as a bad place to live, because it wasn't. The people were friendly and the streets were relatively clean. Besides, at the top of the block Jennifer could make her own life, separated from those below with her stylish, professional pad.

'Click,' went the metal of the bottom step, as her high-heeled boots met with the pavement below. Good to be safely down, she thought, and there she stood for a moment, leaning on the railing as the swirling steps disappeared above.

But this pleasant moment of solitude didn't last long, for Jennifer was soon brought back to reality by the shouts and general hubbub of the early market several streets away.

Breakfast, she thought, I must head for the department store.

2

Arthur Bingham traced a tired finger around the edge of his coffee cup as he looked over the other chairs and tables and out towards the street beyond. Recently his work had been getting him down.

Since the revolution everything seemed far more regimented. The President kept a close eye on those in his internal cabinet, and this meant he had to work beyond his ability and ahead of schedule just to please him.

Arthur was a government detective, that is to say he kept tabs on people and made sure they did not vanish off the radar. A short, stocky man, he had thinning grey hair, bald on top, which he covered by wearing an old-style reporters hat, the type that was famous in the early decades of the twentieth century. He was getting old now, having spent much of his life working for the royal family in the days before United rule, and his age meant that he was not considered the right material for the front line of United intelligence. Instead, he was tasked with the jobs that nobody else wanted for little or no personal gain.

This morning was no exception, although today, instead of trawling the streets of London at daybreak, he had found solace in one of the many cafés and sandwich bars which had sprung up in the capital during the pre- war years of prosperity. To him it was a godsend that small businesses like these, which had at one time only sold sandwiches and baguettes to Londoners at lunch time, had diversified. Now, in order to deal with a national drop in the country's economic prosperity and a distinct fall in customer numbers, many had taken to opening far earlier in the morning and serving breakfast alongside coffee and other hot drinks which complemented their normal lunchtime menus. It provided a place to gather his thoughts and, in many ways, it brought him back to reality and gave him time to think.

Arthur Bingham had been dispatched so early on a dismal and dreary morning to search out a pretty young lady who intelligence sources said was leading a suspicious double life. Lengthy investigation and secret surveillance had revealed that by day she worked as a waitress in one such coffee shop, Strand Sandwiches, but by night transformed into the adored and infamous Forces' Sweetheart, Miss Marmalade. The government had discovered the fact in recent weeks and now they wished to acquire her services.

President Barker had presented Arthur with his most important task to date. Many United

Governments, he said, were secretly planning a series of deployments and offensives aimed at bringing the dark days of war to a close. To do this, certain secret documents needed to be transferred between countries, particularly the United Isles of Great Britain and United France. The problem was to make the transfer without risking discovery.

The Forces' Sweetheart provided the perfect distraction, since by placing the documents on her person and then dispatching her to perform in Europe, the government effectively reduced the risk of sabotage whilst still making a quick and effective transfer. It was an ingenious solution for even the Reformed generals would think twice before launching an attack against the famed Miss Marmalade.

However, the Forces' Sweetheart had already declined the offer, and this placed the government and indeed the President in a very awkward situation. By the time her response came through, things were getting serious. Across the world United forces were taking on the Reformed enemy in strategic battles in which they lost more and more land. To the United leaders it soon became clear that things were coming to a head and they had no time to waste if they wanted to act on their advantage.

President Barker had dispatched Arthur Bingham to meet with Miss Marmalade's regular persona at her place of work and accost her as only a government detective could. And this, he hoped, would be enough to convince her to change her mind. Personally, Arthur Bingham held out little hope that a short conversation between himself and the singer, especially in a place where no one knew of her secret life, could ever succeed. But he did agree with the President that the location of such a meeting and the surprise of his visit would make the Forces' Sweetheart feel somewhat uncomfortable, and that was why he had been here for almost an hour already, reading a newspaper and occasionally ordering another cup of coffee which he hoped would keep him alert enough to continue his waiting game.

For a while it went on like this, with little to break the monotonous silence that accompanied the movement of his eyes across the endless lines of print. In fact, he was considering leaving the shop for a well-deserved cigar, but that was before the doorbell chimed and a strange customer entered.

The man had almost completely concealed his identity, for he wore black from head to toe and a dark balaclava with only a hole for the mouth through which a scruffy beard could be seen. Over his shoulder he carried a large rucksack and as he passed by the table and out towards the back of the shop, Arthur heard him whisper some indecipherable words under his breath.

This new addition to the situation was strangely exhilarating, for anyone walking the streets in such garb was one to watch. So Arthur decided he would sit and wait to see how things progressed. Quickly he folded the paper and wrote a few lines on his clipboard to remind him of the man's appearance. Who knew, such information might be of use later.

Minutes passed and the man did not return. So Arthur, believing he might have passed out though some back door, decided there was time for a cigar after all. Even standing on the far side of the street, he had a clear view through the front window and into the shop, so he would notice if Miss Marmalade did happen to arrive at work. The taste of the cigar was strong in his mouth and it was this addiction that pulled him through the major stresses of his job.

From his position across the street there was just enough distance to escape. Suddenly smoke began billowing from behind the shop, as if something was on fire and it signalled a dangerous warning in Arthur Bingham's mind. Hesitating for no more than a second, he turned to run as the whole street exploded in a ball of fire behind him. Realising he would not get far, the detective lunged forwards to seek cover behind a rubbish skip. His heart was thumping in his chest. The fire ball was a sudden blaze of reds and yellows. Then, as quickly as it had blotted out all that was around, it died away, remaining only in a small corner of the Strand.

The enemy might think twice about attacking Miss Marmalade, he thought as he fell back against a brick wall, but that doesn't stop them waging war against her government.

***

For Jennifer, the war had provided glamour and fame. Her double life had, so far, provided her with many new benefits. She had numerous male admirers, soldiers were all over her and she loved it, even though frivolous relationships were emotional unstable. But, all this was about to change. During the course of the day to come, events would unfold that would change her life forever, and she would never be able to go back to her old life again.

The backstreet in which Jennifer was now walking was dark and damp. The buildings on either side of the cobbled street nearly met in the middle, and they blocked out almost all the sunlight. They were the kinds of buildings you might expect to find in the older academic cities of Oxford and Cambridge but streets like this still existed in London too. They hid in the very heart of the city, between the buildings of glass and stone, and Jennifer headed this way every morning.

The café where she worked was located on the corner of The Strand. This was a popular destination for the rich and famous. The heart of the city's entertainment district. Numerous theatres resided along The Strand, but since the war had begun a great many of them had been boarded up, for some were simply no longer viable. Jennifer soon noticed this and for as long as she could remember her dreams had been of owning one. Miss Marmalade could afford, of course, but Jennifer wanted to make it on her own.

Pausing momentarily in thought, she glanced to her left and finally happened upon the towering figure of Brown's department store. It seemed to be looking down upon her, frowning. But, Jennifer knew, like most Londoners, that Brown's made the best English breakfast money could buy, and she had no qualms about venturing inside.

Considering the hour of the journey to work, the streets were unusually crowded and not with business people either. There were a few wearing dark suits and carrying briefcases, but for the most part they were normal, everyday people, women, children and a spattering of men. It seemed strange for so many of them to be here on the Strand. Jennifer noticed it as she pressed the button for the pedestrian crossing. The lights seemed to take longer than usual to change and when they did a long line of bicycles and hover cars built up at the red light, snaking far past the end of the street, and disappearing out of sight. Wondering what all the commotion was about, Jennifer hurried across the busy street and into the relative safety of the department store.

Inside, the shop was symmetrical, and there were many different areas to choose from. Whether it was books, fashion, or gardening materials you were after, Brown's department store had it all. It was then that Jennifer realised how long it had been since she had visited a store like this and so, walking gingerly forwards, she studied a map of the shop floor. The café, was on the third floor and that meant navigating three towering escalators, a job made tricky by her stiletto heels.

The café was laid out not unlike a futuristic star ship, every surface finished in aluminium and chrome. In the middle of the room two elderly ladies with fishnet hats dished up bacon and beans and Jennifer quickly took her place at the back of the queue. Feeling the distinct lack of change jingle in her pocket as she left the pay desk, she helped herself to a plastic chip which could be inserted into the radio speakers at the table and proceeded to the last vacant window seat. In front sat an elderly man with a black and white border collie, and behind was a middle-aged couple. The man wore dark sunglasses and the woman had strawberry blonde hair.

Jennifer tucked into her breakfast; she was famished, and it wasn't until she was halfway through a runny fried egg that she paused mid mouthful and inserted the small circular disc into a slot in the very centre of the table. Immediately the radio fired up, just loud enough for Jennifer to hear, although much to her annoyance she was met not by the latest chart music but by the voice of a dull and repetitive news broadcaster. At first Jennifer returned to her breakfast, paying little attention to the story being referred to on the radio. She considered turning it off, but had second thoughts when the newsreader paused and began the story anew.

'A Black Day for London' were the stark words that greeted her through the speakers, followed by 'Insurgents Strike Again'. Jennifer tried hard to catch every word, for this was not the kind of headline you heard often in London these days. The radio very rarely referred to the war at all, choosing instead to play popular music aimed at taking people's minds off the dangerous and on-going conflict, and these words clung coldly to the heart.

As one that always longed to be in the know, Jennifer listened intently to the rest of the bulletin, for if anyone were to ask Miss Marmalade about the attack, a foreign soldier, for instance, she would need to know fact from fiction. The newsreader continued:

> Today is a bleak day for London. After a sustained period of peace in the capital, insurgents have attacked a building in the city. At the current time, the location of the incident had not been officially verified, but soldiers, believed to be from the Asian Republican bomb squad, did not appear to have a clear motive. All four were killed on impact and it is known that they were on the list of Republican insurgents who live within a short distance of the city. Intelligence sources say…

Jennifer stopped listening and gazed into the space in front of the table. How could something like this happen in London? The real war always seemed so far away, yet now it was right on the doorstep. No, it couldn't have happened, and in frustration she yanked the plastic chip away from the table so that the radio went dead. Soon she was nibbling on the corner of her toast and listening to those around her. The old man with the dog was humming quietly to himself, and the middle-aged couple were deep in conversation. Jennifer homed in and listened for any gossip.

"I bet they'd been planning it for weeks," said the man, with a mouthful of bacon.

"Yes, I'm sure," the woman replied. "But what surprises me is why they chose this target. I mean, what would they want with such a nice little tea shop?"

"Yes, I know what you mean, darling," came the man's voice again. "It was such a nice little shop. Strand Sandwiches, I used to go there often."

Strand Sandwiches. Jennifer repeated the name in her head until the meaning sank in, and by the time it did, she was already halfway down the escalator.

The street outside seemed even busier than it had been just half an hour earlier, and now Jennifer knew the reason why. Everyone wanted to catch a glimpse of the attack and the remnants of the building, the place where she worked. She had to think fast in order to take it all in; the corner of the Strand just up from Trafalgar Square was blocked off by a police cordon. Even from this distance she could see smoke rising high into the sky and debris spilling into the road. Jennifer momentarily wondered why she hadn't noticed the commotion earlier.

There were more than a dozen fire fighters no more than twenty feet away and she knew immediately what she had to do. Pushing forwards through the crowd, Jennifer was stopped by a burly police officer. She waved her name badge frantically in his face, but he didn't take any notice.

"I'm sorry, Miss, nobody is allowed to pass, by order of the Metropolitan Police."

"But this is my place of work, my job and my livelihood," Jennifer cried out in distress.

"I know it's a shock, Miss, but our primary concern here is to dampen down the fire and try to rescue anyone who might be trapped inside."

"There might be people in there?" Jennifer screamed, suddenly thinking of those she knew.

"We don't know for sure," the policeman added. "So far we haven't been able to get near."

Jennifer's face was a picture of horror. There were tears streaming from her eyes and her hair was a mess. She was only partly comforted when Derek, the manager of the café, suddenly ran towards her, arms open.

"Oh, Jennifer," he cooed. "It's terrible! I don't know what I'm going to do. You don't know how glad I am to know that you're safe." He locked down and brushed the wet hair from her eyes and at that moment Jennifer couldn't bear to look up. He was such a good man and she was just deceiving him.

She pulled away, and as she did so noticed a British soldier in the very corner of her vision. He had shaggy brown hair that looked as if it hadn't been combed in a while and his face was young. He looked innocent. Jennifer couldn't help but stare; even when she heard the policeman's voice in her ear she did not turn away.

"If it's any comfort, Sir, Miss, I have spoken to the President and he says that our troops are already on the trail of these insurgents. There is mention of a deployment of some kind tomorrow morning."

"But what I just don't understand is why they targeted my café in the first place?" Derek questioned. The policeman paused for a moment and then reached up to wipe his brow, shifting nervously. Jennifer couldn't bear it any longer; she turned her had back and looked him straight in the eyes.

"It's me they wanted to kill," she said.

3

Across London's East End, where the River Thames met the swirling expanse of new suburbia, life had taken on a relatively normal pattern and the day-to-day humdrum of modern existence passed by without notice. Marking the middle of this dark land of grey roof tiles and blackened chimney pots was the ageing Stadium of the Sun. Now cracked and broken, the paint peeling, the stadium had once been the love of the capital when it was commissioned for the 2012 Olympic Games, but now it stood alone and deserted. The Olympic village that surrounded it had since been converted into flats and student accommodation, the stadium itself used by the hundreds of football leagues that had grown from the rubble of the FA. People across the country supported their local teams, but there was very rarely any overall outcome to the various competitions.

If you walked past the Stadium of the Sun and headed north along Churchill Lane, turning left into Blair Avenue and right into Cameron Drive, you would reach a stone water fountain. The fountain had been designed as a monument to the armed forces and was surrounded by a series of neatly mown lawns, plotted flower beds and white speckled gravel. The ceremonial garden itself had been commissioned by the Prime Minister as he left office in the year 2013, and it had paved the way for more of the same design to appear during the decades that followed. It was, however, more important now to have monuments that honoured the nation's troops as a whole, and these single stone fountains had since been forgotten.

Cameron Drive, though, was the location of the original fountain, and that made a difference. This particular monument marked the entrance to the East London and Thames Regimental Barracks.

The barracks themselves were cold in contrast to the warm sun of the afternoon. The dark colours swallowed the brightness and it fell, so that the lightest part of the complex was a single grassy courtyard that marked the centre. The courtyard was alive with the colours of the season. Greens, blues and reds danced in the breeze and, as it was surrounded on three sides by the rooms of the various occupying soldiers, the location had become a haven from the strict discipline that existed within the barracks' walls.

It was on such an afternoon, when the sun was high in the sky and a shadow was cast on the ground beneath the oak tree in the furthest corner, that three men had decided to stop beside a window. The fresh air provided an escape from the sticky and humid interior and the three were deep in conversation. The breeze blew silently across the top of the open courtyard and ruffled the dry leaves that nestled in the guttering, sending them fluttering to the edge of the neatly mown lawn. One of the men checked towards the door that led back inside. He was sure he could hear someone moving behind that wall but, satisfied that nobody had actually ventured into the courtyard itself, he turned his gaze back in the direction of his comrades.

"I hear we're jetting off tomorrow. It's a mission that they don't want anyone to know about," said the man on the left. He was in his late twenties and wore a dark green baseball cap far down on his head. Beneath it, could be seen the rough stubble and tired lips that showed he had already done battle in some hot foreign country.

"It's probably just a routine posting like all the others," spoke the second. He was a lot younger and his face showed no scars. As a new recruit, he was surely about to see his first instance of real combat.

"I disagree," piped up the third and final member of the group. "If they haven't made it official yet then it's got to be something dangerous, or stupid. Either way it doesn't look all that favourable for us."

Both the others turned and looked at their friend. They were aware that he was intelligent and so an automatic candidate for leader, but secretly both wished they possessed his ability and thirst for knowledge. And they were right to do so, for Chris himself had experience of the trouble they might be letting themselves in for. It was something that he did not want to mention quite yet.

Staff Sergeant Chris Aston enjoyed the responsibility that came from being in charge. He hoped one day soon to join the SAS and honour the glory of the parachute regiment. But when the opportunity would come along, he did not know.

***

It was the hottest summer on record, one year before war would break out across the world and Chris Aston had just completed his Pass Papers, which marked the conclusion of his education. He had achieved a merit in Law Studies and two distinctions in General Sciences and World History. All of his lecturers considered Chris as someone who could go places, and could have any job he chose. But the grades didn't mean anything to Chris, who had always been adamant about his future career and he knew he could do it with the best grades in the world, or the worst. It didn't matter. Chris wanted to be a soldier in the SAS. But there was one thing that stood in his way, he was still only seventeen and needed his parents' permission. Chris being Chris, he didn't let this get in his way.

Two weeks after receiving his exam certificates, the time felt right to do something about it and Chris wrote a letter to his parents, the letter he had dreaded so much.

Dear Mum and Dad,
I love you both. Please don't worry about me while I work out how to follow my dream. I have taken my savings and for a while I will be staying with Grandma and Grandpa. I will ring you when I have sorted myself out.
Christopher.

And that was that. Chris left home and was a free man. It was a strange feeling, especially for someone who was still so young.

The long lanes that lead to River Cottage wound peacefully in the late afternoon sun. Chris had taken the train to get this far and now he was almost a breath away from gaining that final permission – his grandpa would sign, he knew he would.

A blackbird landed on the tarmac just in front of him. It hopped to the grass verge and tugged a worm from between the blades. It was an inspiring sight and one that made Chris wonder what he would miss most when serving overseas. The London Royals was one of the best regiments in the world and it was almost certain that with the Royals he would tread the sands of some far-off country. What he didn't realise, was that it would happen quite so soon.

The old wooden gate at the edge of the garden creaked slowly open, and Chris was immediately met by his grandma's open arms.

"Chris," she said, "we've been so worried. Your parents have phoned and everything…"

"Valerie, do be quiet," came Ron's voice from behind.

"I know why you're here, young man," he continued, addressing Chris directly now, "and I am proud of you. I will gladly sign your papers and I'm sure you will serve your country well."

"Yes, but before you go gallivanting off to London, you must stay here for a few nights and rest. You need a good home-cooked meal inside you. You will certainly miss that when you are away," said his grandma.

And it was at that moment that Chris realised he really would. He would miss his family, the food and the British way of life that was like no other. But at the same time he would be serving his country and the thought of this made him happier than anything else could.

Two weeks later, Grandpa Ron had signed as promised, and Chris was on his way. By the time he reached London, the papers had already been forwarded by wireless. And so, with only the money in his back pocket and a mind full of dreams, he headed for the Thames Regimental Barracks and for the life that lay beyond.

* * *

Wondering now, Chris studied his comrades up and down. The three most definitely made an odd grouping, but it was Thomas who intrigued Chris the most. He always wore that dark-green baseball cap far down on his head, even in the depths of winter. It was as if he was shielding his eyes from some strange, invisible enemy that neither of the others could see. He always complained that the light was too bright and made funny faces whenever a photo was taken. It must be his reaction to the light, Chris had thought after the same thing had happened on their passing-out parade. Now he had a record of his dear friend standing with him, sword in hand and cap against his chest, and mouth wide open.

Chris had always believed that Thomas would never make it through the tough regime; they had met on the first day of training. Thomas was short and tubby, where Chris was lean and tall. They were almost complete opposites, and yet here they were, standing in the courtyard, ready for what was sure to be the most important posting of their lives.

* * *

While Chris Aston was taking his final exams, Thomas Fisher was at the helm of his father's business. It was a factory that made clocks, and Thomas genuinely loved his job. A few years earlier, his father had been taken ill and as a result had retired from his position as head of the company. Almost immediately Thomas had taken up where his father had left off, and it had been that way ever since. He enjoyed this new challenge, the workers respected him and he, in return, provided them with good wages and working conditions. He was fair, but had a firm hand all the same.

It was on one particular grey and dismal morning, when the sky was filled with the strong sense of approaching rain, that Thomas Fisher was late for work. Because of his position, he did not need to be on time, but he liked to be punctual all the same. This morning, however, had been a catalogue of disasters, and Thomas had resigned himself to the truth that today, he just wouldn't make it.

The entire town seemed to be running slower than usual. The traffic tailed back up Main Street, well past the Church of the Holy Trinity where Thomas often attended the Sunday service, and many of the shops and businesses that stood on each side of the road lay cold and dark, with shutters still closed and no sign of life behind. The problem soon became clear. Two men were standing in a deep hole in the middle of the road, whilst another, dressed in a green reflective jacket, which seemed only to attract the motorists' rage, spun his Stop and Go sign on a tall pole and waited for the vehicles to snake by.

Eventually the traffic lights shone green, then orange, then red, and slowly the tailback started to ease. On the third change of lights, Thomas managed to make it through, his frustration clearing as he continued on his way.

Driving onwards down the country lanes and winding single-track roads that led to his empire, Thomas Fisher quickly began to make up time. But what he did not realise was the urgency with which his late arrival was being questioned up in his office on the third floor. There two men waited patiently, dressed in green and black, wearing berets and the Royal badge. There was a letter there also, on the desk, unopened, ignored. Real life was catching up with Thomas Fisher.

At the factory, he parked his car in the reserved bay, close to the entrance, and made his way up the stairs and towards the office. Marking the halfway point was a large glass window which allowed one to keep an eye on the workforce below. Today things appeared to be carrying on as normal, the conveyor belts were brimming with the watch and clock parts and people were sorting them into piles, while slow-moving robots assembled the final products.

Thomas continued past the window, for there was no need to pause here today. He opened his office door with a click, and saw immediately the two men in uniform. For a moment he hesitated, before turning towards his desk and realising why these men were here.

On the side table was a letter, an important document detailing the requirements of National Service. Thomas opened it and read from top to bottom, twice. He knew what it meant, for it had been all over the news; in these troubled times of conflict reputable young men from across the country were receiving such letters of conscription and within a month they were being transported to the front line. But why him? Surely he could not be considered soldier material? He had a good head for business, but his role at the factory would be of little use in the armed forces.

Slowly lifting the engraved ink fountain pen from the desk and thinking of how he might fight for the good of England, Thomas Fisher signed his name on the dotted line in flowing handwriting, much to his own surprise.

The two men watched and waited. They would take the letter back to headquarters, to London and the Chief of the Defence Staff. Once they had left Thomas Fisher silently locked his office door and fell, face in hands, into an old armchair. He really had signed away his life.

One month later to the day, Thomas arrived at the Thames Regimental Barracks in London. He was briefed on the ongoing conflict in the Middle East that would eventually lead to the war, of which they were now an important part.

Thomas would fight many a battle in the years to come. Modern civilisation was entering a dangerous stage and he knew that the conflicts would not end in the near future. Thomas trained every day for the pitfalls of the future that might await him. He learnt how to fire a gun, and to use other weapons, how to escape an advancing enemy without becoming a target and about life in the battlefield. The first part of his service was gruelling, but it was not exactly dangerous. When the time came for a proper battle, Thomas would suffer greatly at the hands of the enemy.

Reformed terrorist organisations grew strongly in wars early years, using improvised explosives to attack United Governments, they aimed to damage as much Capitalist power as possible. The larger groups were based in Eastern Europe and they concentrated their efforts on the United Isle of Great Britain and United Lands of America.

Thomas Fisher's mother was a barrister for the County Council and his father, upon retirement from the company, had taken on part-time work. As part of their new roles, Thomas's parents had drawn up a Home Security Bill which aimed to control the illegal movement and travel of Reformed citizens for work purposes. Following local trials, this bill had been recommended to the United Government. They wanted to use it nation- wide.

While fighting overseas, Thomas liked to keep up to date with news from home. Two months after he had been drafted out to the Iranian border, his parents and their colleagues were called to London to discuss the introduction of the Law for the protection of the United workforce

But the terrorists were bitter in their quest for destruction, and had martyrs already in the country. They were not happy with this introduction of working caps. A year and a half after he had signed on the dotted line Private Thomas Fisher received a standardised government letter. It came, as such letters did, with the Thames Regimental stamp and a London post mark, but what was written on those pages would haunt him for the rest of his life.

It conveyed in very blunt terms the news that his parents had been among those killed in an explosion on board a privately hired train travelling on the outskirts of London. Eastern European militants had since claimed responsibility for the attack and arrests were being made. He was expected to take solace in the fact that, like him, his parents were doing their bit for the country and its war effort. It did not help.

* * *

Chris looked at his friend again. He could never really understand the memories that were hidden in Thomas's mind. From the outside it had created a wall between the man and the rest of the world; his baseball cap was a physical marker of this. However stupid Thomas's decisions sometimes were, however hard he tried, there was still an air of distinction about him. He would fight hard when the battle required it and Chris had knew he would never give up in the face of a defiant enemy. His skills may soon be put to the test, Chris thought as he considered what their position might be by the time the day was out. We may again have to fight together and almost certainly die together, far sooner than he thinks.

The final lad who made up this trio of brave soldiers was Ewan Roberts. He was different from the others in because he had joined the Regiment at a later date. He knew the others well; they had spent time together training in new forms of combat and had discovered a liking for each other. But, unlike his friends, Ewan's devotion to the cause had been roused completely by chance.

***

London's West End was a marvellous place. Before the war broke out it was thriving with visitors, coach parties and tourists. It was the home of the big-time musicals. If you made it to the West End, you were bound to be a success.

There were theatres on every street corner, each vying for the public's love, and there were many different musicals, plays, and sometimes comedies to choose from. But to Ewan Roberts, it had always seemed like one dream too far.

Ever since he had passed his National Diploma in Media and Theatre Studies at the age of sixteen, Ewan had longed to be on the stage, longed to see his name in lights. Studying at the Royal Academy of Dramatic Art provided a pathway to his first major audition. The Andrew Lloyd Webber Trust was presenting the fiftieth anniversary production of Joseph and the Amazing Technicolor Dreamcoat in London's West End, and the director was searching for talented young students interested in the lead role.

At the auditions Ewan had performed better than his expectations. He had to push his voice to the extreme, but he did well and the director offered him the part. Now began the gruelling schedule of eight performances per week, and the laborious task of keeping his voice healthy.

The musical made a big profit well into the following year, but on the outbreak of war, things changed at a very fast pace. London saw the biggest threat from Reformed troop bombing, worse than any other European capital, and the government had to take action. Entertainment districts faced closure as each evening the lights were dimmed across the city. Many of the West End theatres were damaged in the night-time raids and slowly the actors started to leave; taking new jobs in the war economy or signing up to join the fighting themselves.

It was in this way that Ewan Roberts finally found himself signing up to the Thames Regimental Barracks. Joseph and the Amazing Technicolor Dreamcoat was the last of the big musicals to run in London. But, on the Friday which marked the one-and-a-half-year milestone for the production, the theatre was razed to the ground in one of the heaviest bombing raids ever recorded on the city.

There were several deaths that evening; yet it was fortunate in a way that the blast had centred above the stage and many of the audience were able to escape unharmed. The sets had fallen and the roof had collapsed, bringing several tonnes of heavy mechanical machinery down to the ground and on anyone below.

Staff Sergeant Chris Aston and Private Thomas Fisher were among the army personnel on duty that night, and they were more than surprised to find the famed Ewan Roberts held between two roof trusses that had fallen toward the top of the rubble. As Chris predicted, the poor man spent many months recovering from his injuries.

But the biggest surprise of all came during their routine training at the start of the New Year. They were making their way around the tough assault course, when a still recognisable Ewan Roberts strolled through the gates, heading straight for the Colonel's private quarters.

* * *

Chris had seen a dramatic change in character in the character of Ewan Roberts in the years since he had enlisted. The terrors of war and Chris's own stories had removed the swagger from his character. Presently he wondered what the day would really bring.

"Come on, boys!" he shouted, rounding the room in his own particular style and reaching down for his rucksack heavy case file. "We can't be waiting around here all day, we've got a colonel to please and some orders to be given." His tone was not in the least bit sarcastic.

Chris, Ewan and Thomas had no idea what was waiting for them beyond the gates of the Thames Regimental Barracks and no notion where they would be posted, or if they would even leave the country at all. The only thing they were sure of was that they had many more days of trouble before them, and as they headed onwards together, Chris knew there was great danger and sadness before them.

4

Jennifer was suddenly aware of the enormous effect the terrorist blast on Strand Sandwiches would now have on her life. She no longer had her full-time job, and that meant no regular, dependable wage and very little means to live by. And she was now on a Reformed terrorist group's hit list. It just didn't bear thinking about.

Heading towards Trafalgar Square at the top of the Strand, she pondered over how the morning had progressed. It was still only twelve-thirty, yet the day had passed in the blink of an eye. The strangest thing was that Jennifer knew she would never see Derek again. It was the way things had to be, if she was to avoid causing any more distress to the people she cared about.

For the average business person, shopper, or government official who walked the streets of London that morning or who stood surveying the stone lions at the edge of Nelson's Column, the sight of a young woman dressed in her black-and-white waitressing pinny, with her hair in a mess and tears streaming down her face, running towards St Martin in the Fields, would have been a strange one indeed. But, perhaps simply from their own embarrassment, when the woman stopped by the edge of the pool, they did not even give her the time of day.

It seemed to Jennifer that the only alternative to a life without regular work and a decent wage was to assume the permanent guise of Miss Marmalade, and that meant giving in to pressure and supporting the United Government. However much Jennifer hated the idea, the constant role playing of fame was not her cup of tea and she never had been one to gossip or involve herself in surreptitious activity, it seemed that all she could do now was to accept the path that had been laid out in front of her and make the best of a bad situation.

But then again, if Miss Marmalade was to accept the offer placed before her some weeks ago, she would at least be consistently engaged and would no doubt be well supported in her task. Although how she would explain the way she was currently dressed to her manager, she didn't know.

* * *

The Commanding Officer of the Thames Regimental Barracks had an enormous office in the west wing of the complex. It was twice the size of other rooms and was fitted out with the décor befitting someone who craved respect, and received it.

"I am glad to see that you got my message," boomed Colonel Smith as he paced up and down the room. "You made a very wise decision."

"You gave us no choice, sir," replied Thomas as he adjusted his cap so that it shielded his face from the Colonel's staring gaze.

"Yes, but you are here to protect our great President, aren't you, lads? Surely that's enough to spur you on?" The Colonel hinted a smile, but it never appeared.

"I still prefer to call it Queen and country," Chris broke in bitterly. He had been in this situation many times before and therefore knew exactly what he could get away with.

"Ah, but Staff Sergeant Aston," the booming voice sounded again, "you need to stop living in the past, my friend. The President has been in power for a long time now. The people of this great country voted for the right to become a republic and so we provided. It wasn't hard to jettison Queen Beatrice, silly girl. This is not the Second World War, Christopher, and you need to start realising that." Colonel Smith loved to give speeches and this was no exception.

Chris, however, had already prepared a retort. "You mean the same people of this country who voted for a change in name and for an alliance with other nations that split the world in two, leading to an outrageous war, which could easily have been avoided?" he spat, wondering how far he could push it.

His comrades looked on in amazement and hoped that this downright patriotism would not alter the Colonel's plans. Chris continued: "I agree with you about Beatrice. She wanted a lifestyle of privilege and wasn't bothered about the people. But when I was brought up, King Henry was still in power and he had to deal with the hideous royal hover crash. I know that people rebelled against the monarchy and saw Buckingham Palace as a focus of their anger, but in history at Pass-Paper level, we learned about Queen Elizabeth II and I believe she was the greatest monarch we have ever had."

"You have strong beliefs," smiled the Colonel. "But let's not let this get in the way of why I've called you here today. Staff Sergeant Aston, Corporal Roberts and Private Fisher, you may well become the saviours of this country in your next posting! How does that sound?"

Interesting came to mind, but so did many other words! Chris thought.

"But we've only just returned from a posting, sir! Surely you can't send us back so soon, I mean we are on leave," said Thomas, ever the optimist.

"I am afraid this is rather more serious than that. You see this morning the far end of the Strand was blown to pieces by a terrorist bomb–"

"I was there this morning, I passed by on my way here," broke in Ewan, cutting the Colonel off in his prime. "It was a terrible sight, I couldn't believe it." He finished and noticed Chris gesture for them both to remain quiet.

"As I was saying," Colonel Smith continued, "we consider this plot to be a mixed message from the enemy. Already it is clear that the attack was not sanctioned by a direct chain of command linking all of the Reformed nations, and therefore we believe it to be a specific deterrent to the completion of our future aims. In short, we know that Reformed troops are fighting a losing battle against the United Lands of America in the Middle East. Meanwhile the President of this great United republic, along with the French Government, has been amending plans for a full-scale offensive in central France which aims to flush out the enemy factions which remain there. This, when synchronised with battles and airstrikes across the globe, is intended to bring an end to the war once and for all. Recently, Reformed spies got wind of our plans, and by striking the Strand with a suicide attack, the enemy are effectively forcing us to launch them far earlier than we anticipated. They believe that will give their weakened forces a dynamic advantage." For a moment the three soldiers contemplated the import of the situation: the last push, the light at the end of the tunnel.

"But how does this involve us?" Thomas piped up, asking the question that was on everyone's lips.

"I… well," the Colonel replied a little apprehensively. "The President has asked for good soldiers to lead the attack in France. The head of the armed forces approached me, and I identified yourselves as candidates. The Thames Regiment has a great history of success and with Staff Sergeant Aston as your leader I am sure you will be successful. A large number of our boys are already based in the area to which you will be heading, a mixed barracks in the Auvergne region, and they will soon be joined by those from the United Lands of America and, of course, from Europe."

Chris thought this through silently and looked at the others. Thomas appeared to be hiding under the peak of his cap, while Ewan had turned pale. Chris himself, however, was almost excited about the whole idea. To him it was the chance he had been waiting for, a chance to lead and for others to follow, his chance to prove he was good enough for the SAS.

"But, sir," he began, forcing the discussion of an issue which confused him. "Why launch the attack in Central France? Surely just by breaching the United defences and moving towards the central

Auvergne region, the Reformed enemy have succeeded in their aims to move closer to our government and its intelligence?"

For a few seconds Colonel Smith hesitated, looking around the room from one soldier to the next before replying. "Well," he began, before taking another long pause. "You are right in many ways, Aston. However, there comes a time to show the enemy what you are really made of. The factions of the Reformed army which exist in an isolated area in central France pose no threat to the greater democracy of the United world. In many ways they are cut off from their superiors, having been surrounded in recent weeks by a variety of special United forces, in the same way as the region itself is cut off from the rest of France." Chris nodded; he saw this as a reasonable explanation. "What we really need are soldiers like you who can fly into the very heart of the Auvergne region and flush out these rebels, dispatching as many as possible and forcing the others towards the borders of Switzerland and Germany where they will be met by a further influx of troops from the very Eastern edge of the United governance."

* * *

Nearly three centuries after the Victorian empire, its lasting effect on London was still visible on Drury Lane. The large red-bricked façades and stone arches marked the edge of the pavement, and the buildings that were found here were now so rare that the whole street had been designated a world heritage site, the designs now written into the history books. There was a theatre on the street too, a very famous theatre and one of the last. It too had been built of red brick, and a shower of tiny lights glowed in the evening just above the entrance, to announce whatever was showing.

Above the posters and the tiny neon lights was a small window. It had a red wooden frame and went unnoticed by those passing on the street below. But it let a little light into a dark room, a room that housed a table and two worn-out chairs. It was a room that could only be reached via a small flight of stairs at the back of the theatre and on the door, which opened with a heavy sigh, was a single brass nameplate.

Jennifer peered at the name and smiled. She had been here so many times before, and the thought that the little old man with the balding head still believed he was the best agent in London never ceased to make her smile. Half an hour earlier she had been crying her eyes out in Trafalgar Square, but from the moment she stepped beyond this door she would have to take on the composure and the attitude of her famous alter-ego. Pushing the door open, she looked into the dingy room and was met by a very familiar face.

"Miss Marmalade," spoke a broad Irish accent. "What a nice surprise. But, oh, what is this you are wearing? Could it be a new costume for your repertoire?"

"Erm… you might say that," Miss Marmalade replied, a little on edge. She hinted a smile and immediately her confidence grew.

"Well, I like it, I like it," her manager replied. "Change is always a good thing and with your ascending stardom how could others not agree? But take a seat, take a seat, and tell me why you call upon me so early in the day."

Miss Marmalade pulled one of the battered chairs closer to the desk and took a fleeting glance out of the window and down to the street below. There was an abnormally large number of people pacing up and down Drury Lane, the outpouring from the first terrorist attack on the city in a generation.

Not wanting to think about her current situation, Miss Marmalade turned away, leaned in close and started to speak in that soft subtle voice with which she managed to seduce all the soldier boys. Yet there was something new in her tone, perhaps a hint of desperation.

"I need a favour," she spoke, her lips barely moving. "There's been some trouble for me recently. Something I don't want to go into, but I need to get out of here. I need permanent work." For a moment she wondered if she had come on too strong. Would her agent question why things were not right? It was no wonder she breathed a quick sigh of relief, then, when he smiled his trademark smile and looked her up and down.

"Well, I know you well enough not to ask, darling. There's no shortage of projects for someone of your persona." The ageing man paused for a moment, imagining he saw the invisible wall which had appeared between himself and the beautiful girl he managed. "There are many, many offers arriving in my inbox each and every day. Most of them I ignore, but as your wishes have now changed, I will look at them in a different light. Of course, I have kept the President's personal request open. Perhaps you could take a little time to consider it now that your situation has changed?"

"As I said before, I'm not struck on the idea. But I need something fast," Miss Marmalade replied a little too quickly. The manager raised his eyebrows and then shuffled some of the papers on his desk. "But if you think it's my only option."

A smile lit up her manager's face. "I'm saying you should consider it. The President has asked for you specifically. At any rate, we can discuss it further at tonight's performance. It's a birthday party I believe?"

"Yes."

"And at this theatre?"

"Yes."

"And so everything seems to be in order now?"

"Yes."

"Good."

"Good."

It seemed strange to Jennifer, as she left the front steps of the theatre behind and made her way back to her flat on the edge of the entertainment district, that the meeting with Miss Marmalade's manager had even taken place at all. He hadn't cottoned on to what was happening, but Jennifer still couldn't stop herself from dwelling on thoughts of the café. Nothing that serious had happened to her before and she was thankful for it. Now, though, things had changed. Within days she could be far away, in a desert or on the very edge of the Arctic entertaining the troops, or the land armies. One thing was certain, the proposition which had been made by the President's personal secretary almost a month ago was ludicrous. She would never accept, as it would make her an instant target; the last thing she wanted was to put her life on the line. In fact, it downright scared her, and yet the thought of new work and new horizons excited and thrilled her at the same time.

5

There were many slogans and buzz words associated with conscription. One of the more popular among the soldiers themselves, was 'the life of a soldier is never a dull one.' It wasn't far from the truth. One month you might be fighting close to the historic fields of Flanders, another you might destroying rebel strongholds in southern Afghanistan. If you were very unlucky, your life would be cut short and you would die in battle. These were the perils of the job, and not one soldier complained about it.

At about the same time that Miss Marmalade was leaving the Drury Lane Theatre, Chris Aston, Thomas Fisher and Ewan Roberts were signing their lives away to the cause - the Colonel had made it hard for them to decline. The fate of nations may now rest on their shoulders and even these three good friends couldn't avoid both the responsibility and excitement of their mission. They were informed that their plane left at nine-thirty the following morning, and then sent on their way.

Colonel Smith had hastily organised a leaving party and ensured that Chris noted down that the start time was seven-thirty prompt. It was now seven-ten and Chris was still standing inside the barrack walls waiting for his friends. Thomas was fiddling idly with a black cap while trying in vain to smarten himself up with a dab of L'Amore aftershave. Ewan, however, was dressing suitably for the occasion in denim jeans and a shirt, but he kept messing with his hair until it was exactly perfect. Chris was different. He considered the party no reason to dress up and wore the same old combat trousers and a green hooded t-shirt.

"Aren't you guys ready yet?" Chris spoke through gritted teeth. "It's at least a half-hour drive across the city and we're already late." He drummed his fingers against the edge of the door frame and he stood so that he was halfway in and halfway out, waiting impatiently.

"We need to look good for the ladies," smiled Thomas, finally setting his cap in a suitable position. "At least we have taken a bit of pride in our appearance."

"There probably won't even be any girls there," Chris muttered under his breath. "We're only going because the Colonel invited us."

"You mean laid the whole thing on for us!" Said Ewan, his showmanship returning. This was their cue to leave, for both Ewan and Thomas were wary of getting on the wrong side of their leading comrade.

"Anyway," Ewan continued a few moments later as they were walking towards Chris's hover car, "you know what it's like in London. This is a leaving party; I've been to one before, trust me, the ladies will be all over us..." He seemed to have found a new air of confidence this evening, and as he and Thomas climbed into the back while Chris took to the driver's seat, he couldn't stop himself from giving his friend a hearty slap on the back.

***

The St James's Place Working Men's Club lay on the site of the original London Bank, although the vault and safe had been moved closer to the Parliament buildings many years ago. It was a far from perfect location, its dark and dingy façade and a back door which exited into a dirty alleyway caused it to become associated with London's many criminal syndicates, a haunt for the drug-takers who could never be considered for military service. Alas, in these trying times, it was all the armed forces could afford. Even if it was cleaned up in preparation for the ceremony, it would never be grand enough to befit its task. As she approached the building via the grotty backstreet, its reputation preceding it, Miss Marmalade only hoped that she could bring a little class to the proceedings, however much the sudden change of venue had disappointed her.

The steps up to the entrance of the building were steep and she found it hard to climb upwards in her high- heeled shoes. This particular evening she had decided to try something a little different, with a short blue-and- white patterned dress that left very little to the imagination. The soldiers will love it, she thought.

Miss Marmalade had become accustomed to the attention that went along with being the Forces' Sweetheart. It meant she had many admirers who provided a series of post-show dates, however, she never letting any relationship become intimate.

It didn't take long for her to notice the portly gentleman standing in front of the frosted glass. It was obvious he had been assigned the task of looking out for someone, but seemed to have fallen asleep at the most crooked of angles, his body facing back towards the main hall, while his face was looking out towards the road. Miss Marmalade quickly rectified this with a loud tap of the glass which brought the man to his senses.

"Oh, I am dreadfully sorry," he smiled, fumbling with the lock on the door. "I was supposed to look out for someone arriving but I must have fallen asleep." Miss Marmalade merely smiled and looked beyond the gentleman's shoulders towards the main hall. A crowd was beginning to gather around the stage. "Right," she began. "I am Miss Marmalade and this is the birthday party, I presume?"

"A birthday party?" the gentleman queried. "Oh no, this is a leaving party for the lads who are off to France tomorrow." He pointed towards the double doors and the Forces' Sweetheart immediately made haste.

"Change of venue, change of event," she muttered under her breath while hoping that her manager really had found some full-time work. "Still, it's better than nothing." And with that she headed to the side of the stage.

***

Chris had parked the hover car at the back of the club and was now following Ewan and Thomas towards the entrance. By the time they arrived, the portly gentleman had disappeared inside and as they crossed the threshold from the street, all three simultaneously glanced at their watches to see how late they really were: 8.03.

One of the double doors that led to the main hall had been propped open and from within the sound of a familiar voice wafted out. Chris recognised it at once. So that's why he wanted us here so promptly, he thought. So we could listen to his speech in its entirety. Quickly he gestured to his friends that they should enter silently by the open door and stand at the very back.

* * *

From her position on the left-hand side of the stage, just behind the curtain, Miss Marmalade could see and hear everything. A pompous officer was standing centre stage, speaking into the microphone. He had a very boring voice. The odd words floated back to her, courage, bravery and Thames Barracks, but none of them made any connection. What did surprise her was when three young men sneaked in through the open doors unnoticed. She studied each one in turn: a baseball cap, nothing strange there; combat trousers and tired eyes, perhaps the leader of the group? These were things she could take in at a glance, but when her gaze met the third member of the group, she remained transfixed, recognising him, but unable to put her finger on precisely where from. Drawing her gaze back to the centre, she realised that the pompous officer had stopped speaking and was now gazing out across the audience.

"Good," she whispered with a sigh of relief. Yet what happened next only proved to make a bad situation worse.

* * *

Colonel Smith was squinting towards the back of the room. The speech had gone well, he thought, but he had still to introduce his protégés. Never mind, he conceded when he noticed Chris was standing at the very back of the hall, after this it will be time for drinking and dancing.

"Ladies and gentlemen," he began in his trademark monotone. "Before I introduce tonight's entertainment, I would like to present to you our reason for being here." He looked out across all the faces and grimaced. Why had he invited all these dignitaries, all these officials?

"This morning a terrible attack was witnessed in the very heart of London, one which can be traced all the way back to leading Reformed terrorists. The President declared a state of emergency, and it was under these terms that he asked me to select three of the best soldiers from the Thames Regiment for immediate foreign deployment. Together they will begin a battle which could end the war.

I'd like you to welcome Staff Sergeant Chris Aston, Corporal Ewan Roberts and Private Thomas

Fisher." The hall erupted in a round of applause that echoed about the roof space and it became clear to Chris that they were expected to join the Colonel centre stage.

* * *

When Colonel Smith had made a sufficient fuss of his three young protégés, Miss Marmalade finally took to the stage. There was another round of rapturous applause and the Forces' Sweetheart made her entrance. Leaving the stage by the left-hand side, Ewan Roberts was surprised to find this famous woman on the bill. Although he'd never actually seen Miss Marmalade, he'd heard many stories. Now, though, when the time finally arrived he discovered the girl now standing on stage was the same one he had seen only that morning. What a coincidence.

By ten-fifteen, Miss Marmalade had completed her set and was accepting dance requests. This was her favourite part of the evening, listening to the soldiers and learning their stories as they danced with her. She loved being in control. But later in the evening, while she was standing at the back of the hall chatting with two tall soldiers Chris had met on his first tour of duty in Iraq, all this changed.

Ewan had already had a few too many and Thomas had danced with almost every woman in the hall. But when 'Let's Face the Music and Dance' rang from the speakers, they found they simply couldn't help themselves.

"Care for a dance?" Ewan whispered with soft tones into Miss Marmalade's ear. To say she was taken by surprise would have put it mildly, but then how could she resist a dance with one of the men who would be heading overseas tomorrow, especially the one she recognised?

The music went on and Ewan slipped his hands around her waist. He couldn't believe he was here, with the Forces' Sweetheart, when to him she was nothing more than a normal woman. It was strange for Miss Marmalade too. To her it felt more personal and she couldn't tell if this was a good or bad thing. Without thinking about it, Ewan was soon resting his head on her shoulder and before long he was whispering into her ear. Her scent was heady, and for a moment he was overcome.

"I know who you really are," he whispered bluntly. "Yes," she replied. There was no sign of passion or emotion; she merely waited for his reply.

"I saw you this morning. I recognised your face immediately. You were standing outside that café..." There was a short pause. "...the one that was destroyed in the blast, and I was waiting in the corner. I saw you, except then you were wearing a black skirt and white pinafore. I might never have seen Miss

Marmalade before, but I've seen you. I simply couldn't forget your pretty face."

Ewan had let his hands weave tightly around Miss Marmalade's back, while his head remained on her shoulder as they moved in time with the music. But Jennifer was struggling, wriggling under his grasp, and before he realised she broke free and ran towards the stage door.

Everyone watched her, but she didn't care. What Miss Marmalade had just heard was too much and it wasn't until she was on the other side of the door and away from the dancers, that she felt safe.

Waiting for the double doors to shut behind her she tried to remember where her dressing room was. Now there were people heading after her, but as she skidded down the first corridor and steered herself into the second, she realised they were starting to disperse. By the time she reached the front doors, she was running so fast that she hardly noticed anything around her. Click – a sound that froze in her mind. The heel of her left shoe had broken away from the sole and sent her spinning off balance and into a heap at the feet of a gentleman who had just paused by the frosted glass.

"Oh, I am sorry," she winced, standing up, believing that she had embarrassed herself in front of the same portly gentleman who had shown her in earlier.

"Oh, you always were very excitable," he smiled. "At least I found you in the end; I've been driving around all evening." And at that moment Miss Marmalade recognised his voice. In all the commotion she had completely forgotten to expect a visit from her manager, and yet here he stood beaming down at her.

"Before you say anything," the Forces' Sweetheart began, "there is no way that I will accept the President's offer, it's just too dangerous." Her manager merely stood, his expression unchanged.

"Well then, I suppose it's a good job that I've found you employment," he smiled. "A proper paid job." For a moment they both paused, and then, forgetting everything that had happened, it was all Miss Marmalade could do not to wrap her arms around the silly old fool.

6

The evening seemed to go on forever, but in fact it only lasted a mere few hours. From the very first moment he had stepped over the threshold, Chris knew it was going to be a complete disaster. He knew he would hate the whole affair and that at least one of his friends, most probably Thomas, would show them all up. Standing by the bar deep in a forced conversation with Colonel Smith, Chris heard the music start. He had never really been much of a dancer. Yes, if a girl were to come up and ask him for a dance he would not refuse, but he just hated the way some people acted, the way that Thomas was acting right at that moment.

Throughout the evening Thomas moved around the hall and danced with every woman he could lay his hands on, sometimes getting far too close for comfort. By the time eleven-thirty came around, Chris had moved to the back to stand with Miss Marmalade as she chatted with some of his old comrades. He had to admit that from a distance she was quite a beautiful woman, only not his type.

Ewan arrived on the scene a few moments later, far from sober, and this prepared Chris for disaster number two. At first the pair seemed to be dancing quite acceptably, but about halfway through the second song Ewan whispered something in her ear, causing all hell to break loose. Chris wondered at first where Miss Marmalade was heading to as she broke through the stage door, but he was left with no time to dwell on it as Ewan rushed past him and headed after her, pursued by a small group of other soldiers and officials.

"Disasters," Chris breathed as he pushed through the crowd and headed for the hallway, "always come in threes."

And now, fifteen minutes later, everything seemed to be calming down, or at least that was what Chris hoped. They were sitting in a large box room above the main entrance where there was only a single window that looked down upon the street below. Ewan was standing by this window, an ice pack against the left side of his face. It didn't seem as if he wanted to talk, and the others were not surprised. Chris and Thomas had positioned themselves on two wooden crates by the door and they appeared to be listening intently to a conversation that was taking place just outside in the hallway.

"How is the young lady?" Colonel Smith's voice wafted in through the crack in the doorway. "It's her that my lads appear to be worried about the most. Especially Aston, he couldn't stop apologising for what had happened, though it had nothing to do with him."

"Oh no, she is fine, just fine," the manager spoke, his Irish accent always more pronounced in times of stress. "Although Marmalade won't offer a word on the subject, which kind of puts me in a very sticky situation."

"How do you mean?" Even though he was used to speaking with all sorts of clients, Miss Marmalade's manager sometimes found the simplest of situations soon turned into a nightmare. He took a few moments to gather his thoughts and looked up and down the hallway.

Twenty minutes earlier he had stepped out onto the street to make a phone call to a very important friend. The man in question went by the name of Watson, and he held a prestigious position as the President's personal secretary. The topic of discussion was a slight amendment to the President's proposal, which saw his top secret codes stowed away on board a United plane bound for France. In short, the documents would still be transported, unbeknown to the Forces' Sweetheart. The call had ended with

Miss Marmalade's manager revealing her delight at being found new employment so quickly.

"Well," the President's personal assistant had said slowly, "It's lucky for her that things are moving a little more quickly than we first imagined. A British general posted in the heart of rural France is awaiting her arrival, along with the documents and your three soldiers."

Back in the hallway, the paint on the ceiling was flaking and there was a large patch of damp alongside the obviously plastic chandelier. The carpets were fraying as well, only in the corners, but it was still noticeable. The manager wondered how on earth Colonel Smith could permit himself to rent out this building, proving beyond a shadow of a doubt that all the articles relating to the state of the armed forces' finances in this modern age were in fact true.

"Because," the manager paused before continuing his sentence. "Marmalade came to me in somewhat of a fluster this morning. I was not expecting her, of course, not for another week, but she was somewhat persistent and would not leave until I promised to find her a permanent form of work."

"And this is to do with me because?" the Colonel questioned warily. "Because, as I have already relayed to Marmalade herself, tomorrow morning the President has insisted she take the final seat on the same jet as your soldiers. I have engineered for her a position entertaining the troops in Central France."

Turning away for a split second, Colonel Smith gulped and considered the prospect. It suddenly came to his mind that the British were withholding some kind of intelligence.

"I bet she was very happy about that one, wasn't she?" barked Chris, bursting out of the room, causing the Colonel to turn back in surprise. Following in his wake was a half-sober Thomas, his signature smile plastered to his face.

"I don't think happy is the right word to describe it," the manager answered a little surprised, yet happy for the diversion. "She didn't protest as I thought she might; she agreed to go. She said that it was kind of me to find a placement at such short notice, and that she knew it might be weeks before I could find another if she decided not to go ahead."

"That's a little strange," Chris retorted, cutting the manager off once again. His visions of a troublesome future were beginning to rear their ugly head. Swinging the door on its hinges so that it opened with a bang against the wall, Chris pointed towards a figure slumped by the window with a cup of coffee in his hand. "That," he said, "is the reason why I find it strange. Why would someone like Miss Marmalade want to spend any longer with soldiers like him, someone who obviously caused her great discomfort this evening?"

"That surprised me," her manager replied. "But what shocked me the most, was that the moment before I left the room to make my way up here, Marmalade asked if I could bring that young man back with me. It would seem she wants a private word with him." This time the manager gestured towards the slumped figure.

"There is definitely something strange going on," Thomas replied with a hiccup, the first thing he had said to his friend all night. "I have no idea at all how Ewan managed to land a girl like Miss Marmalade." Chris shook his head and sighed.

***

While her manager tried in vain to smooth things over with Colonel Smith, Miss Marmalade had been sitting in her dressing room deep in thought. Tonight had been a little unnerving, but there was no way she was going to let it affect her future.

So, she thought as she slid her hand around the hot mug of tea and took a sip, this is what it feels like for the secret to be out, for someone to finally know. She contemplated this for a few moments. Yes, he seemed to know who she was, but he'd only recognised her face, he didn't know her name. If she really didn't want the truth out, then Miss Marmalade could just deny everything, and to be safe claim he was too drunk to remember clearly. There was one problem, though, one thing that prompted her to make entirely the opposite decision. It was one simple sentence: I simply couldn't forget your pretty face.

For the second time that evening there was a knock at the door. By now the hands on the clock were showing an early hour of the morning and Miss Marmalade was in no mood for talking. She had tried to explain herself earlier and she doubted that she could do a better job now, especially after three glasses of wine. At the time she had convinced herself these were only to calm the nerves.

"Enter," she said rather hoarsely, preparing herself for the onslaught. The door opened with a click and that strange and familiar face appeared.

"Hello," Ewan began, fumbling a great deal over his words. "Your manager said you wanted to see me." It seemed the effects of the drink had not worn off to any great extent, for he still wore a confident, yet altogether far too silly smile on his face.

"Yes I did," Miss Marmalade replied, dropping her guard a little and almost hinting a smile. It must be something in his presence, she thought again. Just don't get too soppy. But there was no need to worry. The drink they had both consumed more than dispersed any tension in the air.

"What's your real name, then?" Ewan smiled, walking haphazardly towards the desk and flicking the switch for the tiny bulbs that surrounded the mirror.

"My real…"

"Yeah, Miss Marmalade is just a stage name, right? I mean it's nice on toast but that's about as far as it goes."

"Yep, I suppose, but I prefer jam myself." Ewan screwed up his face for a second.

"Miss Jam? That doesn't have quite the same ring…" She couldn't help but smile inside, as a moment arrived and clung in the air. So he is witty and good looking, she thought.

"Jennifer," she then replied hastily. "That's my real name."

"Oh, it's lovely. So is that the one you use in the café? When you are all dressed up like you were this morning? What is the deal with that, anyway?"

For a moment Jennifer couldn't quite believe she was here doing this. It was far too early in the morning to be standing in her famous alter-ego's dressing room and chatting with the first man who was interested in her as a real person. Earlier in the evening, she had convinced herself that at 12 o'clock it would all go pear-shaped, just as it had done for Cinderella. But as the moment passed, she had found a new air of confidence. It was only then that she realised Ewan was looking directly at her, staring into her eyes and waiting for her to reveal all. Deep down she knew that he would not leave until he knew the truth, but she didn't need to worry about it, because for the first time in her life she wanted to tell someone. She wanted to let this charming soldier boy in.

Without a second thought, Jennifer hoisted herself up onto the desk next to where Ewan was standing and began her story. She told him about the flat, her family situation, the pros and cons of modern life in the capital and how she came to be Miss Marmalade. Most importantly, she told him what had happened earlier that day, how she had headed into London on a normal morning ready for work and had arrived to find the place blown to pieces. Then she told him how she had noticed a soldier standing in the furthest corner of the road, silent and unmoving, and then of a visit to her manager and the secure job he had organised for her.

When she at last finished, Jennifer realised that Ewan had been listening intently, and she soon came to realise that he was genuinely pleased to have been told the whole story.

"And I promise you now," Ewan smiled after a short pause. "I will not tell Chris or Thomas anything about our extra passenger." Jennifer just smiled.

"I'd much prefer to see their faces when they realise." This time she positively beamed, so that she found herself drawn into a close embrace with the handsome man before her.

It's only a hug, she thought as they parted again. There had been an immediate connection, both knew it, but neither knew how to admit it. Slowly Ewan moved his hand up and around Jennifer's shoulders. When she in turn drew closer, he smiled and looked her up and down.

"You really are beautiful," he said quietly. "I have to admit I never really understood what the other guys saw…"

"What do you mean?" Jennifer replied, pulling away a little. She was becoming more and more intrigued by this man with every minute that passed. She longed to know more about him.

"Well, I mean, you're stunning, but to me I see you as more than that. Even since I've been here, I've noticed something different, something deeper…"

For a moment Jennifer wondered if the drink was making him say these things. How could he read her so well?

"Aw, I don't know what to say," she replied. "That really is one of the nicest things anyone has ever said to me. It means a lot, Ewan…"

The soldier was only trying to express his feelings in words, but it appeared neither was able to. To her, he was attractive in so many ways. From his messy hair and dark eyes to his awkward smile. He was tall too, she felt safe with him and although he was a soldier, he seemed to have no lack of compassion, unlike the others.

To him, she was the epitome of beauty. It seemed as if everything he had ever loved in the few girls he had known in the past was encompassed within her. Her long blonde hair was gorgeous and her blue eyes almost piercing. They were wide and bright, with long eyelashes that curled up to meet her sparkling eye shadow. To him it did not matter that she was famous, he knew he would love her anyway.

They could not express their immediate feelings in words, or the moments in the dressing room that followed, it was too sudden and new. Instead there was a mutual understanding that feelings were far easier conveyed in a physical fashion. And as the silence between them became unbearable, acting together like two young children, shy and alone in the dressing room, Ewan leaned forwards and brought their lips together.

Jennifer did not pull away and the first kiss was like tiny fireworks erupting between them. From the time they parted everything was different. Now they understood each other, that this new and exciting feeling was shared, that they each felt the same. Jennifer didn't want it to end; she loved the feeling of escape she gained from kissing this man.

"Is this love at first sight?" Ewan whispered, running his hand through her long hair. She smiled and nodded, but at the same time drew away a little, remembering something important.

"Ewan," she said slowly, "there's something else you need to know…" The solider pulled a face, confused. Jennifer took the chance to continue. "I've been approached by the government several times in the last few weeks." It was the wrong thing to say, the wrong time and it would ruin the atmosphere, but she had to tell him. "They want me to carry secret documents for the United Army to France…"

"But why you?" Ewan asked almost immediately, it was the obvious response.

"They think I wouldn't be a target. They believe even the Reformed Army wouldn't attack me because I'm the Forces' Sweetheart." Ewan screwed up his face again.

"Well, I guess that does make a little sense," he said simply. Jennifer was surprised.

"But I didn't accept, I said no every time. I just couldn't take the risk…"

"…that's understandable." Jennifer wanted him to understand in every possible way.

"Do you believe me, Ewan, can I trust you?" This time there was no hesitation.

"Of course I believe and you can trust me one hundred percent. What did I say about keeping our additional passenger a secret?" Jennifer smiled both inside and out. Revealing this and gaining his trust meant everything and it proved he was genuine. But there was even more to come.

"Jennifer," Ewan asked suddenly, immediately looking deep into her eyes.

"Yes," she replied a little sheepishly. There was a moment's pause.

"Kiss me…"

By the time Jennifer listened to his footsteps padding down the hallway, it was all too much. Her mind was filled with so many thoughts of the day's events. For once those footsteps did not mean a horrible goodbye, but instead they led to a world of new beginnings.

* * *

It was half past two in the morning by the time Chris, Ewan and Thomas piled back into the hover car that was parked outside.

"It's a good job I didn't have anything to drink tonight," Chris sighed as the others fought with the seatbelts in the back. "I doubt they would let either of you drive in the Reformed state of Tiwaki, and that's saying something."

"Oh, but it was worth it, though, wasn't it?" Ewan piped up; it was the first thing he had said to his friends since the incident.

"How do you work that one out?" Thomas pondered, dropping his cap to his knees. "There weren't many girls there. I should know. I danced with those who were."

"You're just besotted, aren't you, Ewan?" Chris said calmly as he put the hover car into gear and pulled out onto the road. "I mean just because you get to dance with the most famous girl in London doesn't mean you're in with her. I saw that look in your eyes and I've seen it with so many others before you, one look and she has you. All she has to do is reel you in."

For the rest of the journey back to the barracks nobody spoke. Chris felt sure that he had laid the situation to rest and besides he couldn't be bothered to take it any further. Why should he have to act the father figure anyway? It was just another battle he could do without.

The buildings that remained on London's South Bank passed by like evil giants that blocked out the stars. Once this had been the smartest place in the capital, the location of upmarket apartments and the new business district and each night the buildings had lit up the Thames like giant fireflies. But that was before the war broke out and the President's right-hand man had since imposed a black-out scheme across the city, which he hoped would deter any possibility of a Reformed air attack. Most Londoners couldn't see the point, and Chris especially noted the fact that the country seemed to be digressing. He always maintained that it reminded him of the black-outs from the Second World War which he had studied at school.

And so the journey went on in the same monotonous silence. It was not a particularly long journey, it just seemed that way. It wasn't until they had passed the third traffic light and turned into the circular roundabout that Thomas finally remembered the question that had been on his lips all evening.

"So what exactly did you whisper to her, then, lover boy?" he grinned, putting on a mock French accent. "And what did she say to you in her room? Or not say, more to the point. I've heard she's one of those girls who prefers to get straight to business."

There was a sudden sigh from the front of the car as Chris realised there was nothing in his power that could stop Thomas from behaving like a complete imbecile, and a few seconds later Thomas himself realised he had put his foot in it big time. "I was only joking," he said, giving Ewan a jab in the ribs. "Come on, you're never going to see her again, we can at least have a laugh about it." But Ewan knew this wasn't true, and Chris knew it as well. In fact, it was only Thomas who had forgotten that tomorrow morning, the amazing Miss Marmalade would be joining them on a flight destined for France.

With a last buzz of the engine, the hover car pulled into the empty car park at the Thames Regimental Barracks and the three men clambered out into the cold morning air. The buildings looked grey and uninviting, and as they reached the door on cabin 232, Ewan couldn't help wondering if tomorrow would be the best, or the worst, day of his life.

7

The morning of the deployment arrived too quickly. It was a peaceful morning; a good morning for take-off and that would put even the toughest soldier's mind at rest. Thomas was sitting in the shadows between the door and the grassy square at the centre of the courtyard. A bowl of cereal was perched precariously on his knee, the spoon hanging from his mouth as he stared towards nowhere in particular. Thomas had always preferred the shadows. He came here whenever he was worried or had some moral dilemma to deal with; it was a practice that he had repeated often at the factory. Deep within the shadows provided answers to all life's questions, and that was something he really admired.

This was an important day. The day when he would undertake the greatest task of his life so far, and he didn't know if he would return. At times like these you really needed your inner strength. However, Thomas was brought back to his senses as the tall and imposing figure of Ewan Roberts appeared from a side door. There was no need to make eye contact, both men knew enough to shy away from the previous night's excursions.

"All packed and ready to go, then?" Ewan asked as he perched beside his friend.

"Just a few more things," Thomas replied. "I've got to change into my uniform."

"Yes, of course." And this was where the conversation ended. Neither of them touched upon that deep embarrassment that lurked in the pit of the stomach, the feeling was bad enough without bringing it to attention.

* * *

The ritual that Jennifer had followed each and every morning with an almost unique precision, ended abruptly. From the moment she had heard the radio news-flash in Brown's department store, things had taken a turn for the worse. That was until early the following morning. Miss Marmalade would have hated the whole affair, but for Jennifer it felt real and when Ewan left her dressing room, she felt loved for the first time in her life. It caused her to order another bottle of wine from the bar. By the time her limo arrived for the journey back home, she was giggling uncontrollably. And now, only five hours later, she had missed the alarm call (which she had never done before in her life) and had woken to a mess of tangled hair and a painful headache.

For the first half-hour Jennifer blamed the whole thing on the drink. But now, as she was sobering up and soaking in the light from the kitchen window, she was beginning to change her mind. Perhaps the events had changed her. After all, she was now free of the day-to-day work in the café and would soon be on a flight across the channel destined for France. Perhaps now she could flirt a little, perhaps now she would be able to reveal herself once and for all. Yes, Miss Marmalade could sing and she was a beauty, but that meant Jennifer had these traits and simply needed to learn how to portray them. It was all merely a sense of self-confidence.

* * *

The derelict remains of the Heathrow landing strip had been bought by the army many years ago and the government had set aside funding to develop the area into an estate of up-market town houses to accommodate returning soldiers. The houses, they had promised, would be surrounded by new office quarters and the runway would be restored. But this was at that same time that the government decided to place a bid to host the World Rugby League, something they had stressed would greatly boost the nation's popularity and encourage growth in the economy. The army's hopes were dashed. War had broken out, and before long a recession was looming. The government was losing money fast, and the armed forces were first see their spending cut. The little money they did receive was then ploughed into weapons research and cross-channel communications. Projects like the Heathrow landing strip were conveniently forgotten.

If he was honest, Chris didn't like where they were heading. Sitting in the back of the Ford 900 with blacked- out windows and with Thomas and Ewan on either side of him, he felt slightly humiliated. They were traveling in a style far above their station, he didn't approve.

The vehicle pulled up to the left of a long line of oak trees that stretched far into the distance. Here, Chris pondered for a moment and set his sights towards the far horizon. In the distance a flag was waving in the breeze and behind that he could just make out the towering mass which was the Eastern Generic Power Station, one of the last old nuclear bunkers. The dull concrete structure contrasted with the bright colours of the flag, clearly visible in the gloom. There was a splash of blue, a strike of white and a dab of red. The flag was flying at full mast because today was St. George's day. How ironic, Chris thought when he finally realised.

Ewan could already see the Myria 690 jet plane positioned at the end of the runway, and as their driver hoisted the luggage out of the boot, he felt his stomach lurch with a sudden sickening feeling. This could be his destiny, it wasn't a game anymore, a foolish charade. This, was to be real and personal combat and he soon concluded it was better not to dwell on it longer than necessary.

The doors on either side of the vehicle opened upwards, and the three comrades exited to stand before the line of oak trees. Dressed in full military uniform, they looked abnormally presentable. All wore the berets of the Thames Regiment, while Chris had taken the opportunity to flaunt his double bravery medals. Together they were a symbol of a nation's courage; three friends sent together, to fight for peace across the world.

The Colonel was waiting for them at the edge of the steps, watching as they marched in group formation, not one foot out of line, towards the aircraft which would fly them to their third tour of duty.

"This is it, boys." He saluted as Thomas reached for the handrail and a slight breeze blew against the side of his face. "You are going to fight for the peace of this great land. I wish you good luck and a safe journey. Mark my words, men, if this project goes well your names will go down in history." It was his way of saying goodbye.

There was no one else on the runway that morning, all three too young to have families of their own. Swiftly they made their way into the plane, the dull thud of boots hitting the metal steps matching that of their heartbeats. Then they took their seats in the cabin and waited for the outer door to crash shut, meaning they had no further chance to change their minds. The moment came and went, the door remained open and Thomas began to drum his fingers rhythmically against the window pane.

"When will we be taking off?" Ewan asked, impatiently breaking the repetitious beat.

"It would appear we are waiting for something," Chris replied with little or no tone. "Perhaps the engine has failed and we can't take off after all." His sarcasm was enough to hide the fact that he knew the truth. Ewan knew Jennifer would arrive; they wouldn't take off without her, while Chris had resigned himself to believing she probably wouldn't turn up at all. And so the waiting game continued, until finally their thoughts were broken by the slight murmur of an engine coming to life.

"I guess we're off then," Chris said simply with the slightest hint of a smile. The engine noise grew in volume, a great roar. Over the din, Chris continued, his voice only just audible, "I knew she was never going to come."

"What do you mean?" Ewan began, turning to look out of the window. The jet lurched forwards a few feet and began to gain momentum. By now Thomas had paused, looking with concern at his friends.

"Miss Marmalade," Chris smiled, fully this time. "Did you really think that I was unaware of her joining us today?"

"But I thought…" Ewan began again, before stopping, unable to continue the sentence.

"Ewan," Chris motioned towards the window. "You've been on edge all morning. Take a look at the empty runway. She's shallow, like many girls. Last night gave her second thoughts and she's gone." His voice was deadly serious, and Ewan Roberts had to admit he had been wrong.

* * *

It was half an hour earlier that Jennifer had finally left her flat for the hover car which was waiting outside. She knew she was late, but there was little she could do about that now. A mobile phone buzzed in her right pocket and she slipped her hand down to reach for it. Sure enough and as she had thought, Smithy was vibrating before her. It was another of those pet names she loved to dish out, and for her it detracted from the Colonel's harsh personality. It made him more approachable. The screen flashed once and a voice rang from the speaker. Jennifer immediately cut them off.

"I'm on my way, almost there. I will arrive within twenty minutes; make sure they don't leave without me." Then she flipped the phone shut. It was all she needed to say, for it was bad enough contemplating talking to the boys, let alone their Commanding Officer.

A short while later the hover car pulled over on the brow of the final hill. To the left the hideous power station stood like a blot on the landscape. The Union flag was blowing in the breeze and the runway stretched out like some strange creature cowering in the long grass. At that moment Jennifer suddenly began to pay attention. There was something moving in the distance. Down the runway it went, not at all fast, but it was moving all the same. It didn't take her long to process the information and for panic to set in; the Colonel hadn't listened to her, he had ignored every word she said and the jet was setting off without her. Apparently the driver had noticed her panic, for without a word from his passenger he doubled his speed and raced down towards the runway.

Colonel Smith could sense something approaching at incredible speed, and the decision he had made only moments earlier was now overturned. The hover car was at the far end of the runway and gaining on the jet plane as it lumbered forwards. By now the pilot had slammed on the emergency brakes and was praying that he could stop the craft before it reached the fields beyond.

In a style not unlike that classic hero James Bond, the small black hover car hurtled towards the end of the runway and came to a halt where the grass met the furthest reaches of concrete. Jennifer was thrown backwards with some force. Doing her best to look composed she pushed open the sliding door and noticed how close they had come to certain death. Looking up now, she saw that one of the plane's tiny windows had been pushed wide open.

"I thought you weren't coming!" Ewan Roberts shouted down, smiling haphazardly. "But, what an entrance!"

"Well, I try to impress." Jennifer returned the smile, watching as the electronic steps descended. "Give me a hand then," she continued, climbing two steps at a time. Quickly she reached for the handrail as down below her driver began unloading her luggage. "Time is of the essence, we've got a war to win!"

8

Clouds floated past the windows like balls of candy floss, weightless in the wide expanse of the blue. The fields and farmland far below were knitted tightly together, in a large patchwork quilt that covered the land in every direction.

Now they were up in the sky, the jet began to make steady progress towards their destination. Already they had passed over the English Channel, and far below they had noticed the large cargo ships docking at Dover, and the small passenger ferries tripping across the waves from Portsmouth towards the Isle of Wight. Before long they had reached the shores of France.

France was a changed country; that much was obvious. Close to the coast the farmland had disappeared, making way for the many industrial cities that had grown up since the war had begun. Here was the centre of the country's ammunition production, with mile after mile of grey urban expanse. As they travelled further inland, nature appeared to regain her grasp, as yet unaffected by the advancing industrialisation.

In the cabin, tiredness and confusion had taken hold. Each knew there was little less than an hour of their journey left, and each in turn resisted the opportunity to make conversation. It had begun the moment Jennifer stepped inside the jet and took her seat in the furthest corner of the already cramped compartment. Almost immediately, she noticed the tense atmosphere, and decided it would be best not speak, even in greeting, until the soldiers had dealt with whatever pride or fear was plaguing them.

It was as the jet had crossed the border between land and sea that Thomas Fisher dropped his line of sight from the window ledge and turned to the others. He noticed Chris and the look of disgust on his face. Perhaps his friend was concerned their mission would not turn out to be the great success he hoped. Turning to the left, Thomas now broke Ewan's line of sight. His friend, showed little or no acknowledgement. He didn't even notice the slight smile of amusement appear on Thomas's face as he took a few steps forward, drew back the sliding door and headed towards the cockpit to communicate with their navigator.

"What on earth do you think has got into him?" Chris asked after a few moments in the icy atmosphere.

"I don't really know," Ewan replied, suddenly snapping out of his trance. "Hasn't he always been like that?"

"I'm not so sure. I think there's something going on here, and if we're ever going to see the other side of this impending battle then we must at least work together." Chris had made his point and so turned away, to consult their briefing documents. A flicker of panic appeared across his face for a single moment, but no one was close enough to observe it.

For the first time since their journey had begun, Ewan Roberts plucked up the courage to address the girl sat opposite him. Jennifer, who could have been flattered by such admiration, returned his look.

"Why so quiet, sunshine?" She smiled, momentarily forgetting that Chris was there. "You haven't spoken to me since we left London and it can't be that long now until we arrive."

The soldier paused for a moment, perhaps contemplating an answer, or at least going through the motions in his head. "It just doesn't feel right," he pondered at last, "you being here after everything that happened last night. These trips are usually just for us lads, you know; Chris as the leader, all boys together. And well, it's going to be dangerous, and hell, we might not even make it back. This is serious, Jennifer!" It was as if the thoughts that had been swirling around in his head like a whirlpool in some far ocean escaped from his lips all at once, a river of thoughts, worries and feelings hurtling outwards.

"Look, Ewan," Jennifer started again, this time bringing Chris into the equation so that he turned and looked at them both. "We all know what's going to happen in the end. We are here for one reason; you are here for one reason. The things that we do and the decisions that we make over the next few days, weeks, months will affect our country for years to come. And like you said, it's Chris who's going to lead us there."

"Yes… I… will…" Chris stuttered, surprised at how this woman was taking control.

"We know he will, or at least we hope. We need something to keep faith in, but for now all we can do is enjoy what we have here, soon and before it all changes." Jennifer was proud of herself. All of her life she had wanted to be this way, standing up for her beliefs. But Miss Marmalade had always prohibited it, stopped it stone cold dead. And perhaps through coincidence, or through the mysteries of fate, it was at that moment that the sliding door drew back and Thomas returned to the compartment again, totally oblivious to any of the previous conversation.

"I've just spoken to the navigator," he began, addressing the others with a flourish of his hand. "He says that providing we can find a suitable landing position, we can touch down within half an hour. Now that's got to be good news, so let's stop this moping around. If we are ever going to work together on this, we need to be confident with each other. What we need is for something exciting to happen, something to get the blood pumping." It was the most that Thomas Fisher had said throughout the whole journey and indeed the last that any of them would say for some time.

With a sudden lurch of its engine, the jet plane began to move with such tremendous force that the passengers were thrown back against the metal wall of the compartment. Far below that little patch of sky which they had made their own, the mismatched hills and valleys of rural Auvergne stretched out, a small piece in the giant jigsaw puzzle that was United Europe. Here and there the odd oak tree or an old decrepit barn, long since forgotten, pierced the expanse of green and yellow.

It was another lurch of the engine and a rotation of almost ninety degrees that prompted the vessel to lose altitude and turn in a nose dive towards the fields below. The pilot and the navigator fumbled frantically with an array of buttons and controls, but there was nothing that they could do. In the cabin fear and panic ensued; each of the friends searching frantically for any kind of protection as they hurtled ever downwards to meet the earth below.

Time seemed to slow. The ever-turning loops of the small transport jet, a confused bumble bee in a state of disarray, passed like the simple spins of a roundabout, and when dizziness and nausea set in, it was hard to remember anything at all.

Several things happened in the moments between falling and making impact with the ground. Chris, who had flown before and who had experienced danger, even at this young age, realised immediately that something was wrong. It did, however, take his mind a few moments to process the information, and when he did, his face, now void of all expression, turned the palest shade of white. There was a moment, although it passed without notice, when Jennifer knocked her head against the very roof of what was destined to be their tin-can coffin. It was only a minor bump, something that Jennifer herself didn't even notice at first, yet it was just seconds later that her eyes closed and she gave in to unconsciousness. Her last thoughts were that she might never awaken again. For Thomas and Ewan, the situation scared them greatly. From the moment they felt that first lurch, they had retreated to the very furthest reaches of their minds, to attain some state of tranquillity, where they could reside until the inevitable happened.

And so those few seconds sealed each of their fates in turn. If you had looked upwards, you might have been surprised to see a United jet plane moving with such speed across the sky, for army transport had always been very reliable. Now all this had changed and the evidence was that one lone vessel, making its way towards the mountains of rural Auvergne, had landed in a crumpled heap amongst the cornfields. It bounced slightly as it made impact, tumbling over the crumbling earth.

It was getting late now, and the jet plane should have arrived safely at its destination over an hour ago. Soon others would notice they had not arrived, firstly checking the radio signals before beginning to search. But whether it would be for bodies or for survivors, they had still to discover.

9

The evening was just beginning to draw in around the hillside when something moved within the hedgerow. Sensing that there was no longer fear in the air, the creature, a beautifully preened male peacock, strutted out into the open and padded across the soft ground. In the air was the smell of death and destruction. This the peacock understood. It also knew that this was human destruction.

To the far left of where the creature now stood, high on its scrawny legs, lay the great mound of metal carnage. A plane without wings and a tail piece which had been thrown the length of the field upon impact. The site, although horribly dangerous, now felt peaceful.

As the sun took one last look out across its kingdom before disappearing behind the hilltops, the peacock began to call, all at once and very loudly. Perhaps it had been startled by the moon's sudden appearance, or by something else. Whatever it was, the poor creature was left totally disorientated. For a moment it hesitated, waiting for its senses to return and then silently and suddenly, the peacock, with its head hung low, left this strange and newfound kingdom to return to the safety of the hedgerow.

* * *

Black, pitch black. Not a sound to be heard and nothing to see. But if you concentrate, home in on your senses, you might just hold onto what little grip you have on life. In the black you can see nothing, and so you concentrate on what you can taste and hear. Fear in the air, a strange taste on the lips. You've tasted it before, but you can't pinpoint where. Your brain is not working correctly and you've lost all sense of memory. Nothing exists beyond the here and now.

Concentrating even harder, you try to hear. To the right of you is the regular breathing of another person. Their breath is strained, but they're breathing at least. And this discovery spurs you on and slowly you begin to remember. Friends, arguing, smiling, and laughing. You have no recollection of why such things happened, but the memories are there.

A picture of a landscape viewed from high above flickers before your eyes. For a moment you wonder if it's all a dream or some horrible nightmare. Only now do you discover your sense of perception has also been damaged, and you suddenly find yourself laughing inside your own head. A voice and a face fills your mind, but the image is faded and the voice is far away. Slowly, the breathing you can hear labours and the laughter takes control. You cannot fight against it because, after all that has happened, you feel safe lying here in limbo. And you realise that you don't want to fight, you don't want to survive. The laughing empowers you, quickly taking over your mind. And then it stops, as suddenly as it began. Your last thought is of peace and well-being. You're safe now, no more laughter and no more tears, just the blackness and the beauty that lies beyond.

10

For Chris, there was only ever one outcome, one conclusion, and that was to survive. If he were to die, he would die in battle. He would not die here, a passenger on a solitary jet plane, where no one cared if he existed.

There came a point, he couldn't tell when, that he found he could open his eyes and slowly adjust to what was around him. Firstly he noted the darkness; not only within the compartment but also outside. There was a crack in the roof, and through it a million tiny stars danced. It was ironic, for heaven could have been where he ended up. Secondly, he noticed the injury. For a moment he feared the crash had caused him such injury that he could no longer feel the pain. The only real evidence appeared on his right arm, which was bleeding in several places. But, his life had been spared.

It was clear to Chris that the force of the impact had thrown the jet some considerable distance. Perhaps the tail or the cockpit had broken away from the main body. It was only when he pushed weakly upwards that he discovered the true extent of the damage and felt the thumping pain in his head. The roof of the compartment fell away from the rest and he used his better hand to create a hole big enough to crawl through. Then, although the pain was close to unbearable, he pulled himself up to the top. Exhausted, he fell back against the crumpled metal. There was nothing he could do now, yet he had to go on.

Creating the opening had begun a chain of events. As he pulled himself up through the space, Chris realised it had been raining in the time between the crash and now, not only because it fell in large streams from the cracks, but because he could taste it in the air. The cold water was fresh and clean, yet he could smell death. This was a sudden sensual overload which caused him to look back down into the compartment, where he noticed a pair of eyes in the gloom. They were full and round in the darkness and that meant he was no longer alone.

An urge to shout out was all Chris could feel building up within, as the flash of something in his head reminded him that there were three others lying back inside the metal casing.

"Hello?" he called hoarsely down into the darkness, panic setting in. "Are you alright?" It sounded so pathetic, his mind dazed such that he couldn't remember the name. Time passed as Chris waited, unable to draw his gaze away. Then from within, a slender, pale hand surfaced above the metal edge and the soldier squinted to see if the body was clear.

Believing that what little debris there was had avoided crushing the helpless figure, he took her left in his right, supported the weight, and pulled Jennifer up through the crevice and into the light of the stars and the moon. At once he realised how vulnerable and cold she looked in the pale moonlight, her skin white, highlighting the dark red of her smeared lipstick. There was a cut on her right thigh where something had pierced through the material of her dress and this was still bleeding slightly. Her face was terrified, and that seemed to scare Chris the most. Here was one of the most famous women in the world, reduced to a helpless, childlike state.

"Oh, Chris." The sound was so faint and it passed through barely parted lips. But Chris heard the plea and responded by wrapping her in his arms to keep the nights chill at bay.

"I don't… don't… know what we can do," he stuttered as tears formed in his eyes and fell upon the beautiful woman's dress. "I just… I hope that nothing awful has happened."

* * *

Several hours passed and slowly Jennifer began to regain some strength. Together, although they were both severely weakened, she and Chris sifted through the wreckage for their friends' bodies and belongings. They were witnesses to so many dreadful things that night and they began to realise how truly grateful they were to be alive.

With some sharper pieces of wreckage, Chris had managed to open the crevice further and allowed the moon's haze to fall upon the two crumpled figures that remained. Thomas and Ewan were injured far worse than either Chris or Jennifer. Thomas particularly, having been knocked out by the look of a gash to his forehead. Chris made sure that both men were laid safely and as comfortable as possible under the cover of some nearby trees before heading to search the remains of the cockpit. Jennifer remained, her bright blue eyes filled with tears, as she sought comfort close to the dark form of her dearest companion.

As with any tragedy, survival is the uppermost concern, but it can be stripped from you at any moment. Chris realised this first hand, when he paced towards the tangled remains of the cockpit and stared down on the lifeless shapes that lay there. Entangled amongst the controls over which they had once had so much power, the pilot and the navigator had given their lives for the job they loved. This was, as Chris had always said, no longer a game. Two brave men had lost their lives in a bid to save four other souls. And Thomas could have been standing alongside them in the cockpit. His too might have become another life lost to the cause.

Chris had never thought deeply about the consequences of war before, he was a brave man but he didn't like to think about the harsh reality. Now he had no choice. The proof of the lengths to which men will go to honour their country lay before him. As he moved away from the wreckage and noticed the slight breeze in the air, Chris made the decision there and then to plan, continue and to never give in. For if there were people left on the planet who could end the Great War through struggle, he would make sure he and his comrades would be the ones.

* * *

For several hours after they had escaped from death, Chris and Jennifer talked through what would happen next. They spent a great deal of the night in quiet conversation, and by the time the moon reached its highest point, they finally happened upon an idea.

Chris had worked out early on that it would not take Colonel Smith long to realise the jet was missing and when he did, he would alert the French United forces who would begin to search for the wreckage. That being the case, if the crash site was discovered it would not be inhumane to leave the poor dead souls in their final resting places. Chris did not like the idea of being discovered. This mission was by no means secret but he knew that the fewer people who knew about it, the easier it would be. Even if the French troops were fighting on the same side, he was here to do a job and he would complete it.

He was also aware, however much he hated to admit it, that something about the crash was all wrong. In the years since the war had begun, military leaders had ensured a complete overhaul of the new United Army. That had led the United Isles of Great Britain to become the leading power in modern warfare design. Knowing this, Chris was adamant that they would certainly never let anything happen to their leading soldiers, not by accident. But what about by force?

The inner workings of any military organisation had similarities, but the Thames Regimental Barracks was perhaps a little different from the rest. Remembering now, Chris realised how Colonel Smith had been quick to accept the President's proposal to post fine young soldiers overseas. In fact, he had waved them onto the jet and away with little planning or preparation. Perhaps he had, behind closed doors, spoken to his French counterparts, but it had been left to Chris, Thomas and Ewan alone made sure they were well equipped. Most importantly, Chris had said, they should each carry a newly developed GPS holographic map. This was a thin computer screen, about the thickness of a piece of cardboard that had long since done away with the conventional OS maps.

Jennifer was tending to Ewan as he started to get accustomed to his surroundings, while Chris kept one eye on Thomas.

"I've been thinking about things," he motioned in Jennifer's direction, breaking the silence. "About how any of this could happen. It can't have been an accident, we all know that."

"What are you suggesting, then?" Jennifer asked, intrigued.

"Well it's the whole establishment isn't it? Nothing's as it used to be, and the world is corrupt. It's all about money nowadays. I mean it was before, but a human sacrifice still meant something back then. I'm just not sure what Colonel Smith meant for us…" Chris finished, his face grave and disappointed. Jennifer couldn't respond for a moment.

"Are you suggesting that he wanted us killed?" she gasped.

"I believe it would have been viable for us to be out of the way, yes. Especially me. I could be a great a danger to him, to his plans."

"But just hold on a minute," Jennifer murmured, trying to work the whole thing out in her head. "Are you sure about this? It just might have been an accident, after all. I know it's unlikely, given the situation, but we've got to consider the possibility." Deep down, she knew she held a loathing for the Colonel just as much as Chris, but didn't want to jump to unjust conclusions.

"Well, I suggest we do our best to make sure," Chris finished, looking up towards the sky for the briefest of seconds. "I have our GPS holographic maps, I recovered them from the wreckage along with our belongings, but amongst the papers and our rations and clothes, I found something else, Jennifer." Chris was speaking seriously, as if the Forces' Sweetheart had something to hide.

"What are you talking about, Chris?" Jennifer questioned, slowly considering anything that might incriminate her. No, she couldn't think of anything. Chris remained, staring forwards, just above Jennifer's head.

"I think you'd know exactly what I found, if you stopped to think about it."

"I'm afraid not, Chris, but I would be interested to know how you think I've compromised your mission…"

The atmosphere between the two had changed immediately. There was tension now and apprehension, where before there had been a mutual understanding.

"Well, right now," Chris said, "I think it's better if I don't reveal too much. In the morning, hopefully Ewan and Thomas will be well enough for us to move out of here. Then we'll look at the GPS together and only then will I reveal what I've found. I feel it would be best to keep everyone in the picture, so that we all know where we stand..."

Jennifer remained silent; she was overwhelmed by Chris's sudden change of direction. In her eyes, he was taking things way out of proportion. At times he was a very hard man to understand, and now Jennifer realised it was best not to try. For Chris, who had led a band of men to war, and would still have them in the best state of mind while they were fighting, it was simple. In amongst the wreckage, as he pulled their belongings away from the crash site, he had found a very interesting object hidden inside Jennifer's sheet music and set lists. What compelled him to look there, he didn't know. But he was happy that he had done so.

* * *

The comrades spent a very cold night in the fields of Central France. The weather conditions were far harsher than they had been used to at home, with a strong wind chill that shook them to their core. Chris had decided early on that it would be best to take turns in keeping watch. He would take the first shift while Jennifer rested, and then they would take turns until sunrise.

The night's bad weather gave way to a glorious sunrise for the dawn and it looked to remain a clear day. Chris had been right in his predictions. In truth, there was a vast improvement in their situation by late morning. Ewan and Thomas felt physically stronger, even though their injuries were not completely healed. As he leaned against the old tree that was their refuge and watched, droopy-eyed, as the sun shone above the distant hills, the soldier was thankful for this, as today they had a lot of work to do.

Before long, Jennifer began making breakfast. She considered them very lucky, for they had escaped not only with their lives, but between them they had recovered some of the supplies and possessions that had been on board when they came down. It meant that Jennifer had a change of clothes, while the others had recovered ration packs that would provide nourishment for many days to come. But the Forces' Sweetheart had also spent a lot of the night unable to sleep, worrying instead about what Chris might reveal in the morning. But when a bleary- eyed Thomas moved his head upwards and acknowledged them for the first time, it was soon forgotten. He was no longer as ill as they had first thought, and that was a great relief.

"Nice sky," he muttered, his words a little slurred. "Where are we?"

"The plane came down." Chris spoke calmly, drawing his friend's hand across the various cuts and scratches. "We were lucky to get out of it alive." To Thomas those words were like an invisible key.

"We didn't lose anyone, did we?" He fumbled, somehow a little stronger.

"I'm afraid the pilot and the navigator didn't make it, Thomas, but the rest of us are okay. Ewan is a little dazed still, but so far Jennifer and I have been able to get most things sorted."

"And speaking of which," came another voice from behind, as Ewan walked towards the pair. "You didn't explain why nobody has come to find us yet?"

Chris was silent for a moment. "I doubt they'll come, Ewan. Or if they do, it won't be until they realise that we haven't arrived. I don't know for certain, but we needn't waste any time hanging around here."

His friend contemplated this for a moment. "I guess that's why you left the bodies then," he replied.

"We can at least hope that they pick it up as a lone jet with no passengers, yes," Chris finished. "Or at the very least, let's hope they leave it be. Those who come to find us could be friend or foe; we have no idea where the enemy are placed. In any case we don't know where we are going from here, so it should be harder for them to find us." Here the Staff Sergeant paused to consider how best to phrase his next sentence.

"We can soon make use of our GPS holographic maps, which are only a little damaged. However, I'm afraid there is something I need to discuss with you all first."

"That doesn't sound good," Ewan said weakly.

"No," Chris replied, but it would be much worse on an empty stomach.

And so, the four friends plodded over to the campfire and warmed their hands on the flames. The sparks that danced up towards the sky drew Thomas towards the warmth and he stared intently, as if there was some lost secret held within those flickers of light.

Jennifer had rigged up a makeshift stand from some metal piping Chris had recovered from the wreckage, and upon it stood a large metal mess tin filled with boiling water and a slowly expanding ration pack. The porridge that was eventually shared between them wasn't bad, considering the situation. Chris by now had grown used to what he called an acquired taste. It was always either a little dry, or far too soggy. But it was food just the same, and it gave them the energy that they sorely needed.

It didn't take long for their thoughts to wander back to the matter at hand. Before they were ready to leave the wreckage behind, and before they even questioned the GPS holographic mapping devices, they had to find out what Chris had really discovered. Their leader drew them together in an open corner of the field; he appeared to be carrying some form of document. It turned out to be a folder, and when Jennifer saw it, she recognised it immediately.

"Chris, what are you doing?" she said worriedly, looking from the soldier's face to the document and back again.

"Don't pretend you don't know what's inside," the Staff Sergeant replied, as Ewan and Thomas looked on in confusion.

"He's going to sing us a song." Thomas smiled sarcastically, trying to bring a little light-heartedness to the situation. Chris scowled at him opened the folder. Quickly he sifted through the papers until he found what he wanted. It was a small black book. Jennifer looked immediately confused.

"I found this," Chris began, clearing his throat so as to be heard clearly, "when I was clearing our belongings from the wreckage. Many of Jennifer's things had spilled out all over the cabin and among her papers, notes and sheet music, I found this book." Ewan moved forwards, interested now in what Chris was going to reveal about the girl he'd fallen for.

There was a moment's pause before his friend opened the book at the middle. "It's full of secret codes and intelligence about the enemy. The book is false and in the middle it houses a secret screen."

Jennifer was suddenly as white as a sheet; Ewan rushed forwards to embrace her, and then took a few steps back as he caught his comrade's expressions. They were shocked, appalled even, particularly Thomas, who could not understand at first what Chris was trying to say.

"But … but," Jennifer began, she herself unable even to believe it. "I told them no … I … I said I wanted nothing to do with it." Her voice was weak, it sounded so far away.

"It certainly looks that way to me," Chris replied simply. His words cut like knives.

"Jennifer," Ewan said quietly, unable to look at the girl's face. "Jennifer…" It was more than he could take and, walking away from the group, he struggled to take in the thought of his love being deceptive. The shock was visible on everyone's faces, for this gave a whole new meaning to their mission and indeed their lives.

"I don't know what else to say," Chris said hoarsely, as the book was passed from person to person. There was no denying it, inside was a small computer screen which housed a world of secret intelligence. "When I found it, it led me to question our whole purpose. Were we even meant to survive?"

"I don't think so," Jennifer whispered. "I bet he had it all planned out. He wanted us out of the picture."

"But how do you know that," Thomas said, disgusted. "How do we know you were not in on the whole thing and that somehow you were meant to get out alive?" The Forces' Sweetheart swallowed, her face still pale.

"Chris, Thomas, I had nothing to do with this. Months ago, a government official approached my manager to ask if I would be willing to carry documents on a secret mission. It was a stupid idea, my manager wanted me to do it, but I refused straight away. I simply can't do the whole dangerous thing, it's not me." Somehow telling the truth in this way was the hardest thing she had ever done.

"Yeah, nice cover-up," Thomas continued. He hadn't believed a word that she said. Chris remained silent, perhaps thinking through the whole situation.

"They pursued me for weeks," Jennifer said finally, her head was bowed in embarrassment. "I kept telling them no, but they just wouldn't stop. They were asking me even on the night before we left, but there was no way I could have accepted. If I was in on the idea, then why would they have placed me on the plane?"

"She's right, guys." This time the voice was different, as Corporal Ewan Roberts returned to the group with a profound vision. "She was telling me this when I was in her dressing room..." Chris was now ready to respond.

"If Ewan says it's true, then we can't doubt his word, whatever our personal convictions." Jennifer breathed deeply, as if a great weight had been lifted off her shoulders, and she embraced the Corporal who had protected her through chance and mutual understanding.

"What it means, though," Chris continued, "is that someone wanted to kill us, or more to the point wanted to destroy the secret documents at any cost. I believe the only person who would know enough to do such a thing is Colonel Smith."

"But why would he kill us if he's on our side, I mean the intelligence is United..." Ewan found it hard to believe their colonel could do such a thing.

"I must admit," Chris mused, "that confused me. But whatever intention the Colonel had, there is no denying that he was the one to place us on the jet, he pushed through the deployment and then okayed Jennifer's position alongside us, perhaps to incriminate her." Ewan had to admit his friend's notion was well thought out.

"We've got to get... to get... to get out of here," Thomas stuttered, the only valuable thing his brain could manage to deliver.

"Yes, and we must keep the intelligence away from the enemy at all costs," Jennifer added.

"You're both right." Chris took the lead again, for this was all he knew how to do. "If this is what he planned to happen, then it's likely no one will have informed the French authorities about the crash. But I bet there were plenty of onlookers." Chris was panicking now. He didn't want to be seen. He didn't want to be hauled into the British Embassy and made to explain something that he did not understand. They needed to make a run for it, leave now, and never look back. "It's probably best if we remain oblivious to the fact that Jennifer is carrying the device. Leave things exactly as they were supposed to be and act surprised when the item is eventually found. That way we will, individually, remain as safe as possible." Ewan didn't like the fact that Jennifer might be in danger if they were captured, but there was little he could do about it now.

Picking up a GPS holographic map from the ground at his feet, he studied the position in which the jet had fallen. The screen was cracked in several places, and many of the controls were inoperable, but it gave them an idea of their location. Of course, the biggest problem was that it was standard protocol to remove the location of barracks or any buildings or locations relating to the armed forces. Both the United and Reformed Armies were wary of the fact that such devices might stray into the wrong hands. From here the group of four needed to find the nearest barracks, and with none positioned on the map, although they knew one must be close, it would be that much harder. They may have crashed completely off target, but it was all they could do, and the map clearly showed a little village further to the east and a road stretching to the south. Now they all knew the jet was heading south when it started to lose altitude, so that direction might just lead them closer to the French barracks.

"What we will do," Chris spoke loudly and clearly, "is split into pairs and take two different compass directions. Thomas and I will head south along the road until we find civilians to ask directions to the nearest army barracks, while Ewan and Jennifer can head east and try to locate the village pinpointed on this map." They each nodded their heads in turn, and shook hands as a form of agreement.

"But how will we keep in contact?" Thomas questioned, his normal speech now returning as he calmed down. This time Ewan fielded the question. Chris smiled.

"Well, when me and Jennifer reach the village we'll wait for you to contact us. The barracks will surely have outposts in the nearby villages and you can use those to give us directions. By splitting up like this, we double the chance that we will find civilisation."

"Unfortunately," Thomas said, again it was sarcastically, "these GPS holographic maps will be no help at all. This one's frozen and the other three were destroyed in the crash."

"Well, we'll just have to make do then, won't we," Chris replied. "Don't leave the village, Ewan, or if you do, always return," he said simply. The other soldier nodded again and pulled Jennifer closer. There was no doubt in his mind, splitting into pairs was the only option, but it didn't stem the worry about what was to come.

Before they left they needed to share out provisions and create a plan. They watched in amazement as Chris produced a variety of personal items. He had found his penknife and it had since done him good service chopping off bark and freeing their torn backpacks. Jennifer was stunned to be handed her own signed photographs in their original plastic casing, while Ewan and Thomas were delighted when their own personal items were produced before their eyes. These reminders of home would make the coming journey more bearable.

Soon possessions, rations and equipment had been divided between them. By midday, when the sun was at its high, they were ready. Their uniforms had survived the impact surprisingly well, while Jennifer was now wearing jeans under a skirt which had been cut to stop it trailing along the ground. Over her shoulders, she had created a shawl from one of the unused backpacks. It was rough on the skin, but it kept her warm. All in all they looked a strange group, standing in the far corner of a French field, close to the wreckage of their transport.

But their minds were sharp and their hearts strong. Soon Chris and Thomas were pacing away towards a gap in the hedge at the field boundary. Quick goodbyes were always the best, it left no time for sadness or remorse. Chris had become adept in the art of quick goodbyes.

Jennifer and Ewan, however, were not the same. They stood beside the oak tree and watched the others go. They stayed there together, rooted to the spot, until Chris and Thomas had disappeared from sight. Then, taking each other's hands and turning away from the wreckage, they began that long journey towards the hope that lay beyond the furthest hills.

11

Even with the best of navigation skills, the toughest of soldiers can find themselves lost in some foreign field, amongst foreign trees and on foreign soil. This was the situation that Chris and Thomas had been battling for several hours. At first, Chris believed that they could do no wrong on their expedition, for if they followed the road to its end he was sure they would soon find civilisation. But he had been wrong. The road had led them round twisting corners, narrow bends, through fertile farmland and past a deep patch of dark forest. But they had found no form of human life.

In fact, it was only on the third day of their journey, after spending two uncomfortable nights sleeping under hedgerows, that Thomas noticed a few scattered dwellings on the horizon. They had just passed out into the open, when a small cottage and a dilapidated barn became visible. They didn't seem to be that far in the distance; maybe they could reach the buildings before the day was out?

Perhaps it was the thought of a huge leap forwards that spurred them on, or that they might now find a little direction in this strange world, whatever it was, the pace of the two, walking across the deep green fields, increased considerably.

An hour went by, and then another and slowly the buildings got closer. Now they could almost see the flakes of paint falling from the front door.

"If we can just get to that cottage," Chris called to Thomas, who was trundling on a few metres behind while trying fruitlessly to dodge every rabbit hole, "they might be able to give us directions to the French barracks." Although the ground became more and more boggy, and the grass grew taller, they made steady progress and soon the comrades came upon a large and prickly bramble hedge that marked the field boundary.

"How are we going to pass through?" Thomas questioned, quickly looking right and then left as if watching a tennis rally. From his point of view there was no way ahead.

"There's a solution to every problem," Chris answered. He appeared unfazed, and was not even that tired from their long days of walking. He showed no visible signs of fatigue.

Taking his penknife from the pocket of his rucksack and flicking the blade so that it sparkled in the sunlight of the late afternoon, Chris Aston began to cut away at the brambles and thorns that faced him. He was pleasantly surprised to find how easily they fell away, for most of them were dead to begin with.

It didn't take long to hack a clear pathway, although by no means an easy job, and by the time he was through, thorns had cut into the palms of his hands. But he could see the ditch below and he knew they could easily jump across it, passing their rucksacks on afterwards. Hedge negotiated, they stood in the cottage garden and immediately saw that the building might be deserted. Grass had grown to knee height through the gravel, while the branches of trees grew thick against the windows and flowers drooped down towards the ground the last of the light sucked by the weeds above. But they had come this far and they were not going to return without knocking at the front door.

Chris rapped hard three times. For a long moment there was no answer, and they were about to turn away when a voice called out from within.

"'ello." It was a surprisingly deep voice with a thick French accent. "Who eez there?" Thomas heard the latch and the lock, but he didn't think for a moment there might be any sort of danger lurking there behind.

The door opened inwards with an eerie creak and there stood an ageing man with a thick grey beard and deep-set eyes. At his feet growled an angry bulldog for whom the open door was a release. Immediately the creature bounded forwards, a look of evil across its features, but it only jumped at them in turn, leaving dusty pawprints all across their tattered trousers.

The man looked at them without care. His eyes were hard and filled with malice, a cold and uninviting stare. He spoke through gritted teeth; his lips were almost completely closed. "What eez it zat you want?" The man addressed Chris eye to eye, while Thomas tried in vain to prise the bulldog away from his sore feet. "This eez private property," he continued. "And you are trespassing on my land."

Chris took each and every situation in his stride, and this was no exception. He realised there was something familiar behind the glaze of the old man's stare. He saw the same emptiness, the same sadness that he had only witnessed in the eyes of his fellows. This was familiar; and any sense of worry evaporated.

"Were you a soldier?" he asked bluntly, hoping not for a reaction, but simply some form of recognition. Thomas was intrigued by his friend's tact. He stood there waiting for the man to reply, wondering where the situation would take them next.

The man in the doorway, who before seemed so hard and bitter in his approach, withdrew a little.

He did not understand how the young man knew, but surely there was no point in denying it? Eventually the expected response would arrive.

"I… I…" he began, stuttering over the words. "… 'ow do you know?" Chris pondered over the question.

"Well, when you have been through it," he began, never drawing his eyes away, "when you have fought for that cause and endured far worse than unspeakable pain, you begin to develop a sense, about others who have done the same."

Thomas looked at his friend for a moment and wondered how he could have felt such things. Yes, they had fought alongside each other, but he had no such sense; he continued because he had to, because it was his duty. "In the eyes," Chris continued, realising that it only made sense in his own mind. "It's in the eyes that you can see it, some unbearable pain and emptiness that you will know if you have lived through it. It sounds silly, but it's really as simple as that."

The man smiled, his face warming with that simple movement of his lips, and slowly he reached out a hand in greeting. His guard had dropped; they had passed the threshold that was his emptiness.

"I am Lieutenant Jacques Beauchamp, third division en ze French Infanterie de Marine, I mean light infantry," the man said. "It's been a long time, and I 'ave a tendency to forget things."

"It comes as a matter of course," Chris replied, taking in the derelict cottage and its surroundings.

"Oui, well you got to learn to live with eet. But I can keep zis little place in good order, and myself too."

Thomas stared at the lieutenant. Chris shot him a glance, and Thomas shrugged his shoulders. Maybe this man was mentally unstable, he wasn't getting involved. Turning away from the others, Thomas kicked the dusty ground with the toe of his boot and wondered how they had ever got so desperate that they needed to ask an old soldier with obvious mental scars for shelter and directions.

"Have you no family, Monsieur Beauchamp?" Chris asked, hoping to help alleviate his squalid conditions.

"Non, zey 'ave all passed on, or left. It eez just me 'ere and ze dog for company, just as I like it."

"We're looking for the nearest army barracks," Thomas interrupted. The smile fell from the lieutenant's face and he drew a little further back into the cottage.

"Oui… Oui… well I should 'ave known zat you were. Zey are around 'ere, just over ze 'ills, you're not far at all. But I 'aven't been down zere in many years."

"We knew we were close," Chris responded quickly, so as to stop Thomas from ruining the situation any further. "It's just that we are tired from walking and we really wanted somewhere to rest for the night before continuing." He felt he had to rectify the situation, set it out simply.

"Ah, well," the old man began again. "I can 'elp you with zat. If you keep eet to yourself zat I am 'ere, I 'ave food inside ze cottage and room for you to sleep through ze long night ahead. It eez nothing much but you are soldiers, of my own breed and I will do all I can to 'elp. There eez an old phone line in ze cottage, I shall ring ahead and warn of your arrival. But eef they start to ask questions, you must keep quiet."

"If you want it that way," Chris said. He watched the lieutenant move from the doorway and followed him into the cottage, "we will never speak again of your generosity." Thomas had a funny look on his face, but he followed obediently, shutting the door behind him and leaving the bulldog barking on the other side.

"Zat may be," the lieutenant warned as he led the way through tiny rooms where plaster crumbled from the walls and old newspapers were piled to the ceiling. It was no more than Chris and Thomas were expecting. "I will give you some advice. Be careful, keep your back covered, and never trust anyone. Ze life of a soldier is a dangerous one. If you want to save yourself you may 'ave to sacrifice someone else, eet eez ze way of ze world and I know it."

For a long time afterwards, Chris wondered about those words. They rang around and around in his head like a prophecy, which was stupid because he had heard it all before, many times. But this was different; now it felt real and raw, after all they had been through there was still a real chance that one of them might die. Battles could be just around the corner, and the best that they could hope for, again, was survival. These were dangerous thoughts too, so Chris tried to place them in the back of his mind, lock them away and concentrate on getting a good night's sleep, something he had missed in the long days before. It would be a welcome escape, a positive distraction, and he would lose himself in it.

* * *

Time spent lost between one rolling green hill and the next can easily cause confusion after walking continuously for several days, sleeping under the stars with only the hedgerows for company.

The journey north, for that was the direction in which they believed they were heading, led Ewan and Jennifer down towards the bank of a river at the bottom of a cornfield. There, the water was cool and clear. They could see stones on the bottom and tadpoles swam silently between the reeds. It was peaceful, and like a lot of rural France, sandwiched between the green of the hills and the field crops. Very often the pair had found themselves walking for hours across the same terrain, so that it seemed as though they were getting nowhere at all. This was when they thought about the others. Time and again they wondered if they had made it to a military base.

The ripples in the water reflected the light from the sun, high on its journey towards noon, and Ewan took a moment to focus upon the woman lying beside him.

"Are we ever going to find the village?" he asked in frustration, his eyes now meeting with the striking blue glow of Jennifer's own. She too was frustrated with their progress, and it was merely by reading her expression that he realised they both knew it might be some time yet before they discovered a direct route to the promised location.

"We've been walking for three days, Ewan," his partner spoke with a little caution in her voice. "If we don't find it soon, then we've been walking around in circles. We've got this map, but all that's done so far is send us in a general direction and the nights sky is never clear enough for you to even try and read the stars!" They thought on the same wave-length. Another thing that they had in common.

"But finding this river has got to be a good sign," Ewan remarked, taking her hand and dropping it playfully into the cool water. "If we follow the path of the river, then we'll eventually find civilisation. And if we come across a road, then that's even better."

Jennifer leaned over and kissed his forehead; it was her reassurance. What else could she do? Ultimately she knew he was right, but it was so difficult to take in; the sudden change from her city life and his youthful exuberance scared her. That morning they had eaten some dried fruit and drank the last of their instant hot chocolate. It was not enough. It didn't set you up for a day's heavy trekking and she knew as well as Ewan, that it couldn't go on this way for much longer. Jennifer was almost too tired to think.

"I suppose we can give it one more push," she whispered in his ear, bowing to his wishes. "If we follow the river until it reaches a road then we should be okay. But we need to find shelter today, for food and for a good night's sleep, if nothing else."

Ewan looked up again and saw the comfort in her face. "I'm glad you agree, because I trust you. But this place, it's just so beautiful. It draws you in."

"You're tired, Ewan. We both need a decent night's rest, and I'm afraid we'll never get that until we reach the village," Jennifer finished and locked hands with him. They were in this together and would be until the end. The soldier nodded again. She was right. She was usually right, and she had been his rock since they'd left camp days and nights earlier. Where would he be without her? Such a strong woman and here he was being a coward. A soldier should be born to lead, he should take charge. But in their current situation, he found he just couldn't do it.

On the opposite bank tall grasses grew that provided cover for the pair as they walked. Each small step was tiring and the river meandered first left and then right so that it felt as though they were never moving forwards at all. But in time the grasses petered out and the flow of the river began to slow. They passed an ox-bow lake, where the river had cut through the fields and left a curve of water clear and still. They drank, and rested for a short while, trying to conserve what little energy remained.

As they again trudged wearily on, following yet another meander in the river's path, they passed a rickety wooden bridge, a simple way to cross from one bank to another, and as they walked further still, field after field of grazing sheep and resting cows. Cows lay down when it is going to rain, but for Jennifer and Ewan, two lonely travellers, the indicator went unnoticed and their pace slowed yet again.

Rounding the next corner and almost ready to give up, a familiar sight met their eyes. It was one which convinced them there was still hope and reminded them of the glory of home. Along a dirt track and towards a small brick bridge, which they could just make out in the distance, trundled a rusty red tractor. Big on its wheels, it appeared to be moving at a very slow speed, which meant that they just might be able to catch up with it.

Ewan was suddenly filled with a new burst of energy, which propelled him forwards. Here was a glimmer of hope and he was going to grasp it with both hands.

"Come on, Jennifer," he smiled, dropping his heavy rucksack at his feet. "This is our chance." Jennifer followed suit, their belongings and what had been their lifeline for so many days lay discarded at the water's edge and together they set off at a jog towards the little stone bridge.

Although they were tired beyond belief, their exhaustion did not show. They knew that if they didn't reach this trundling tractor, it could be the end. They might never escape the fields of France. Together they ran down towards the little bridge, waving their arms in the air hoping that the driver would see them.

Their prayers were answered, as the tractor slowed and before long, came to a complete stop.

Ewan could not contain himself when the cab door opened and a tall, dark- haired man jumped down from the seat.

Jennifer noted how dashing he looked, but shelved the thought immediately.

"'ello," the man beamed, neither worried nor scared of the approaching strangers. "Quoi? What are you doing 'ere?" Realising these were not French natives, the farmer drew upon the very little English he knew, and it was then that he noticed Jennifer. She had to be the most beautiful girl he had ever seen. Scrambling from the riverbank and up the grass verge, she was finding the going difficult. "Mon dieu! …you look so, très malade … ill. What 'appened to you?"

"We have no time to explain," Ewan said in a slow and emphasised response, bringing up the rear and finally joining the conversation at Jennifer's side. "But we could do with your help." He felt a little worried about being so blunt with this Good Samaritan, but it would be useless to waffle when they needed help so badly.

"Well, I can ze you need 'elp, mon ami… especially when such a, belle fille, looks so tired and pale." Jennifer was strangely pleased to have new male attention; it reminded her of Miss Marmalade's professional life. Her head told her to flirt with the man to get what they wanted, yet her heart made sure that she stayed true to her loving companion. "Eef you don't mind me asking, where are you 'eading?"

"Well, we were…" Jennifer broke in without a second thought before being queried by a very cautious glance from her companion. "…needing to get to the nearest village, yes. We're actually looking for the French barracks which we've been told are located in this area."

The farmer smiled and leaned against his tractor. "Well ze good news is I can 'elp you… I mean to say… eet iz not exceptional to ze un militaire walking through ze fields with such a magnifique jeune femme… beautiful woman… now eez it? No?" It appeared the farmer was playing a game, trying to work out exactly what the two travellers were up to.

"I'm afraid the information is confidential. I'm sure you understand," Ewan said matter-of-factly.

"Je vois," the farmer replied, raising his eyebrows. "But when I zink something strange eez going on… When you 'ave been travelling as long as eet appears you 'ave, zen I zink you need to give me a little more … information."

Ewan was flummoxed. Once again the opposition had got the better of him, and as he looked from Jennifer to the farmer and back again, he realised that neither of them was very pleased. "I tell you what I'll do," the farmer began again, taking Jennifer by the hand and leading her towards the cab,

"I will take you to ze village, but from zere you are on your own. I do not know vat you are doing, garçon… but you 'ad better make sure you look after zis belle fille, because I never could resist such a beautiful face."

Ewan fell completely silent for the first time that afternoon. There was nothing else worth saying and it was foolish to waste his energy trying. Quickly he nodded and looked around them. They were in the middle of nowhere, surrounded by fields; the nearest village could be miles away. They had no chance of reaching it on foot before sundown, and Ewan was forced to admit he had been wrong.

"Okay," he murmured almost inaudibly as the farmer smiled and opened the cab door, helping Jennifer to climb inside. Then, he jumped down from the road to the riverbank and headed off in the direction of their waiting belongings, leaving Ewan to follow behind, slow and tired, while Jennifer giggled inside the cab, realising just how eventful their little journey had become.

12

At the end of a long dusty track which led through the middle of the village was a large old farmhouse built from local red brick. It had large bay windows on the front which looked out over the main street and small windows at the back from which there was a view of the pasture that lay behind. The paint was peeling off the walls and the cement between the brickwork was speckled with tiny air holes. There was an old wooden gate at the front of the yard, and behind it a small black and white collie dog padded up and down, keeping watch on all who passed by.

This was very much a working farm. A mile up the road, the cows were grazing in the fertile fields while piglets squealed at their sty door and waited for their mother to feed them. Inside the house, traditional cheeses were produced in the dairy, while meat was cured in the pantry. The farmer himself was a middle-aged man of perhaps fifty years, with a balding head. He wore the same blue overalls and flat cap all year round. He was well known in the village and spent many an evening in the local café. The main focus of the villagers' attention, however, were the farmer's twin daughters.

Renée and Belle were stunning young women, well-educated and destined to go far. Both were extraordinarily talented singers and they longed to be trained, but on their father's small income it had never been possible. The girls didn't let this get in their way, though, and with their earnings they would venture together into the city to keep track of the changes in fashion and adapt accordingly. The girls voices, auburn hair and flirtatious humour, made them irresistible to the local boys. Their father, however, kept an eye on his daughters for he didn't want to find them compromised by one of the many farm labourers; he had husbands already in mind for his girls.

Jonathan and Andrew occupied the large manor house further along the country lane and prided themselves on being directly descended from the French royal family. Although the family's power had been relinquished a century before, it didn't matter, everyone knew their history and respected it. The aristocratic young men couldn't resist the twin sisters' charm or beauty, and before long they had been besotted.

On a bright afternoon in the middle of the previous summer, when the farmer had been employed on the land at the back of the manor house, he'd noticed how the boys felt. The farmer saw an opportunity to secure his family's future and within a matter of days, two weddings had been arranged for the following year. Jonathan and Andrew had accepted the proposal immediately, but little did they, or the farmer, know that as the month of the wedding drew nearer, events would unfold that would prevent the loveless marriages arranged by their father and change the twins' lives for ever.

Dusk was beginning to settle as Belle Lavètte made her way back up the dirt track that led to the farm. Her long auburn hair was hooked back into a ponytail and as she passed by the window of the village café she pouted and admired her reflection in the glass. Belle looked somewhat flushed, though, as if she had had a close encounter. It was true that she had discovered something very interesting, and she couldn't wait to tell Renée about it.

The gates of the farmyard grew closer by the second, and in her excitement Belle ran the final few metres up the stone pathway. She found the front door open as usual and from the pantry wafted the smells of traditional French bread, made freshly that morning. Belle bounded into the kitchen and called out her sister's name several times over. Their father was still out in the field and there was no chance that they might be overheard.

"Renée, Renée!" She shouted, as her sister padded lightly down the hallway. Renée appeared before Belle in a short white dress fastened with a belt around the waist and finished with tiny golden sunflowers embroidered at the edges. She was a picture of beauty. "Renée, Renée. You will never guess what I 'ave discovered!" Belle was grinning from ear to ear.

"No," her sister replied, taking little or no interest in what was being said. "Let me guess. You have found another set of love birds cavorting in our barn, no?"

"No," Belle replied even more impatiently this time.

"That was this afternoon, and besides, I couldn't see who they were, just dark figures huddled close. But now… now, I think I worked out who it was. I found this – t-shirt, ripped up." Belle reached for her satchel and pulled out the remnants of a pink-and-blue stripy vest top. She looked pleased with herself. "Renée, there has been someone down there and I am the one who found out about it."

"And what's it got to do with us?" Renée pondered the question carefully while playfully twirling strands of her golden hair between her fingers. "They are only getting a bit of what everyone wants, no?"

"But on the way back," Belle protested again, "I was thinking about this emblem I saw on a bag in the barn… it must be his… and I knew I remembered it… the United Army is red, white and blue… he is a British soldier, Renée … fancy that, a British soldier in our little village, eh? And… And, the girl with him … she was the prettiest girl I have ever seen."

"I thought you said it was dark, no?"

"Oh… well… well," Belle was jumping up and down frantically trying again to reach into her satchel. "He must have dropped this when he was climbing the ladder into the loft. You will see what I mean!" She handed her sister a torn photograph of a beautiful young woman. Renée sighed and looked towards the far end of the room.

"He is taken then and she is beautiful, little point in trying."

"No, no. Wait, there is more…" Belle just couldn't control herself. "I was thinking that he cannot stay in our barn forever. So we have the right to go and tell him… And… And…" Belle moved closer to her twin sister, whispered in her ear and they both giggled uncontrollably.

"More soldiers, eh? Oh, Belle, you are not as silly as you seem… If there are more, then we are very lucky girls. We have to go and tell him right now." Belle looked deep into her sister's bright blue eyes and was glad that she understood.

"It is a good job that I came to get my sister, she always knows what is the best thing to do."

* * *

In amongst the hay it was easy to forget everything other than the relationship between two people who just happen to be in the same place at the same time. For Ewan and Jennifer, their relationship was never official. It merely grew over time into something both of them wanted, but neither would admit to. It was never planned for them to bed down amongst the rafters of a hay barn, but fate intervened and they found themselves diverting to a path on which they never set out.

The previous afternoon, for it was getting late even before Ewan and Jennifer had been discovered at the roadside, the farmer in the rusty red tractor had entered the village by the church and trundled down towards the centre of the village. There was no denying it, this village was certainly quaint. The buildings were held together with large stone pieces and striking wooden beams which adorned the exteriors. Both Ewan and Jennifer noticed that in this community everyone was friendly, for people waved and smiled at the farmer as he passed by.

They soon reached the centre, and as the little red tractor slowed to a stop Ewan jumped down and looked around. There was no obvious choice of direction, so they would simply have to go on their instincts. For a while they wandered through the backstreets hand in hand, but as the evening began to fall they realised that they needed somewhere to rest for the night. They had considered several locations in passing, but many of them seemed, at best, rudimentary. In fact, the real solution, a small hay barn at the top of an overgrown path, could easily be considered the best of a bad bunch. It looked watertight, warm and provided privacy from the outside world. This was something they could only have dreamed about during the cold nights they had spent since leaving the crash site, which seemed a lifetime ago.

Together, they dragged their belongings off the road, their bags heavy at their feet, before climbing rickety ladder to the hayloft. There behind some old barrels which Ewan guessed were full of wine, Jennifer found a pile of old sacks which they could use as a blanket, and she began to create a makeshift bed amongst the hay.

They slept far better than they imagined they would, waking from a dreamy daze when the sun was already high in the sky. It was not surprising, given they had endured many sleepless nights, and Ewan could not resist the tempting smile on Jennifer's face which drew him back to her side. Soon after they had awoken he had felt compelled to check that the coast was still clear. But her hand on his, reminded him that such necessities were really not as important as they first appeared.

At some point, Ewan must have woken again for a few moments. He was still half-asleep, yet he noticed two important things. The first was Jennifer's arm resting right across his body, her long hair tickling his cheek, and the second was a pair of eyes squinting up at him from the dark below. Surely it was just a hallucination and his quick retreat to the realms of sleep forced him to dismiss it. But he was wrong, silly even. For as his eyes fell shut once more, he instinctively drew in close to the woman lying beside him.

The eyes which had surveyed the sleeping man turned into a tall and tanned figure with auburn hair. She tiptoed towards the ladder and climbed up as quietly as a mouse. Peering over the top of the hayloft she saw two people lying in the hay, covered sparingly by the old sacks. This was all that the girl needed and she slid back down the ladder and skipped towards the doorway, no longer caring if the couple above were to awake and discover their visitor.

* * *

Ewan was woken with a start. Sure that someone was shaking him roughly back to the real world, when he opened his eyes he was shocked to find two giggling faces staring down at him. It took several seconds for him to grasp the situation, but when he did, he realised its consequences. He didn't know who these girls were but he had to get rid of them before they woke Jennifer and they both had to face the consequences that came from sleeping together in a farmer's hay barn.

"Hi," Ewan yawned, still dazed by the situation. The girls smiled sweetly, replicas of each other. Twins! "...Erm, I know this isn't the best situation in the world... but can you just... erm... wait down the ladder for me?"

"No," both girls replied together, their smiles not faltering for a moment.

"No?" Ewan queried, suddenly finding himself blushing uncontrollably.

"We want something from you," the first of the girls said simply, placing her hand on Ewan's shoulder and turning to her sister. "What are you going to give us in return for making use of our barn?"

Ewan found the situation embarrassing, and it didn't help matters when Jennifer began to stir next to him. "Look," he whispered through gritted teeth, pulling up the old sack. "I can make it up to you – we just needed somewhere to stay for one night – and maybe you can help us as well." The twins thought about this for a moment.

"Oui," they replied in unison and Ewan wondered if they were constantly going to talk like this, "but only if you promise, and I think we 'ave given you quite enough already, no?" Then the twin on the left whispered something to the other and slowly they began to back away towards the ladder. They were only halfway down, when one of them shouted up again.

"Oh, and by ze way, we 'ave found your little picture and your girlfriend's ripped-up t-shirt. Zey must 'ave fallen out of your bag, a pity, no?" Both twins giggled uncontrollably again at this last remark, before jumping down from the ladder.

Ewan looked around the hayloft and considered his options. There was no way to avoid the twins, and in any other circumstances he wouldn't have minded in the least. But their current situation was embarrassing, and these auburn girls had a point; he was once again in the wrong. Beside him, Jennifer turned in a sleepy stupor, now almost awake. Her beautiful blue eyes opened slowly, and her golden hair fell across her face. She was the picture of innocence here amongst the hay. She rolled over under the covers and looked up at her companion and only then did she realise something was terribly wrong. Ewan was sitting bolt upright, his eyes darting around the barn before finally meeting her own gaze.

"What's wrong?" she whispered, reaching for his hand and yawning.

"Jennifer…" he began, before thinking about what he was going to say. "…Jennifer, there are people here. The people who own the barn…"

"What do you mean… how did they know we were here?" Ewan thought about this for a moment although he hadn't even considered how the twins had found them, it seemed less than important.

"I don't know Jennifer, but they did. I just woke up and they were there. It's embarrassing, for them to see us like this. But I managed to convince them to wait down below until I had warned you."

"Oh," Jennifer replied, pulling the sack tighter around her body, clearly nervous. "Well, I guess we need to go down and see them." Ewan nodded, still a little stunned, and reached behind the nearest barrel. His hand fell against a pile of soft material, and he was relieved that the girls had not taken their clothes and hidden them. That would have been the icing on the cake.

Both of them dressed in silence, assessing the situation. Love can overpower rational thinking, but where else were they expected to sleep the night? Ewan jumped down the ladder first, and stood opposite the twins. He didn't say anything. He didn't want to. In the half light of the barn he merely looked at their attractive faces and wondered about them.

When a sleepy Jennifer dropped down from the ladder moments later and stood beside her strong-willed companion, the twins began to giggle again. Her hair was a mess and she wore no make-up, but she was still as pretty as the picture Belle Lavètte clutched tightly in her hands.

"So, who are you?" she began, first addressing Jennifer, before motioning to her sister who moved to stand beside Ewan. "You 'ave got to be very important to 'ave a stack of signed photos ready to 'and out to ze first soldier willing to 'and 'imself over to you."

Ewan immediately felt guilty and his face flushed with embarrassment. Renée Lavètte was not a silly girl and the moment she noticed his discomfort, she placed an arm around his waist and drew their bodies closer.

"I'm Miss…" Jennifer began, sensing she had no alternative other than to reveal her true identity to these girls.

"No, Jennifer," Ewan interjected, blocking her words escaping. Belle turned to look and Renée raised her eyebrows in surprise.

"Now, now, silly soldier boys 'ave to be punished." She smiled knowingly, turning her head so that she was eye to eye with him, before grabbing his face and kissing his lips. It was a long-lasting kiss. "Mmm," she grinned, her eyelashes dancing before him. "Does she kiss you like zis, soldier boy?"

Jennifer wasn't having any of it, these girls were cheeky, and she would stand her ground.

"Look, I'm Miss Marmalade," she sighed, watching as Ewan's face fell. "And this is Ewan Roberts. He is a soldier in the United Army based at the Thames Regimental Barracks in London. We're nothing special."

The twins gasped, seeing this was perhaps a big mistake. "You mean to zay zat you are ze Mademoiselle Marmaláde?" Belle shrieked, looking again at the photo. "You know, I would never 'ave guessed zat."

"Yeah, well now you know," Jennifer replied simply.

"And if you don't mind, I'd prefer it if you'd remove your clammy little hands from my man." She was almost glaring at the beautiful Renée, who by now had dropped to sit by Ewan's side, equally returning her dangerous stare.

"Look, it was an easy mistake to make," Ewan said, realising he had to do something to ease the tension building between the three women around him.

"We never even noticed at all," Belle said blankly, "and, well, we wanted to make you feel zat little bit maladroit, awkward, about sleeping in our barn. We come 'ere when we want to escape from Papa and we never dreamed zat anyone else would use eet." This was an obvious lie, yet it sounded wholly convincing.

Jennifer faltered for a moment and noticed a chink of light seeping in from the dusty window. It must be so warm outside, and she almost wished they could be sitting together in the sun. She longed to be back with the others, with Chris who would look after them and Thomas who could make her laugh, while she and Ewan fell passionately in love. Playing the bad cop took her way out of her depth.

Ewan wanted to escape, to take Jennifer and run, but of course he couldn't. They had spent too many nights alone, and it was important they reached the French barracks in the next few days. Don't leave the village, Ewan, Chris had said the last time that they were all together. But surely things had changed now? Was it still possible to stay here? The girls might be bad, but they could also be fragile, broken even, and that could be their ticket to freedom.

The whole barn shook with a rumbling vibration that woke Ewan from his daydream. He saw the more talkative of the twins disappear through the open barn doors, and the next thing he knew she was calling back to them.

"Belle, Belle eet iz Papa, we 'ave to 'ide from 'im." Her sister's reaction was immediate. Grabbing Jennifer by the arm, a look of terror across her face, she ran towards the doors, leaving Ewan to reach for their backpacks and follow suit. Outside Ewan saw the root of their problem. At the far end of the track a middle-aged man wearing a flat cap was approaching on a rickety old tractor that made deep tracks in the soft earth. Perched on the footwell was a grey-haired sheep dog, and sticking out of the trailer behind was a dangerous-looking pitchfork.

Belle whispered something in Ewan's ear that he couldn't understand. She urged them past the barn and towards a gated field that neither Ewan nor Jennifer had noticed. Here they jumped in turn through a gap in the hedge, not knowing what they would find on the other side, and prayed for their freedom.

They landed in a pile. There were stinging nettles and brambles all around them and the contents of their backpacks felt less than comfortable, but there was nothing they could do. Here they were hidden from view and, knowing this they waited until they heard the dilapidated tractor crunch back into gear, turn around in the track and head back to the village.

13

There is a pool of water high on a mountain which overlooks the valleys below. The mountain is not high. It forms part of a range that stretches round in a great circle. The views from the tallest peaks are spectacular, while the water from the pool is clear and clean.

Thomas was not at all surprised when, during the evening that followed their encounter with Lieutenant Beauchamp, Chris had suggested they should leave the old man after dawn the following morning.

That night they had taken refuge in a dark room at the back of the cottage. The walls were crumbling and there was a strong smell of damp. The ground was hard and they did not sleep well, but it was shelter and protection from the elements. Chris was not foolish, and if his experience had taught him anything, it was that Reformed skirmishers would search an area meticulously and with great caution, if there was a reason for them to do so. He continually worried that the alarm had been raised since their escape from the wreckage, and that someone knew they were missing. Thomas thought so too. He had been posted overseas with Chris several times in the last year and had studied his friend closely. He had learned that his comrade was always precise in his approach and that he preferred to work alone. Thomas often wondered if Chris was lonely, if this hard outer shell hid some emotion with which even Chris dared not do battle.

By the time morning really did arrive, the grass was wet with dew and the pair were far into their journey towards the French barracks. They had headed out past the cottage, covering the fields that lay beyond and walking up and down the hills that followed. For a while, the landscape was rich with vegetation. They avoided those places where crops had been set, but walked slowly through the pathways made in great towers of barley, glad of the cover it provided.

Time passed slowly for Chris and Thomas, as it had done on previous days, with only long periods of walking and no way of telling the time. They were left to chart the passage of the sun across the sky, noting when it reached the second quarter that afternoon had arrived. At lunch, they ate plentifully. It was not the best food, Lieutenant Beauchamp being no Michelin-star chef, but it filled the longing in the pit of their stomachs.

They gradually started to notice changes in the landscape. The fields gave way to rockier ground, and soon they came upon a huge drop in the land, the edge of a hill that led down towards a flat and barren plain. Beyond that, mountains rose up in the distance. As they made for the mountains they saw there were no tall peaks, snowy tops or rocky crevices. These were green and round in shape, looming up large above the empty plain. From where they stood, the drop seemed impossible, yet both men knew this was their only way forward, for there, nestled at the base of the green peaks, towards the middle of the plain, was a mass of square buildings arranged in an organised fashion. At last they had found their prize, and Chris had to give the French generals credit. The barracks were perfectly hidden.

They began the dangerous descent slowly, and after a period of gingerly climbing backwards down the steep slope, used the branches of trees for support and passed their rucksacks from one to the other, Chris Aston and Thomas Fisher finally reached the foot. From here the expanse of the plain loomed even larger than it had done from above and now they had to trek right across its length.

As they began to walk across the hard ground, the gates of the barracks loomed up before them, tall and black against the blue of the sky. The whole area was heavily fortified. Chris had guessed it would be, but what they hadn't realised was the extent of the fortifications. The metal fencing stretched far into the distance, both to the left and right, topped by thick coils of barbed wire. This fence was impossible to climb, lucky then that the soldiers did not have to.

The guard on duty at the front gates looked bored. He leaned heavily against a wooden post. For a while he remained in that position, unaware of the soldiers who were now making their way towards him. Chris and Thomas found this highly amusing, and when the guard finally saw their approach, they were surprised to see him stand bolt upright with his gun positioned over his right shoulder as he saluted.

"He knows we're soldiers, then," Chris whispered as they walked forwards. Thomas nodded in agreement and they both smiled. The French barracks may have looked impressive, but the soldiers appeared to be less so.

* * *

Five minutes later, through the first gate and past the officers' car park, Thomas was sent in one direction while Chris was shoe-horned into another, a young soldier leading the way. He felt no animosity about this; they must have split them by rank, he a staff sergeant and Thomas a mere private. In any case the old man had told the communications office their names and rank in advance. It was an informed decision.

Chris passed offices, bunk houses and then a cafeteria before reaching an open green space. Then the soldier who had been leading the way, saluted to Chris and headed off to the right. Chris felt sure he could get used to everyone saluting him, it made him feel important. Across the grass, there was an opening between two trees and through it he could see Thomas being introduced to other soldiers. They were kicking a football from one to another, and it didn't take long for Thomas to become involved. Chris smiled; at least his friend seemed happier now.

He decided that he needed to find the centre of activity. That way, he could enquire about Colonel Smith's French counterpart, the man in charge, and then, with that out of the way, he could begin to look for Ewan and Jennifer. He would keep his promise, that much was certain. Ahead of him the path ended at a muddy field and to the left there was a large concrete expanse, a parade ground. It would be silly to head back the way that he had come, so the best option appeared to be branching off to the right, in the same direction as his guide had disappeared.

At first his chosen route led ahead in a straight line, but soon more buildings appeared and Chris began to take time to look around him. The path was narrow and where there had been grass on either side of him there was now tarmac. Red-brick structures stretched out along the length of the pathway. These were the newer buildings; he could tell they had received considerable investment. They had large, double-glazed windows and blinds that hid whatever lay inside, while the door to each building had its own primary colour so that taken together a rainbow stretched out before him. Well, the French are famed for their artistic tendencies, Chris laughed as he contemplated the thought.

Now the new tarmac gave way to a gravelled path. Chris began to kick his heels, propelling small shards of stone across the grass. To his left he had reached the end of the smart buildings and was now greeted by a wire fence marked with a bold notice. He read it with interest and didn't notice as another person walked up behind him. He read:

Training Ground:
Grade IV Personnel only. Proceed only when accompanied by a registered professional.

Suddenly a cold hand caught the side of his neck and Chris thought for a moment that he was about to be throttled. He jumped round in surprise.

"Are you Staff Sergeant Aston?" The voice was low and deep, the kind Chris might have expected from a soldier who had undertaken many a dangerous mission.

"That's me," Chris replied hoarsely. He took on his dismissive tone and immediately went into defensive mode, looking the man up and down. He wore a uniform, just like his own, United forces. His hair was thick and black, and combed away from his face in a style that was popular in the 1930s. He had the French forces emblem pinned to his chest, and the United European Medal took pride of place on his top pocket. He looked sinister, and could have easily passed as a member of the old Italian Mafia.

"Well, Staff Sergeant Aston," the man breathed long and deep, "our soldier should have warned you not to stray." The man stopped for a moment, looked his prey up and down, and then added: "...especially into the private quarters."

Chris smiled uncomfortably where he stood and looked back up the alleyway between the buildings.

"I didn't know," he sighed finally, knowing better than to launch into an argument. "We are all soldiers here, and I thought I was left to get my bearings alone." The man's stare never faltered, and it hit Chris's and bore down to the root of his soul.

"Be that as it may," he wheezed, his voice dropping even deeper than Chris had thought possible. "I see it as taking liberties, considering you're a guest here. If you were under my command, I would be overseeing your discipline for the matter." Chris winced and leaned back against the wire fence, he was not used to this, someone questioning his authority. "But," the man finally looked away, glancing further down the alleyway, "the Major General thinks differently to me, and I have to respect his views. He asked me to come and find you, and to take you to his private quarters for a meeting. However, looking at the state of your uniform, Staff Sergeant, I think we had better make a diversion to the store room first." And with that the man paced off briskly back towards the crossroads, occasionally glancing over his shoulder to check Chris was still there, following like a dog on a lead, and soon enough both captor and prey disappeared around the corner and out of sight.

14

Behind the gate and hidden from view by the overgrown hedge, four young people sat, cut and bruised, on the slope of a hill. Together they had managed to escape the tangled brambles and stealth-like sting of the nettles, but they had fled in such earnest that they could never have made it out unscathed. Each had uttered a sigh of relief when they finally heard the rickety old tractor turn and head back towards the village. Ewan's mind was swimming.

"So, just run it past me again," he asked, moving his hands up and down his bruised legs. "Why are we actually doing any of this? What is it that your father has done?" Belle Lavètte winced and glanced at her sister; surely it was time to reveal the truth? This could be their escape.

She pulled a handful of grass from the hillside and began twirling it around in her fingers. Not looking up, she began to speak in a hushed and timid voice.

"Well, Papa, 'e 'as ze old fashioned values." Her voice was so different to how it had been only an hour earlier. "'E thinks zat we want ze same things as 'im and we will settle down and stay 'ere on ze farm." Belle stopped, and for a moment it looked as if tears were forming in her blue eyes. Jennifer sympathised with the story, yet she wondered how much the old farmer really knew of the world.

"It's like that wherever you go," the Forces' Sweetheart replied, placing her arm around the French teenager and gently brushing the hair from her eyes. "They come from a different generation, parents I mean, and it's hard for them to understand the things that we want. At some point you simply have to fly the nest–"

"But Papa," Renée butted in, staring straight at Jennifer as if she were the wisest woman in the world, "'e thinks 'e can plan our lives for us, when 'e does not know what is 'appening in ze world. I 'ave seen it, sometimes me and Belle, we stay up late at night and we watch ze news on ze television, we know what is 'appening to ze world."

Ewan felt it inside. So far the conversation had given him no reason to speak up, it wasn't his place to question. But war affects everyone, and sometimes you have to face up to the consequences and the facts of life.

"This war," he said, so suddenly and plainly that it sounded almost normal, "World War Three has been going on for four years, and there is no end in sight. What are we fighting for? Nothing. Merely the solution to a never-ending problem. Man has a desire for conflict…" Renée and Belle looked to the floor, they understood that it was happening, but they couldn't imagine how it might feel to be a part of it.

"Our papa," Renée sighed, tears falling, "'e wants us to get… se marier… married."

"But that's not so bad," Jennifer smiled, seeing the happiness that might enter the twins lives.

"No," Renée wept, tears falling faster now, "'e… 'e…'e 'as picked out an 'usband." There was silence for a moment, as each of them considered what had just been said.

"But what… why has he done that?" Jennifer asked, struggling to comprehend the situation.

"Surely you have your own minds, and you're more than old enough to make that decision for yourselves," Ewan chipped in, glad of the distraction from talking about the war.

"Oh, we are always telling 'im," Renée murmured her accent slipping into a deeper, thicker French. "But 'e never listens. 'E 'as always been ze same. 'E is overprotective."

"Eet iz because Mamma died when we were still so young," Belle continued emotionlessly. "'E thinks we need 'is protection and guidance."

"Well you probably do need protection," Ewan muttered, shrugging, "but for a completely different reason." Renée smiled for a moment, looking far into the distance. She moved her body in closer to the soldier, finally resting her hand against his thigh.

"Oui," she agreed, her expression changing so that she looked almost puppy-like. "We need protection from zis, zis war. But we need protection zat comes from outside of ze village." At that moment, Belle Lavètte suddenly stopped, frozen. She let the clump of grass that she had been playing with fall to the ground. Then she turned to look at the others sitting close to her on the hillside. Jennifer's arm was still draped loosely over her shoulder and her cheeks blushed with the excitement of her thoughts.

"Can we go wiz you?" She grinned and looked from Ewan to Jennifer and back again. "Eet iz ze solution to our problems."

"No, absolutely not," Ewan replied instantly, and it was only then that he noticed the tight hold Renée had of his body. "You don't even know where we are going."

"Well," Renée replied, thinking hard, but growing more confident with every passing moment. "You are a soldier, and she iz Mademoiselle Marmalade, ze Forces' Sweetheart. You are lost in zis village in ze middle of France, so I zink you might be 'eading to ze nearest United barracks, to be safe, no?"

"You… you know where the barracks are?" Ewan replied in surprise, now understanding that these twins might just lead them to victory.

"Oui, we do," Belle replied eagerly. "And we will fight and defend ourselves. We want to learn ze courage of men as lovely as you." Jennifer shot her a horrified glance and Belle blushed.

"We would do anything." Both girls smiled and Jennifer realised that she really would have her hands full if they decided to let these girls come along.

"Come on, Ewan, I'm sure they will not be any trouble," she concluded, by no means sure. "And if they can lead us to the barracks, and to safety, then that's got to be a good thing."

Ewan sighed and leaned forwards. "Okay," he muttered, "I guess you can come along." Before he had even finished speaking, both girls jumped forwards and began planting kisses all over his face. When they came up for air he added, "But first you need to collect into your own house, take clothes and provisions, and then before we go very much further, I want some more information on who your father wants you to marry."

"Eet's a deal," Renée giggled, leaning in to kiss him again. Behind her, Jennifer looked on aghast.

***

Back at the farm all was quiet, but the doors were locked, the girl's father thinking that locking them out would teach them a lesson. Renée tried the front door whilst her twin, padding as lightly as possible, tried the back. But Jennifer had spotted an open window, wide enough for one of the twins to squeeze through and reachable if they climbed on Ewan's shoulders. They wasted no time, Belle opting to shimmy through the tight space before the rest of them ran for shelter behind the front wall until she returned.

Belle Lavètte landed on a battered old sofa, as she knew she would, and raced towards the stairs. Up she jumped, several steps at a time, deciding first to head for her sister's room, where she could grab backpacks and a pile of her sister's clothes. She left drawers open and clothes scattered, but that didn't matter; they were never coming back. Next she passed her papa's room, where she had the ingenuity to grab several faded shirts and a pair of trousers which she was sure Ewan desperately needed. She was about to follow along to her own room, when she froze mid stride. She swore she could hear something, a noise downstairs. But by now it would be too late. Whoever was there had made it into the house.

Taking a deep breath, Belle Lavètte pulled her body back against the wall and edged along towards her own room. There was no going back now, and all she needed were a few more things.

***

Outside, Renée, Ewan and Jennifer watched in silence as the battered red tractor drew up into the yard. It was fate, perhaps, that the twins' father had returned. Now they were stuck, with Belle trapped inside.

"She could be in real danger," Ewan whispered, reaching out towards the wall and moving back behind the oak tree that overhung the road. "But if we stay silent and hidden he has no reason to suspect that we are here." Renée Lavètte squeezed her eyes shut.

"Where will she be?" Jennifer whispered urgently in her ear.

"Upstairs," the twin mouthed, and Ewan knew what they would have to do.

***

The room was a mess, drawers flung open, cupboards empty and a bed covered with clothes. Belle had stuffed what she wanted into the backpack already. Now she was looking for something far more important. Rummaging through an old wooden box she found it, right at the bottom. Placing it quickly around her neck and then zipping up both bags, she pulled one over each shoulder and made a beeline for the stairs. She skidded around the last corner and was about to jump down when she realised that her father had beaten her to it.

A strong and imposing figure, he stood at the bottom of the stairs with a rolling pin in his left hand, beating it hard against the palm of his right.

"You have been a very bad girl, Belle," he said. "You and your sister." He grimaced, his voice low as he moved further up the stairs. "Are you are trying to escape from me, like your mother did all those years ago?"

Belle screamed suddenly, as her papa lashed forwards. Then she started to cry. "But Mum died," she protested in French. "You are wrong, Papa; you don't know what you are saying."

Her father pulled himself up several more steps, his face covered in sweat, and his smile was grim. "I wanted your mother out of my life. She was gone, merely a memory, and so I told you she had died. It made things final." And with that he raised the rolling pin high and made a second strike forwards at his teenage daughter, sending her fleeing in panic.

Belle screamed again and ran to her sister's room, locking the door shut behind her. The others were outside; she knew they could hear her. Her father banged repeatedly against the door, his voice louder than ever. "Come out, Belle! You are like your mother and I know you would come back. I made a promise to Jonathan and Andrew and I don't intend to break it. You're staying here, in the village." He banged once more, a great thud this time. And then came silence. He was waiting.

There was only one thing that Belle could do. From the window, she could see the others standing below. Figuring that they must have heard her screams, she rapped against the glass. They looked up in surprise, in time to see the single pane shatter, sending shards of glass down towards the ground. The noise roused her father, and he hammered again on the door, before Belle heard the sound of his footsteps and his heavy breathing moving down the stairs. She didn't have long; soon he would be outside, where he could set himself on Ewan or the others.

Moving the hooks of the ladder against the window ledge, Belle checked they were secure before shouting down to Ewan, who had dragged the others out of the way to avoid the falling glass. She dropped the two rucksacks first, Ewan and Jennifer catching them with ease, and then with one last look around the room, she felt around her neck to kiss her mother's necklace, and then turned to ease her legs out over the edge. As soon as the wooden rung slipped under her, she knew it had been a bad idea.

***

The others looked on in horror as the wooden ladder crashed to the ground beside them, and they saw Belle swinging from the window ledge, holding on for dear life.

This time it was Renée who screamed, just as Ewan ran to stand directly beneath her terrified twin. Jennifer closed her eyes and placed a hand over Renée's, whilst Ewan looked up, realising that Belle would not be able to hold on for long.

"Jump," he shouted. "I'll catch you." Behind him Renée screamed again, but Belle knew there was little else she could do. Ewan was a soldier, he was strong. And it was not that far to the ground. Squeezing her eyes shut, Belle Lavètte let go, and found herself falling into the strong and warm embrace of United soldier Ewan Roberts.

15

There is, men say, only one thing that can keep you sane in battle and that's the thought that you are fighting for the freedom of everyone at home and to save the lives of your comrades. It is not every man for himself, as some may think, but working as a team, that will ultimately bring the peace for which a soldier always searches.

Chris knew this. He believed it and lived by it. But that was before he had signed up for World Service. His dreams of joining the Parachute Regiment of the SAS had to be put on hold for a while, but he knew he would get there somehow. It was this that spurred him on and gave him the will to fight the battles that he didn't always believe in. The government of the United Isles of Great Britain, where Chris had his home, was corrupt, and there was nothing he could do about it.

Pacing the cold concrete corridor, Staff Sergeant Chris Aston 73236 was deep in thought. The sound of his steel-capped boots hitting the concrete floor bounced off the walls. It was a monotonous sound, not unlike the ticking of a clock, the waiting game Chris was now playing. You could never rush anyone and it was useless to try, he had come to realise that. He also knew that it was impertinent to call upon one's general or commander without prior warning. And so he would continue to wait until something brighter appeared on the horizon.

Racking his brain for anything that might help him to deal with his current situation, Chris leaned on the dark- brown water pipe and picked at the peeling paint. He felt calm and refreshed after a shower and dressed in his new uniform, yet he was less than pleased about his run-in with the mystery soldier. Who was he to tell him what he should do?

A thick metal door opened with a sound that broke through the silence. Must be bullet proof, or bomb proof, Chris thought as he pondered the rivets. And as he did so the figure of Major General Sir Adam Du Tale appeared in the doorway, casting his shadow out along the concrete passage.

The Major General, a man of experience and stature, was in fact slightly built for a man of his position. Standing at only five foot four inches, he was a great deal shorter than Chris had expected, and it was his protruding belly and not his tall physique that caught Chris's eye.

About sixty years of age, he had dusty grey hair under his dark blue cap. His eyes were tired and hard, and he seemed to have a peculiar way of staring at his men. His posture was pompous and officious although the average soldier would quite plausibly tower over him.

Gesturing with his right hand, Major General Du Tale prompted Chris into the office and to take a seat amongst the dahlias. Chris immediately noticed how grand the room was compared with the corridor outside. It was lavishly furnished, with a dark-red carpet and two large glass chandeliers. There was a plasma screen on the furthest wall and a large oak table in the middle. Chris, happy that this was where their meeting would take place, pulled one of the chairs from the table and sat down. Beside him was a large space into which Adam Du Tale drew one of the comfy armchairs, took a seat, and began to speak.

Du Tale had an immediate air of authority which worried Chris, since it was reminiscent of generals he had known in London. Such times were best forgotten.

"Well, well, well," the Major General began, taking a sip from his glass. "Chris Aston. We weren't expecting to see you here so very soon." Chris fidgeted uneasily in his seat and wondered if this man knew something that he didn't. For a few moments there was silence. Du Tale appeared to be planning his next move. "Between you and me," the Major General continued in a voice that was more a suppressed shout than a whisper, "we, that is myself and other leading commanders in this area, have been keeping a close watch on Colonel Smith from the Thames Regimental Barracks in London. We have long suspected that something untoward has been going on under his watch."

Chris found that he was not as surprised as perhaps he ought to be. Here was Du Tale confirming his suspicions. Colonel Smith had never been the most approachable of characters and, in London, Chris and the others had begun to realise the colonel had rather more enemies than supporters when it came to his military tactics.

"We do believe, Staff Sergeant Aston, that a certain air accident in which you were involved was no accident at all." So he knew about the jet crash, and now he was suggesting, as they themselves had done only days before, that Colonel Smith had planned to kill everyone on board. Chris suddenly realised how foolish they had been to expect that such an incident could remain undetected or Colonel Smith's role in it.

With a great sigh and a lot of effort, Major General Sir Adam Du Tale hauled himself from the chair and turned to face an open glass door which Chris hadn't noticed. He beckoned for the young soldier to follow and led the way out onto an open patio. Chris looked back and wondered at the difference between exit and entrance. The exit of the building was not unlike that of a quaint English country house, those Chris remembered from his childhood. There were metal-framed windows and wooden shutters, each painted in a rich red. Beyond the patio Chris took in views across a river and towards mountains thrust up in mismatched patterns from the ground, great piles of earth in greens and yellows, where flowers grew on the slopes and pools filled the great rims of the summit.

"I see you are as impressed with this view as I was upon first arriving at the barracks," Du Tale began again, his voice carrying on the wind. "That's the Chaîne des Puys, a wonder of French beauty and the stronghold which may just win us the war." The view was almost surreal, even as they were standing before it, and both men knew that such beauty would easily be ravaged if a battle were to take place.

Chris couldn't help but notice how the fresh air had changed this man. He was far calmer now and Chris himself had relaxed to the point where he might even enter into a conversation. After all, he felt sure he would need as much detail as possible before he could make an accurate and informed decision about his future.

"What you must understand, Chris, is that war is all about money. For years, centuries even, there have been people who supported the fighting simply because they could make a profit from it." They were now walking amongst ornamental rose beds and as the Major General paused for breath, Chris wondered where the conversation was taking them. "Now, out of all those people who can make money from war, the arms race in the First and Second World Wars was where industrialists earned their profit, not to mention the many businessmen in the Middle East during the three Iraq wars; there are many who make bad the money they earn, so to speak."

Chris thought about this for a moment and considered the possibility. Du Tale appeared to be a smart man, and his ability to communicate was top-notch, but all that he had said still left one question unanswered. Why? Chris could not work out why this man, with his English peers and English ways, had any need to question the legitimacy of war or, the nature of those men who had been placed in commanding roles.

"But why is any of that important now?" he asked, speaking for the first time. The question sounded wrong, stupid even. But Chris knew that there was no other way around the matter.

"Because we want to win the war, soldier," Du Tale replied in a matter-of-fact manner. "And we have a great many supporters on our side. They are willing to help us achieve our goals; however, we need to overcome certain obstacles that lie in our path. One such obstacle happens to be dear Colonel Smith from Thames." Chris was about to enquire further, ask what Colonel Smith had done that was so awful, and gather the gossip even, when something untimely broke his pattern of thought.

For a moment he listened. It started at first way off in the distance, the slight buzz that could easily be mistaken for a hovering glider, passing over the barracks out towards the hills beyond. But the noise didn't fade. Instead it grew in volume, a great whine of high- and low- pitched sound, not unlike a fire alarm. Or perhaps an air raid siren?

"I'm sorry about this," Du Tale called over the din, motioning towards the upper windows of the building they had just left. Chris felt sure that he would soon need to resort to lip reading if he wanted to understand anything that the Major General was saying.

Overhead, the noise of the alarm still reverberated around the buildings as Du Tale directed Chris towards a concrete wall at the back of the rose garden. The wall marked the edge of the patio above and was quite a considerable height, which made Chris wonder how steep the steps they had climbed down minutes before really were. As the pair walked past the many beds of flowers, their petals quivering from the vibration, Du Tale seemed blissfully unaware of the bedlam going on all around him. Several high-ranking soldiers had run past them, yet the Major General chattered on, knowing full well that Chris could hear nothing.

In the middle of the concrete wall was a large metal door painted in a dark red with rivets all around. It was marked 'private' and sealed with a coded lock. The Major General punched in a few digits, watched as the catch gasped and the door swung in on itself to reveal a dark world beyond. It thumped shut behind them and the noise from outside ceased immediately.

"I am sorry about that, Staff Sergeant Aston," Adam Du Tale called through the musty darkness. "I fear things are moving a little quicker than we anticipated." He clicked the lights and the vastness of the room was revealed. "That was the hover raid siren, by the way. Very effective. A nuisance, mind you, sends the soldiers into an awful panic." Hover raid. To Chris it sounded so matter of fact and yet it meant so much more.

In the furthest corner of the room a phone was ringing on the wall. Du Tale looked from Chris to the wall and back again, apparently realising that it could be urgent. While the Major General talked in hushed whispers into the receiver, Chris took in the bunker and hoped Thomas had gelled well enough with the other soldiers to stay safe. Knowing Thomas, he would be fine, yet a horrible pang of guilt settled in Chris's stomach.

It was now obvious why the door to this underground bunker was marked private. It was another of Du Tale's secret hideaways and this one, although far more sparsely furnished than the first, was still regal and grand and was filled in the centre with glass display cases. There were posters on the walls, different designs on every side and Chris felt compelled to study one, before reading the slogan that covered it and finally understanding the room's real use. By now Du Tale had finished on the phone and was walking back towards the soldier who took one last glance around the room and stepped back from the poster he was reading.

United Front Against Nuclear Terrorism was the slogan and underneath in fancy red lettering it read: The end is near for Reformed forces and decisions must be made now… Join your fellow me, and fight for the independence of the world.

Du Tale placed a hand on Chris's shoulder. This room was the hub of the French deployment plans and, looking around him again, he noticed the colours of each glass case. They corresponded to the countries involved, the stars and stripes of America and the red, white and blue of glorious Britain. Du Tale moved towards Chris again and began to speak.

"I did not want to have to bring you here." His voice was much more sincere than before. "You did not need to know about this yet. It was not the right time. But as I said, things are moving quicker than we ever imagined they would."

"And who was that on the phone?" Chris retorted angrily, his resentment swelling between them. It was ironic that Du Tale had not wanted to bring him here. The outcome of the jet crash was much the same, twice now he had been part of something he shouldn't.

Du Tale stood for a moment, thinking, before taking Chris by the shoulder and guiding him towards an open glass cabinet where tiny multi-coloured men were positioned on a map of the world.

"It was the Major General of the United American Army," he said simply, pushing some blue soldiers forwards on the map with a plastic shovel. "The Reformed troops to the north of Old Pakistan have been fighting bitterly against our men for several months, creating a blockade in the Khyber Pass and fighting off attacks from any United forces. But, in the last few days, the men have been tiring and have become sluggish in their behaviour. I have just received word that this morning American troops managed to break through the east of the blockade and gain some vital territory."

Chris contemplated what the Major General was saying and he understood just how insignificant he, Ewan, Thomas and Jennifer really were in the great scheme of things. Soldiers from both sides were dying every day, and yet they had believed that it was some great miracle that they had survived. What if they hadn't? They would just be more numbers in a book, the list of the war dead totting up.

"Is that a good thing for us, then?" Chris queried, looking down on the map of Europe where a gaggle of tiny soldiers were positioned next to a mountain range and a series of small buildings marked Chaîne des Puys, France.

"It is great news, soldier. But it means we need to move into phase two of our plans. And that makes things a little more difficult." The room was suddenly quiet and Chris wondered why they had not been disturbed if the situation outside was still so serious. Had the alarm stopped? He could not hear it, yet he was sure this bunker was soundproof anyway.

"Phase two," Du Tale coughed again, drawing the soldier's attention, "involves all United forces working together to win the war. We've done some provisional research, which is how we discovered the problem of Colonel Smith and how we came to realise that the biggest of the many battles taking place across the world would centre itself right here in France. The Chaîne des Puys, Staff Sergeant Aston, I told you it was a special place and it could just win us the war."

Chris wanted to ask more about Colonel Smith. Why did the Major General keep bringing him up in the conversation but not say anything more about him? But now the familiar sound of the phone broke his concentration. Brilliant, Chris thought as he watched Adam Du Tale pick up the receiver and acknowledge whoever was on the other end. This time it had to be a serious conversation, and Chris was not at all surprised when the Major General looked more than a little worried as he arrived back at the glass cabinet moments later. But Chris had been wrong, at least in part, for now the Major General had some interesting news.

"Firstly, Staff Sergeant Aston, do not worry about your friends. They were picked up at a bridge not far from here by one of our informants. He knew one of them was a soldier and was worried when they wouldn't give him any information. He felt it best to contact us directly and we are now keeping an eye on them. Personally, I feel they will be able to make it here on their own." Chris grimaced; he wasn't so sure. "And secondly, you must follow me outside for a moment."

The large door opened freely from the inside, and Chris noticed was how dark it had become. The sky was overcast, and the Chaîne des Puys had faded into an eerie mist. Du Tale was about to say something, when a bleeping noise from his pocket stopped him in his tracks. "No signal in the bunker," he smiled, as he flipped open the lid of the holographic phone and read back the message in silence. It was as if he already knew what was going to be displayed on the tiny screen. It was not good news. But, without the slightest suggestion that something was amiss, he flipped the lid, slipped the phone back into his pocket and turned to Chris with a ghostly smile.

"Aha, Chris! The joys of war are upon us," he boomed and Chris couldn't tell if he was being ironic. Given what he had discovered in the space of the last hour, anything seemed possible. "You know, Staff Sergeant Aston, you really did arrive just at the right time. Now you can watch the fighting from up here, or you can take part in the battle. The decision is entirely up to you."

16

Minutes after Belle Lavètte had fallen into Ewan's capable arms, the group were on the move once again. Jennifer had raised the alarm, watching as the dilapidated tractor fired up once again and headed back out towards the road. They had no choice but to run, and so they did with Ewan still carrying a numbed Belle tightly in his arms.

They had barely reached the end of the street, before a traditional blue-and-white police car, the Gendarmerie had been sceptical about the new hover car design from the very beginning, came speeding up towards the farmhouse, parking so that it blocked the entrance and the only available exit for the twins' father, who was desperately trying to pursue his teenage runaways. As they rounded the corner, the sisters took one final look back towards their family home, and watched with a mixture of surprise and disgust as the portly farmer was handcuffed by a Police Officer and marched towards the back seat of his awkwardly parked patrol car.

The little group disappeared. Renée reached into her pocket for her tiny holographic phone. She waved it before the others and they suddenly realised.

"I didn't see you phone the police," Jennifer said, stunned.

"I work in mysterious ways," Renée protested, giggling.

Ewan smiled, brushing hair from Belle's closed eyes and adjusting his arms so that he held her more comfortably. She really was unusually delicate. "And the day's not over yet."

"Oh, but Belle," Renée cooed, looking at her sister's limp body. "She fell from such an 'ight."

"But she's breathing," Ewan replied. "I felt her pulse, and when we get a little further from the village we can rest and wait for her to come round."

"Yes," agreed Jennifer, who along with Renée was now carrying one of the very uncomfortable backpacks that Belle had managed to fill before her escape. "Besides, we're going to need somewhere to bed down soon, and it will give us a chance to change into the clothes that Belle has managed to find for us." Her words alerted them to the evening darkness which was slowly beginning to draw in.

For a while, they walked in total silence, each knowing their situation was now all the more dangerous, none knowing the right thing to say. Neither Ewan nor Jennifer had any idea when they would see Chris or Thomas again, as they had done the wrong thing, strayed from the village, so if they were to come looking for them, they would not be there.

"We have friends at the barracks," Ewan said suddenly, breaking the silence and stopping dead in the middle of the road. "They told us to wait in the nearest village and they'd come and find us."

Jennifer turned and walked back to Ewan, leaving Renée standing alone. She could see the tiredness in his eyes, and the fear. This man was heroic, a world away from the person she had met on the dance floor and seen outside the café only days before. She loved him now, more so after what they had been through.

"Chris and Thomas will be alright," she whispered, looking at Ewan in the same way she had done the night in her dressing room. He melted instantly. "Chris is a born leader. I bet you they've arrived already, and soon they'll be out looking for us, whether we're at the village or not."

Ewan's gaze dropped. She was right, of course, but it didn't stop him from missing his comrades. He had never been separated from them like this before. "First the crash, then the endless walking, and now this," he breathed. "So much has happened in such a short time."

“I know,” Jennifer said, forgetting they were not alone. She was quite suddenly brought back to her senses.

“I thought I knew zis road,” Renée called, poking her head out from around the next corner. “Along ’ere, eez a turn off, and zen we shall come to ze new stables, and zey are owned by ze very men our papa wanted us to marry.” Her look was almost devilish.

“But, Renée,” Jennifer protested, sounding not unlike Belle, “surely you’re not suggesting we stay there for the night? Not after the way you found us this morning.” But the French girl’s expression did not change.

“Zat is exactly what I am suggesting. Eet would be ze perfect way to seal ze deception, no? I would like to take at least one thing from zem.” And with that she disappeared again, leaving Ewan and Jennifer bewildered.

They had already begun to follow, when she shouted to them again. “And you ’ave to tell me about zis crash. When Belle is awake, I want to know everything.”

***

It was much later. The day, which had been bright, gave way to a torrent of rain that lashed down upon the roof like a hail of bullet fire.

The stables themselves were surprisingly comfortable and it had been easier than anticipated to break open the front panels and sneak inside. Now they were searching for warmth amongst the straw as they tried to restore their energy. Belle Lavètte came round, but a while she was groggy and could not bear to talk. The others, for fear of upsetting her, felt it was best to leave such discussion. They would come to it, all in good time. Instead, Renée had made sure to extract every last detail from Ewan and Jennifer about the crash, their journey and everything that had led them to this point. They talked quietly for long periods, with Renée checking the time on her holographic phone every so often, surprised that time was moving so slowly.

When they grew tired of talking, they finally committed themselves to sleep. Jennifer had locked herself into Ewan's embrace and Renée hugged her weak sister close, but they soon found that their surroundings, were close to unbearable. They were sleeping on a hard uncomfortable floor and in the end realised sleep was no longer an option. They had decided to venture out into the night air, tinged with a chill left by the departing rain. Now they were standing together in the dark, looking up at the stars that filled the night sky.

"I still do not see how you could 'ave walked all zis way after an accident d'avion..." Belle whispered meekly, "when I was, out like a light, and after only falling from an upstairs window. Eet must 'ave been a terrible experience."

"It was horrific," Ewan replied tightening his grip around Jennifer, not wanting to discuss the topic any longer.

"Soon you will be back with your friends," Renée added. "And we can all work together to do ze best we can."

There is something about the night time, everything is so much colder and darker. You feel the need to seek safety. The night is for those with something to hide. But yet, there is a hidden beauty. Here a full moon shone down, a million tiny stars flickered in the heavens, and light glowed from the top of a distant hill.

"If you look carefully," Belle breathed, almost silently, "you can see ze lights from Montrebone Manór." She looked at her sister and they both closed their eyes for a moment. "Zat's where ze brothers live," she added. "Zey are rich, powerful, and we 'ave no desire to marry zem."

"Life is strange," Jennifer agreed. "I mean look at the situation we are in now."

"We want to escape," both twins said in unison, their auburn hair caught by the moonlight. Renée turned to Ewan before continuing. "Perhaps now iz ze best time, with ze stars to guide us. We often visit the cliff edge, we know ze way."

Ewan breathed deeply, tasting the dampness of the air, and then looked around at the others. The roads would not be dangerous at this time of night, and if they wanted to get to the barracks without being seen, it was a good option.

"Let's go," he mouthed, looking back towards the stables. "Get changed, grab your things. We've already eaten, let's go." He felt like an officer, he was in charge. He felt like Chris, it was strangely exhilarating.

Together, they changed in silence, Ewan glad to replace his old army uniform with the clothes Belle had taken from her father. He unpinned his badges and placed them on the chest of the worn woollen shirt so that people would still recognise his rank. Jennifer easily squeezed into a tight pair of jeans and a long t-shirt that she knew immediately belonged to Renée, and the twins found by coincidence that there were matching jumpers in the backpack. Soon they were ready and they set off down the road, carefully shutting the doors of the barn behind them.

The twins were right, the stars provided more than enough light to guide them down the winding roads. With the landscape still in darkness and their movements hidden by shadow, they made quick progress.

The road they were walking on soon came to an end and Belle followed low hedges before reminding Renée of a gap that led to a rocky track. The track took them across fields and through a narrow patch of woodland. Walking close together, the twins lead the way, while Ewan and Jennifer, hands locked tightly, brought up the rear.

It was not long before they reached the path to the cliff edge. The hill sloped gently upwards, leading to a steep downward incline, which Chris and Thomas had negotiated only the previous day.

By the time they stopped to look out over the plain they were almost too tired to continue. Rain lit up the mountain range and Ewan felt a connection; they would be safe here, they would come to no harm.

"Wow," he whispered in awe as both Belle and Renée grinned back at him.

"You see why we come 'ere, simply to look," Belle replied in earnest.

"This eez ze Chaîne des Puys mountain range," her sister continued, and pointed at the group of mismatched buildings at the foot. The barracks. At last. "We might 'ave to go down backwards."

Instinctively Jennifer squeezed Ewan's hand tightly. There was magic here and they could both feel it. For below they knew their comrades were waiting for them.

17

There's a small stretch of land that runs between the Chaîne des Puys, where the grass is long and the ground is flanked on either side by two tall mountains. It is a peaceful place, where trees grow randomly wherever seeds have fallen. The nature of such a landscape made it the perfect location for the headquarters of a Reformed offensive against the French.

At the far end of this hidden stretch and behind a clump of tall evergreens, Reformed troops had built a makeshift hut from fallen logs and branches. There were representatives from all of the Reformed countries, and many had developed their own language which they used to communicate. Many of the leaders spoke in English, but that was now considered the language of the enemy, and if you wanted to remain popular, you spoke anything but English and French.

To build even this small ramshackle one-room dwelling, the soldiers had to work in the dead of night, the black of their uniforms hiding them under the stars. The location was far enough away from the nearest United French barracks, on the far side of the mountain range, that there was no need to worry about being discovered. The French knew there were Reformed troops in the area, but like all United forces, they would not launch an attack until necessary. However, it still took the Reformed troops several long weeks to complete the dwelling between the trees. Now it was finished, and ready for use.

All factions of the Reformed Army within the immediate vicinity were marching towards the Chaîne des Puys ready for battle. The Reformed forces in Europe were now thin on the ground and their governments were in debt from the costs of such a prolonged offensive, but those in charge felt the end was near and even at this late stage, that a Reformed victory remained certain.

* * *

Chris made his decision in that split second. He was a soldier and some had called him a born leader. He had survived the carnage of a United jet crash, along with three other comrades, and he figured it must have been for a reason. He was going to fight as he had always done, with the fate of the world hanging in the balance. But first, he needed to be reunited with his comrades.

Staff Sergeant Chris Aston and Major General Sir Adam Du Tale were walking rather more briskly now, back along the paths that led towards the centre of the barracks. The private quarters were almost deserted, everyone was preparing for the onslaught of defensive action.

"I will be fighting for your side, sir," Chris said simply and with the authority required for such a situation. "But before I do, I want find my comrades." The Major General turned to look at him, a grin appearing on his face.

"Good choice, Christopher," he wheezed, his grin never fading. "I am prepared for the approaching battle, as I'm sure you are. I shall collect Private Fisher myself and will give you a room in the quadrant from which you can organise yourselves. Your other friends will be directed there when they arrive."

Chris thought about this for a moment. It sounded like a good idea, but how were Ewan and Jennifer to cross the barren plain, presuming they made it that far? "How will they cross safely into the barracks?" he queried, realising his worst fears were following him, that again they might all face the threat of death. "Surely they'll be captured, or worse, killed?"

This time the Major General didn't turn back. "Chris Aston," he replied thoughtfully, "you worry far too much. The plain is facing towards the Chaîne des Puys. The barracks were designed so the mountain range backed onto the private quarters. The front entrance is one of the safest in the complex." Chris chuckled to himself. "So, Christopher, if anything is destroyed at the height of the approaching battle, it should only be my collection of van Gogh paintings. There would be no human sacrifice at all, at least not in the grounds of these barracks." The Major General seemed ready for anything. There were so many other questions that Chris wanted to ask him, but somehow it felt inappropriate.

As the pair rounded the final corner and headed towards the parade ground where Chris and Thomas had separated earlier in the day, every soldier in the barracks was turning out in full uniformed colours; hundreds of men lining up in regimental pattern.

At the front of the open courtyard Chris saw a small wooden lectern, a microphone, and a set of speakers. He was about to turn right and take his place with the other soldiers, when the Major General spoke to him again.

"I am afraid you are going to have to come with me, Staff Sergeant," he said calmly, taking Chris's arm. "This address is rather important and I feel you will be surprised at what I have to say."

Chris was unable to resist and together they approached the lectern, aware of the noise several hundred United soldiers could make in a confined space. They were all chatting amongst themselves, yet they kept a watchful eye on the front, awaiting their orders. Chris followed Du Tale forwards, and suddenly there was silence.

"Attention!" shouted a voice from the left, and together the men saluted Major General Sir Adam Du Tale.

"Friends," Du Tale began, his voice echoing around the quadrant like the great British leader, Winston Churchill. "There are bleak times ahead. You will know this, as for many, many weeks we have been planning the inevitable battle that is to come. Reformed troops are now approaching faster than we first thought. In these dark days of war we have been forced to implement our plans far, far sooner than we would have liked."

Chris was not at all surprised by the Major General's oratory skills, but he felt more than a little nervous standing beside him, looking out over so many pairs of eyes.

"I have assembled you here today, to brief you on the way ahead and prepare you for the days to come. As I speak, Reformed forces are descending on the Chaîne des Puys and we now know they have assembled a makeshift headquarters somewhere in the immediate vicinity. These men are growing weak; their governments are in grave debt. If we can succeed in destroying their strongholds, here and across the world, areas in which they are not familiar; which they do not call home, then we will be in with a very good chance of ending this terrible war once and for all.

Do not misunderstand, this offensive will be dangerous and you men will be fighting on the front line, but you will be protecting and fighting for the very future of these lands. What happens here, amongst the glorious mountains of the Chaîne des Puys, will change the future of this world. Together we will surely see those who have wronged us brought down."

The Major General stepped back from the lectern and a great roar erupted from the regimented crowd. These soldiers had an obvious respect for their leader and they hung upon his every word. Chris, meanwhile, had still received not the slightest clue as to why he was standing beside Du Tale at the lectern. But all of his questions would soon be answered, in one clear demand, that would lead him in a definite direction.

As soon as Du Tale began to speak once more a hush descended for a second time. Chris realised they would now return to their old ways, fighting for their country, against one enemy, as it had always been.

"Well men," Du Tale's voice boomed, "my valiant men, you have both pride and courage in your souls. There is no way I could let you fight alone. We are four hundred here in this complex, and you will be split into two groups to be led by the two most experienced officers I could possibly place in such a position. Together, they have a wealth of experience; individually, a pride that will see not one of you men fighting in vain. Now those of you in companies A through to D will be led by Commandant Jean Andrew Babineaux…" At the mention of this name several shouts went up from a group of soldiers to the left, and Chris watched as the tall, dark and imposing figure that he had run into earlier in the day approached the front of the quadrant. Seeing him in a fuller light, he looked more like a distinguished fighter with many gleaming medals on his chest.

The Major General was smiling broadly and waving at particular soldiers whom he recognised, as he welcomed Babineaux to the stage. This man appeared to be held in as high regard as Du Tale himself, and his manner was as arrogant as that of a man of much senior rank.

"A very warm welcome indeed for Commandant Babineaux. He is a seasoned leader who will do well in battle. You can do no better than be under his command.

For those of you in companies F through to I, I have both an interesting and wholly fruitful surprise for you. Some of you may be aware of two British soldiers who arrived here earlier today; many of you will have met Private Thomas Fisher. But, as great a soldier as Thomas may be, he has a counterpart." By now Thomas, who Chris had seen three rows in, appeared to have melted into the crowd of men, shying away from the limelight. Up at the lectern, for the first time in his life Chris wished that he could be doing exactly the same thing.

There was no escape for him. "I hope you will join me," the Major General continued, "in welcoming my choice; a man of some years' experience, a talented leader and a man I trust to bring you expert guidance in the dark days to come: Capitaine Chris Aston." For seconds there was a hideous silence. Chris was confused, why was the Major General introducing him as a capitaine? He knew it was a French rank, but he was a British solider, why introduce him as anything else? A few muffled claps echoed around the buildings, but it was a far cry from the thunder of applause that had welcomed Chris's counterpart to the stage. He felt sick, quaking in his boots before a group of men for the first time in his life, and unable to understand what the Major General wanted of him. He wondered how he would ever be able to lead them to victory. But there was no need to worry, for as Chris looked out across the men who would soon be risking death, something remarkable happened.

From the very centre of the group, Thomas Fisher had emerged from a gaggle of men and was looking up at his friend and comrade.

"He is a born leader," he shouted, his voice ringing high above the silence. "He saved my life and the lives of others who I know you will meet in due course. And you will be proud to be led by Capitaine Aston when you realise that he saved the life of one of our most important and influential personalities." His face was red with effort and he was laughing too. "Just you wait!" And then he began to clap, as loudly as he could, and soon others were joining him, welcoming this unknown man who had been chosen by Du Tale and was willing to risk his life for them. And Chris couldn't help but smile back, as two hundred feet pounded against the ground to echoes of: "Chris, Chris, Chris."

Commandant Babineaux's face was a picture. He had never contemplated being beaten on home soil. But now he truly was. And Chris appreciated that the days ahead would not be as hideous as they had first seemed. "Enough," Major General Sir Adam Du Tale's voice roared suddenly, more happy than angry. The silence returned and the speakers crackled with his voice. "I knew you would take kindly to both your leaders." He paused for a moment and acknowledged both Chris and Babineaux, before tightening his gaze. "Now, men, pay attention. Reformed troops are approaching fast. Their morale will be boosted by an increase in numbers and the possibility, however slight, of triumph in the battles to come. Before us are the glorious Chaîne des Puys. The night is beginning to draw in now, and beyond the private quarters, between us and the approaching enemy, is a fast- flowing river. You will know this, of course and it will work in our favour. So get some rest now before we head out into the battlefield tomorrow. The enemy will not reach us before sunrise, of that I am confident." And with that, they began to disperse, heading off in small groups to their own bunkhouses.

Chris was about to greet Thomas, when he felt the Major General's clammy hand on his shoulder.

"Well done, soldier," he whispered into Chris's ear, turning him around on the spot. "Nobody here need know about your past encounters with Colonel Smith. Merely do as you have always done." As he finished, Chris watched Babineaux return. Thomas was walking patiently in his wake. "Thank you, Commandant Babineaux," Du Tale smiled and then he was dismissed. "Now boys, like Colonel

Smith, I feel that you are our future, the key, so to speak, of our intelligence force.

A little while ago, I was in talks with the President of the United Isles of Great Britain about sending some high- quality soldiers to fight here in the mountains." Chris and Thomas looked at each other, lost for words as they realised it was Du Tale who had engineered their deployment and Colonel Smith who had taken a liberty in removing them. "I know it's late, but before we all allow ourselves a little rest I need to show you to the room that I have been promising, so that you know where it is if your friends were to arrive in the early hours of the morning, say."

There was a mysterious twinkle in the Major General's eye, as he led the two men away from the lectern towards a high wall at the far side of the quadrant.

"I'm sure you understand the sudden way in which I introduced you earlier Capitaine Aston," Du Tale continued as they walked. He seemed to enjoy referring to Chris by his new title. "As you are now serving in France, certain changes have to be made. I want you to lead two companies of men, and for that you must hold a certain rank. Therefore I have bestowed on you the non- commissioned rank of capitaine, with your pay remaining at its original level." Chris wasn't sure, but he nodded anyway. Experience had taught him that when soldiers were given a non-commissioned rank, it was invariably hard for them to make the transition, continue to associate with their former comrades or even be accepted by their new colleagues. Chris had a strange feeling there would be a certain animosity towards him now.

When they reached the wall they found a door which blended into its surroundings; dark, damp and peeling; one that could easily have gone unnoticed if you had no need to use it. The room on the other side was empty save for one large table and a single light bulb hanging from a ceiling cord. It looked not the least inviting and Chris was not surprised.

"I know it is a little bland at the moment," Du Tale said, his smile fading. "But I will arrange for diagrams, posters and cabinets to be moved here from the war rooms. It will help you with your planning, I'm sure."

Chris smiled weakly and Thomas nodded. "Yes, sir," they said in unison. In truth, they were too tired for all of this now and besides, the Major General had promised they would be reunited with Ewan and Jennifer before anything else took priority.

"Well then, you know where it is," Du Tale said meekly, wiping his brow, and directing them out of the room. "Shouldn't be too much of a problem when your friends arrive." He stopped outside the door and breathed in the fresh evening air. "Things went well tonight, boys. Thank you." Finally he pointed to the right and added, "You will be sleeping in that bunkhouse. Head off now. Private Fisher will show you where to go, Chris." They nodded and the small group parted company.

"You've got to tell me what's going on," Thomas breathed as they reached the entrance to the bunkhouse.

"Tomorrow, Thomas," his friend replied. "When Ewan arrives with Jennifer then we can talk everything over." And with that they entered the small wooden building and found their bags waiting for them on the bunk beds they were to share.

18

It was late, but Thomas found he couldn't sleep. He'd been awake for hours, lying on his bunk in an unfamiliar country, thinking only about the day ahead. For a while, when they had first arrived at the bunkhouse, it had been almost impossible to sleep. Instead they spoke in hushed whispers while the light bulb hummed and flickered. They discussed the evening's events, and Chris confided in his friend how worried he was about the task he'd been given, while Thomas mumbled sleepy encouragement.

Chris had eventually nodded off, but Thomas remained wide awake. Checking that the other bunkhouse residents were sleeping soundly, Thomas kicked the underside of the mattress above and hissed, "Chris, wake up!"

A soldier in another bunk turned in his sleep, but didn't wake. Silently, Thomas watched as a pair of feet dangled over the edge of the bunk above and Chris slid down the short metal ladder.

"I'm awake now," he whispered as his feet padded to the ground, "but I'd prefer if you never did that again, you have big feet!"

"Where are you going?" Thomas asked, pulling the bedclothes away and getting up to stand beside his friend. He pulled on a dressing gown, tied it at the front, and looked Chris up and down.

"I'm going for a walk," he replied, grabbing a thick sweater from his new kit on the table and pulling it over his head. "I need some air." Thomas didn't even bother to answer as Chris opened the wooden door and headed off down the steps. He merely followed him out into the chill evening.

Outside, they quickly saw they were not alone. They had exited the bunkhouse into a central square, surrounded by a cluster of other small buildings. Dotted all around them were other groups of two or three soldiers. Some were smoking, while others were talking quietly, the furthest deep in conversation.

Chris wondered if this was a routine gathering or if others were unable to sleep. Did these men share his own worries? Were they fearful for their lives as he was, or the lives of their friends?

Setting off with Thomas at his side, Chris began a circuit of the square. They passed the group of soldiers who were smoking lazily, and Thomas eyed them as Chris nodded in greeting before carrying on. Did they know he was their commanding officer? Or perhaps they were in the company to be led by Babineaux. Before long Chris had reached the far side of the courtyard. Thomas took a deep breath.

"When do you think it's likely Ewan and Jennifer will arrive?" he asked. "It will be good to see them again." "Sometime in the morning, I hope," Chris replied, stopping and turning back to his friend. Thomas nodded, surprised at this curt response. It was only when they were halfway back to the bunkhouse that they heard voices shouting from behind them.

"Chris! Chris!" came a deep voice through the night. Chris turned on the spot to see a soldier they had passed moments before, and another beckoning to them from the corner of the square. Reaching the pair, Chris thought them striking individuals indeed; both wore their United uniforms, one was very short with brown hair, while the second, the man who had called, was well built with dark hair that may once have been styled into an afro, but now lay limp around the soldier's ears.

"Alan Waldow," the man said, extending his hand in greeting, first to Chris and then to Thomas. "And this," he smiled and patted his friend on the back, "is Brian Callowman."

"Pleased to meet you," said the second. "You'll be our commanding officer in a few hours' time."

"Good to meet you," Chris replied, his mind struggling to compute information, due to his lack of sleep. "And this is my good friend and comrade Thomas Fisher." The two soldiers smiled.

"Oh, we know Private Fisher," Brian chuckled, slapping Thomas on the back. "We met him earlier today. Your friend has quite a personality."

"Yes, that would be Thomas," Chris smiled.

"What brings you out here in the middle of the night?" It was Thomas who had enquired, tired of people discussing him as if he wasn't there. Alan Waldow looked hard at the new arrivals.

"When we can't sleep we come out here to talk things over. Sometimes the guys have a kick about. It takes our minds off things." The young soldier paused for a moment and suddenly his jaw dropped, as if there was something important that he had forgotten to say.

"What is it?" Thomas asked, kicking the ground. Brian grimaced. "I'm sorry, we forgot. Commandant Babineaux was up here a little while ago. He asked us to come and find you…" Chris shuddered at the thought of what his counterpart might want. And he'd kept him waiting.

"He said something about Du Tale greeting some friends of yours," Alan continued. "Said they'd arrived about an hour ago, a chap and three girls."

In this tired state Chris's mind worked slowly. In fact, it was Thomas who asked.

"Three girls?" he said. "Ewan was with Jennifer when we last saw him, so where did the other two come from?"

"Do you know where they are, Alan?" Chris replied worriedly. Again the soldier smiled.

"Babineaux said they had all gone to the washrooms for a shower." The two soldiers stared at each other, thinking the same thing.

"Where's that?"

"Head back towards the courtyard and follow the signposts!"

Chris nodded, and was about to leave when he grasped something. "You're both British, aren't you?" he asked, surprised that it hadn't dawned on him.

"Indeed we are, Midlands born and raised," they both answered. Everyone smiled.

"Good," Chris finished. "Our French friends would be a little less tactful."

* * *

They found the washroom easily enough. It was a long, plain building, located not a great distance from their office base in the quad. In the darkness Chris was beginning to develop a mental map of the complex.

There were no soldiers out in this part of the barracks, perhaps because it was located further away from the bunkhouses or they didn't want to risk being caught by Du Tale. It was particularly exhilarating for Thomas, as for once it looked like they were breaking the rules.

"We'll take one each," Chris said simply. "Ewan will be in here somewhere."

Thomas needed no further instruction. Inside, the shower rooms were damp and humid, with several cubicles and very little space to move. Thomas could hear the sound of running water, and as he turned to investigate, he almost walked straight into a pretty girl with auburn hair. She wore a simple blue dress and her long hair was damp against her shoulders. She was tall and slender…

"…French," Thomas breathed as the girl began to talk.

"Renée, Renée… Eet would appear zat we 'ave found our first soldier boy." Her accent was astonishing, deep and strong. The first girl smiled, and Thomas heard water stop, and the catch on a door, before a second woman exited the furthest stall, a towel wrapped around her body, another holding her hair to her head.

"Oh, Belle, you were right." This time the second girl smiled, more perfectly than the first, and Thomas was suddenly conscious that he was looking at a pair of French twins. "Take 'im outside and wait for ze others while I put on my clothes," she added before disappearing back into the stall.

Outside again, the chill in the air hit sharp against Thomas's face. He knew he was blushing and was glad of the dark. Then he saw that Chris had emerged from the opposite side with a very wet and bedraggled Jennifer, and Ewan, who appeared to be wearing strange clothes that barely fitted him. The look on his face said it all.

"Well, we made it," he smiled, looking from Chris to Thomas. "It's good to see you both!"

"Care for an introduction?" Chris replied warily, his eyes first on the auburn girl in the blue dress, and then on another, so much like the first, as she emerged from the entrance beside them.

"Of course," Ewan smiled. "This is Belle Lavètte, and her sister Renée. They are twins."

"I can see that, Ewan. This is no game. You're probably not aware, but tomorrow we begin fighting against Reformed forces. It's a dangerous operation, and there are a mountain of things that I need to explain to you and Thomas before dawn breaks."

"Why so serious, soldier boy?" Belle giggled, walking towards Chris. "Eet sounds like fun." He took a few steps back and grimaced. In time he might come to understand these French girls, but right now they were a danger.

"It's serious. It's life and death and I'll be leading the troops. Now, Jennifer," Chris looked at the singer and she nodded politely, "I have to take Ewan and Thomas to discuss strategy. If I walk you girls to the Major General's office, will you be able to look after yourselves from there? I'm sure he's found beds for you, and in your case, Jennifer, it will be safer."

"Yes," she smiled, moving to stand between Renée and Belle. "That should be fine." As she passed by the soldier, she added in her quietest whisper, "I'll have a word with them while we're there too." Chris smiled and realised just how much he had missed the company of the others.

"Guys, please wait here," he warned, turning to address the pair. "I won't be long." He was about to direct the girls, when they were interrupted by another soldier. This time the solider wore a dark uniform and several large badges on his chest, which suggested he held a position of some importance.

"I'm sorry to interrupt," he said briskly, "but I've been instructed by Du Tale's internal leadership to search through the girls' belongings." His voice held the utmost sincerity.

"But why on earth would you want to do zat?" Belle asked in protest, suddenly pulling her own backpack behind her and away from the soldier's grasp.

"I was just about to ask the same question," Ewan interjected, looking the man up and down. He seemed genuine, but had not yet stated his intentions.

"I'm afraid I'm just following orders," the soldier continued, moving a little closer to their grouping. "If it's any consolation it's primarily the singer's backpack they wanted me to rummage through." Ewan pulled a strange face while Chris and Thomas watched with interest. Unbeknown to the twins, the others were putting on a highly elaborate show. As Chris had said just before they left the crash site, remain oblivious and act as if you know nothing at all. That way you will avoid almost all trouble.

"If he really needs to search my backpack, then I'm not going to stop him," Jennifer said suddenly. It was as if everyone else had forgotten she was there. "I mean it's not like I've got anything to hide." Behind her Chris nodded, as she turned to wink at them from the corner of her eye.

"But does it really need to be done tonight?" Chris queried, moving to address the new solider face to face. "I'm afraid so," he replied quickly, moving forwards to stand directly beside Jennifer. "Now, if you'd kindly hand over your bag." Gingerly Jennifer reached behind her to grab the backpack which was propped up against the outer washroom wall.

For at least five minutes they watched in silence as the soldier tipped the contents of the backpack out onto the cold hard concrete and examined each item in turn. Mainly it was a mixture of her clothes, toiletries and the empty food packets she and Ewan had consumed on their journey. But there were also sheets of music and lyrics in a thick pink folder, and it was only here the solider suddenly slowed in his examination of every object.

"Aha," he shouted, shuffling through a series of sheets. It appeared he had known all along what to look for. "I knew it."

"But what on earth is that?" Jennifer asked in mock surprise, as she watched the soldier stand up to full height and open a small black book. It was a joke in itself that this soldier didn't cotton on to their cover-up. "I don't remember putting that in there."

"That's what they all say," the solider replied in earnest, as his eyes moved backwards and forwards across an open page. "This is just what we've been waiting for." Suddenly things were getting that bit more serious.

"Just you hold on a minute," Chris breathed deeply, moving to stand directly behind the soldier. "What exactly is it that you think you've found." The man before him merely laughed.

"Why our secret documents, of course. Major General Sir Adam Du Tale was informed days ago that they would be transported alongside the Forces' Sweetheart."

"So is that the reason they brought our jet down?" Thomas questioned, "because Jennifer was holding some secret documents."

"It certainly seems that way," Chris replied almost immediately, now giving Jennifer a strange look.

"No, no, that can't be right," Ewan continued, moving to stand beside the girl he loved. Behind them all, the French twins giggled with delight.

"Oh, Belle, I do love ze gossip," Renée smiled. For Chris, enough was enough.

"Whatever happened, happened," he said, bringing to an end their conversation. "I think it's about time I took the girls away and gave Jennifer some time to recover. She's obviously shocked." He was right; the Forces' Sweetheart had turned as white as a sheet, again.

Quickly Chris paced away from the group, before signalling to the girls that they should follow. Then once they were together he proceed to inform the twins of the interesting deception. They giggled again and Chris realised that they had pulled it off; they were free of the documents and the guilt that hung over them. It left their minds clear to concentrate on the impending battle. They talked as they walked and soon they had disappeared. Following in the same direction was the soldier that carried the newly discovered documents. He did not wish to remain in what he believed to be a compromising situation any longer than was necessary.

"I'm glad that's over," Corporal Ewan Roberts said, turning to face Thomas. Together they started to gather Jennifer's belongings which were scattered across the ground.

"Well, at least we're rid of the documents now," his friend said, "and you've learnt that she can't remain an angel forever, which is probably quite a good thing…"

***

When Chris returned to his friends, he found them waiting impatiently. It had taken him far longer than he had hoped to introduce the girls to Du Tale. There was a lot of explaining to do and questions to ask, many of which would have to wait for another day.

Quickly they headed into the building, flicking the lights and closing the door behind them. The same musty smell remained and the one large table still stood in the centre. Moving forwards and placing a pile of folded sheets there, which had been given to him by the Major General not ten minutes earlier, Chris began to speak.

"Well, Ewan, how are we? It is good to be back together, is it not?" Ewan could sense something sinister in his friend's voice, some kind of evil intent.

"Yeah, it's really good," he replied, knowing that his time as a leader was over. Chris was now in command again. "In fact it's pretty amazing considering only days ago we were entangled in the wreckage of a United jet with little or no hope of survival." His hair was still wet across his forehead and he looked innocent as the light hummed above them.

"Yes, well, be that as it may," Chris continued, now noticing that Thomas was eyeing them both eagerly. "You left the village when I had specifically told you not to." He was calm at the moment, yet his temper could rise at any time. "And you brought French twins along for the ride. They have no place here, Ewan, in a dangerous theatre of war."

His friend contemplated the fact, figuring in his own mind how best to reveal the truth. "It would have been just as dangerous if they had stayed in the village," he said simply. "Jennifer and I, we rescued them from their abusive father. We had no choice."

There was silence for a moment. Chris played with the words in his head. Instinctively he knew that now there would be no need for anger, no need to use force.

"Well then," he replied finally, placing his arms around his two friends and guiding them gently towards the table, "that is different." His voice had changed, and it was as if they were talking as they always had done. "Now," he began again, reaching for the papers that he had placed on the edge of the table. "Thomas has asked me to explain a few things." The young private nodded, before adding.

"When we arrived here, Ewan, I was sent off with the other soldiers. Chris was taken away to meet the Major General and given a position as commanding officer for several companies."

Ewan found it hard to believe. He had almost forgotten what it was like to be a real soldier. While he had been meeting and greeting girls, and jumping between village barns with Jennifer, his friends had been preparing for war and for a battle that was right on their doorstep.

"You're going to have to explain all of this to me," he said worriedly, watching as Chris unfolded the largest piece of paper in the pile.

"I'll make it simple, Ewan," his friend replied. "Listen carefully." Both Ewan and Thomas leaned in close, ears pricked, for they knew this information would be important. "This is a holographic map of the Chaîne des Puys, the mountain range that you can see behind the barracks, and over the next few days, battles will be taking place not only here, but across the world in strategic locations, in order to try and bring this war to a head."

Chris watched as his friends nodded and looked down at the holographic map before them. It was displayed a variety of marks and arrow directions. "These marks show the locations in which Major General Du Tale will want us to position our men. We will be taking supplies with us and because I will be commanding four companies of men, I will be marching each to a separate location, with secondary officers then taking control and the three of us remaining together and fighting with H Company." He took a deep breath before adding, "At least, that's what Du Tale told me when he handed the papers over. You may also wish to know that I've been given the non-commissioned rank of capitaine. That's because on paper, I have to be at a certain level before I can lead a company of men." Ewan's face fell, as he too appeared to realise the difficult situation which the Major General had put Chris in.

"It won't affect the way we look at you," Ewan said, "but you'll get a lot of animosity over it." Thomas nodded and Chris was glad of their understanding. "But why you? Why Capitaine Aston? Why not a leading French officer?"

Chris smiled and chuckled to himself. "Believe me, Ewan, there is an egotistical French Commandant in charge of the four other companies. And to answer your second question, I feel we are simply part of a very large plan. You see, Major General Du Tale told me that he and his officials have been studying and tracking our dear old Colonel Smith for some time. It would appear that he is up to no good. I don't know what he's been doing, but it appears that when Du Tale asked for three British soldiers to be deployed to the Chaîne des Puys in order to lead a new and dangerous offensive, Colonel Smith saw it as a chance to be rid of three very experienced men." The latest revelation was shocking for everyone and they found it hard to comprehend.

"Hold on a moment," Thomas asked, trying to remember back to the night before their deployment. "Colonel Smith told us that the President had asked for us specifically." The look on this face was one of confusion.

"I feel it was merely a ruse and a ploy, used to convince us to sign on the dotted line," Chris said meekly.

"But that must mean that the Major General–" Ewan struggled over his words.

"Exactly," Chris smiled, breaking his friend off midsentence. "The Major General has been following us for some time now. And personally, that is the only proof I need to convince me that we are far safer here than we ever would have been back in London." The others nodded. "I also believe that it would be quite beneficial for us to do some planning before morning."

For some time following the conversation, they stood around the table discussing how the day would pan out. Of course, they had been through these motions many times before, back in London, but then these had been merely hypothetical. This time it was real and far more serious. The holographic maps that Du Tale had provided for them were in-depth and detailed, showing not only the terrain of the Chaîne des Puys, the locations where the French Government believed the Reformed troops would attack first, and the slightest rocky outcrop that might provide cover during a face-to-face battle, but even direct routes back to the barracks, through great areas of open scrubland with only the trees for cover. These were escape routes if they so needed them.

Chris soon developed an expert skill in planning and preparation. Early the previous day, he had been worried about the offensive, but now, it appeared that Du Tale had provided him with a fully formed plan and all he had to do was implement it.

As the three British soldiers continued to discuss tactics within that small, damp room, the sun began to rise above the mountains and the eight hundred soldiers who had spent their last night in comfort began to rise and prepare themselves for deployment into the field. Inside, Chris, Ewan and Thomas had no way of measuring the passage of time, and so they were quite surprised when there was a knock at the door and a gentle hum of expectant excitement began to rise from outside. Thomas was the first to reach the door, opening it wide to see a somewhat fraught Jennifer standing on the steps, surrounded by an ever-expanding group of soldiers, and looking expectantly into the little room.

"Miss Marmalade, we love you!" were the shouts echoing from the crowd. "Sing for us, Miss Marmalade, we love you." Thomas looked on in surprise and grinned as he remembered they really were friends with one of the most influential women in the world. His warning the previous day had paid off.

"Chris, Ewan," he called, "I think you had better see this." Quickly, both men raced over to the doorway and looked out upon a scene of complete infatuation. Jennifer was dressed in a short, flowing, flowery dress; Chris knew it did not belong to her.

"It appears that they have recognised you as the Forces' Sweetheart," he said weakly, "I did wonder how long it would take."

"Yes," Jennifer replied timidly, looking around. "I'm really not used to all this attention. My manager deals with this, not me." She smiled and suddenly her face fell "But it will only get worse; the Major General said that Renée, Belle and I are to be nurses. We will look after any injured soldiers out in the field." Chris approved. He knew Du Tale had a sensible head on his shoulders, and this task would surely keep the girls away from any further trouble.

"Inside, now," he added finally, as Ewan ushered Jennifer into the small room. Then he raced to push the door shut behind them as the men surged forwards. He was just about to close it completely, when he saw a familiar figure approaching through the crowd. The soldiers backed away quickly as their Major General paced forwards towards the doorway. Immediately it was open again and Du Tale was speaking.

"Chris, I didn't think you would take this long," he said, all of a fluster, not himself at all. "Things are beginning, Chris. The time is nigh. I have taken your friends to the hospital wing, and now I must lead you to your men, Capitaine Aston. Bring the others with you. I will deal with these." He gestured towards the crowd of angry men which was by now slowly dispersing and Chris barely had time to gather his thoughts before they were out of the little building, down the steps and off to meet their destiny.

"Men," Du Tale roared to those who still remained, hoping to get another glimpse of their idol, "to your companies, AT ONCE!"

The soldiers began to run in every direction, and Chris smiled to himself, for at that moment he knew that with Du Tale he would always be safe. "Oh, Miss Marmalade…" the Major General said surprised as he turned around and found himself eye to eye with the beautiful woman, "…erm, I mean, Jennifer. What are you doing here? Off to the hospital wing with you now."

Managing quickly to kiss Ewan on the cheek and wave to her friends, Jennifer headed off to reunite herself with Renée and Belle, shouting until she was out of sight. "Keep yourselves safe, I'll be thinking of you. Don't let them get into danger, Chris; I know you will be a great leader." Even Chris felt the tug at his heartstrings as the Forces' Sweetheart finally disappeared and Ewan's heart dropped from his chest. This was it; there was no going back now.

"Now then," Du Tale said finally, marking the end of it all, "Chris, Ewan and Thomas, come with me." And silently the three men walked with the Major General, towards the waiting soldiers.

19

The French had not fared well in the war to this point. The split between countries and the backhand alliances did not suit them. But there was nothing they could do about it and so they had to stand as one nation and survive whatever was thrown at them, together.

A particular problem for the French Government in the years before United rule were their neighbouring countries, those who were supposed to be allies. Germany was heading towards United rule, with job losses the like of which had not been seen since the late 1920s and a mass evacuation of troops stationed in every current battleground. Germany had always been very prompt at preparing for war and the French had grown accustomed to the fact that a precursor for the beginning of a conflict was, more often than not, the Germans' call for rearmament.

While Germany worked on a battle plan and led its people towards the light of a new republic, the rest of Europe remained eerily silent. Italy, the

Netherlands and many of the Baltic States were playing stalemate. It appeared that no one country was prepared to make a tactical move before another. But while for the most part Europe remained quiet in the years that led up to United rule, France still had to deal with its most problematic neighbour.

The English Channel had, so far, been big enough to separate France from Britain, a country in the upthrows of anarchy and revolution. But the Anglo-French relationship was a dangerous topic of discussion, especially amongst the United leaders who had banded together in the face of unspeakable evil.

These two European powers had been in almost constant conflict throughout history, fighting against each other to gain an upper hand. Even in the years that led up to United rule, when relations were somewhat cordial and cooperative, each country regarded the other with a little wariness on their own part, due quite substantially to their individual historical differences.

Britain was considered iconic, and many were shocked that a monarchy which had lasted well over four centuries could once again be overthrown by a simple regime change and the power of the people. But in modern society was it really that much of a revelation? After all, the British monarchy was one of the last remaining in the world, and indeed political revolution was by no means a new invention. The leaders of the new RAP (Rights for the Average Person) political faction had many influences to draw upon, communism, fascism and, of course, the exploits of Oliver Cromwell and the Parliamentarians who had succeeded in creating a republican commonwealth in the seventeenth century. In essence their ideas were effectively the same, with the newly elected president wholeheartedly embracing the idea of United rule and then promoting it with an avid success to leaders of the other European states.

It brought Britain in line with France as both were now ruled as United republics. But even this was not enough. With the onset of war and rearmament fracturing discussion there was an increasing suspicion between the two leaders; despite this, they had no option but to place their trust in each other.

* * *

Several years and the majority of a war later, Colonel David Smith was sitting at his desk, his office placed high above the streets of London. He had chosen never to be located at the Ministry of Defence, for he could do without being constantly compared to every bureaucratic half-wit who held a similar position. He was a man on his own, important and a leader in his field. No, it was far better for him to locate his offices high above the streets of Soho. After all, he was the colonel of the Thames Regimental Barracks, only the greatest in the whole of these United Isles.

Colonel Smith was certainly a man who lived for his own personal achievement. But like many in highly respected positions, the Colonel sometimes abused his power. In fact, he was considered by many to hold a very personal secret close to his chest.

Pausing mid flow and looking up from his keyboard, Colonel Smith glanced at a pile of letters stacked neatly beside him on the desk. Many of them would be unimportant, he was sure, just the routine checks that he must complete on certain case files, standard letters from the President sent out to everyone in his position and catalogues detailing the latest equipment that he could now purchase for his men. But even though the contents would be tiresome and boring, he knew there was a real need to check each and every letter, for he was still awaiting some important news.

Quickly reaching for the pile he realised he'd been right; there were letters from the President and several thick catalogues, but hiding between them and almost at the bottom of the pile were two letters air-marked France and an official document sent first class from Lennons Bank Plc. The latter was strange, for David Smith knew that all of his banking was completed online. He had never had any problems before.

Reaching forwards to pull his penknife from the centre of a pot which contained a variety of coloured pens, he made light work of opening all three letters, and opted to read the official document first.

Dear Sir, it began in the usual formal tone. *I write to confirm that your most recent payment has not been completed, as of the date…* Colonel Smith scratched his head. This had never happened before; all of his payments went through on time. That was the way his office ran on a day-to-day basis. Surely it could not be that important? Later, he would ring the bank himself. Next he reached for the first of the airmail letters and was surprised to find inside a newspaper clipping and a frantically scrawled note. He recognised the handwriting almost immediately, but the newspaper clipping, that was a surprise.

Read the attached, it said simply, *and I think you will find that all our efforts have been thwarted. The road from this point onwards is very slippery.* And it was signed with a simple initial, the letter 'B'. Colonel Smith tossed the note aside quickly, and began to read the newspaper article with a far greater interest. What could he be talking about? The plan was certain to succeed, it was almost guaranteed. But as he read the headline and looked at the photograph which accompanied it, his face fell.

DOMESTIC DISTURBANCE IN FRENCH VILLAGE: FARMER ARRESTED

There was a picture of an elderly man, thinning hair, handcuffed and standing beneath a broken window, while in the background he could just make out three dark figures running in the opposite direction. It was an amateur shot from the scene, taken by an onlooker, and two of the three figures were unrecognisable. But the third, who was carrying a fourth in his arms, was unmistakable.

"Ewan Roberts," the Colonel breathed, still staring at the photograph before him. "So they did survive." Colonel Smith was shocked, to say the least. For years he had been in this job and nothing had ever gone wrong. His life of luxury had been secure and yet now there was a single seed of doubt fixed between the pages of his life. Thinking quickly now, eyes darting around the room, he reached for the second French envelope and paced over to the window. There, he looked down over the streets of Soho and marvelled at the plight of the average Londoner, more careful in these dangerous years of war. For a moment he wondered what it would be like to swap places for just a day. To be normal for once, with no high military position, and the expectation that was inevitably placed upon you.

The Colonel sighed deeply, his head in his hands, the tired lines beneath his eyes suddenly more pronounced, and was about to open the second letter when there was a hurried knock at the door.

Wondering what all the commotion could be about at a time when he could really do without it, he flung the letter down on his desk in a fit of temper, sending the contents spewing halfway across the shiny surface, and paced towards the door, pulling it wide open. Quickly a minor official darted into the room, shuffling from side to side expectantly.

"What is it now, William?" David Smith questioned with disinterest. The young official looked pale as a sheet.

"Well, sir," he began, trying not to catch the Colonel's eye, "I've just received a message from France. Fighting has begun in earnest against the rebel Reformed troops stationed across the Chaîne des Puys. Tomorrow there begins a full-scale offensive across the world, aimed at winning the war. The Reformed troops are weakening, sir, but our men are as strong as ever–"

Colonel Smith was angry. There was a look of thunder about him, streaks of lightning behind the eyes, and his response broke off the official mid-sentence.

"What?" he boomed, staring the man directly in the face. For a few moments he stood there literally quaking with anger, and then suddenly his resolve changed and he weakened. He wiped his brow with the back of his hand, tufts of grey hair pushed back against his forehead. And this time he spoke far more meekly. "Why wasn't I told about this?"

The small and timid official merely shook his head, not knowing what to say. "There is one more thing, sir," he muttered. The Colonel sighed but did not stop him. "The President called a few minutes ago, he wanted to know why one of our most superior jets went down in the middle of French territory, close to several Reformed strongholds, and why he was not informed about it. I told him, I… told him, I didn't know."

"Thank you," Colonel Smith grimaced at last, swallowing hard. "Now if you could leave me alone for a while…"

"Yes, sir. Of course, sir," the official smiled, backing out the room, pulling the door shut behind him. He seemed glad the whole ordeal was over. Walking back to his desk, Colonel Smith dropped into the chair and dialled a few digits into the phone with his podgy fingers. The computerised voice on the other end of the line sounded tiny and far away, yet it confirmed his greatest fears.

'Payment ID: 2561921… Payment month and transaction… July – Reformed Forces of China,

General Yee Ling Chow… Payment status: Transaction unsuccessful.'

The Colonel slammed the phone down hard and once again buried his head in his hands. Things could not get any worse. His story would soon be over and the war would soon be won. His side would be victorious, and yet he would not be happy. The reward he had been promised all those years ago would not come; he would be bankrupt, desolate and without a purpose. It didn't bear thinking about.

But perhaps there was still a way to save himself. Wiggling the wireless mouse, he clicked open on a 'new email document' and thought about the best way to explain things. Dear Mr President, he began, but found himself unable to continue. Beside him on the desk, left unnoticed in the panic that had ensued, was the second letter. It had exactly the same postal address as the first, and was lying next to the neatly opened envelope, its message clearly visible.

The net is drawing in, David. It will not be long, you are in our sights. Treachery and deception is a court-martial offence, may I remind you, and I do not think the President would approve. We have several of your soldiers here. They are safe and well after a disturbing aviation accident for which we both know you are responsible.

Until next time. Du Tale.

20

They were to be stationed furthest from the barracks, as Chris discovered moments after they had been grouped together that same morning. He was introduced to the companies which he would be commanding, and then they were briefed on the aims of the offensive and the exact location within the Chaîne des Puys to which they would be deployed.

And now they were here, occupying the space between two great green mountains. From what Major General Sir Adam Du Tale had said, it appeared that they were stationed on the opposite side of the mountain range to the enemy and that meant that if they were able to push through, Reformed troops would approach through a small gap to the left and meet them head-on.

It was early in the afternoon and Chris was sitting with his back against the soft earth of their trench. Ewan and Thomas flanked him on either side and just beyond the top of their self-contained hideaway they could see tall blades of grass dancing in the breeze. The exposed earth was damp against their arms and the sun beat down upon their faces. Here they waited with bated breath, just three men, while before them several hundred stood on the front line.

"Well, I guess we just have to pass the time until the excitement begins," Thomas said, kicking a pile of loose stones across the length of the trench.

"If you listen carefully," Chris replied, tactfully reminding his friend of their current situation, "you'll be able to hear that the fighting has already begun." Sure enough, far in the distance the rattle of machine-gun fire echoed around the hills and every so often an explosion broke loudly across the distance and rocked the very ground they were sat upon. "What we've got to remember, Thomas, is that the enemy don't care. There are no morals in their society, or at least not those that respond to human suffering."

Ewan leant across the pair and reached for his gun, an AP-78 assault rifle, only the very best in modern warfare design. Silently, he clicked it open and slid in a tiny computerised chip. Their weapons were already loaded with a good amount of ammunition and that meant they could hold off reloading until it was essential, while the computer chip controlled the rapid fire rate and secured the lock-in sight that would provide the perfect aim.

"These people," he added, securing the gun closed, "were responsible for that horrible terrorist blast in London. They nearly killed Jennifer and how nobody was injured, I'll never know." He paused for a moment, looking around. "For this reason and this reason alone, I intend to destroy as many of them as I can."

Chris nodded, for he understood his friend's motives. "Oh, and Ewan," he said rather suddenly, "I think it's a good job you have primed that weapon of yours. We might need it very soon indeed." And it was at that moment that a small plane passed noisily overhead. Painted dark red, on the underbelly of the cockpit was the emblem of the Reformed Army of the World. That was a dangerous white circle, with the symbol of an atomic bomb in the centre. They had not yet used such weapons, but it was only a matter of time.

All three turned to look at the same time and almost immediately they ducked down further into the trench. They were wearing their camouflage cover, so remaining hidden wasn't a problem. However, the plane was moving slowly, and they knew this meant it was scoping the landscape; heat sensors would be checking for any life down below. Crossing between the mountains, the plane headed in the direction of the front-line fighting. There, the three soldiers watched as a United fighter jet appeared out of nowhere, and a fierce gun battle soon ensued.

"We've got to get there," Chris mouthed. "We can't just sit here." And both Ewan and Thomas knew he was right.

* * *

On the same side of the mountain range and a little closer to the front line, Renée, Belle and Jennifer were overwhelmed by every aspect of war. They were volunteering in the medical tent as requested, and were surrounded on every side by the injured and the fallen. They had no training and they were not prepared. But somehow it didn't matter. Jennifer took her commands from the leading medical officers and then she conveyed the task to the twins. They were to comfort the men, provide a friendly and reassuring face which would make them smile, while at the same time they could perform minor first aid and replace bandages on various dry wounds.

"We've had word that a group of soldiers will be heading this way," the officer called to Jennifer, who immediately came rushing over, her hair pushed back with an Alice band. He had the slightest French accent, yet he spoke impeccable English. "There was an explosion our end not so long ago and several of the men involved were rather badly injured. There are others with superficial wounds, and I was hoping you would be able to take care of them." He smiled and Jennifer nodded. It was like speaking to her manager all over again. Except this time, she had more faith.

"I'll do my best, sir," she replied, looking around the crowded room. "There are a few in here that I was tending to earlier." Having said this, she moved in closer and whispered directly into the officer's ear. "I don't think they are going to make it, sir."

The officer thought for a moment before formulating a reply. "Well that's a fact of war, my girl," he said gravely. "I'm afraid there is nothing we can do." He paused again. Like Jennifer, he whispered. "But if they don't happen to make it, we're taking the bodies through there to be identified." Quickly, he pointed towards a gap on the furthest side of the tent which was covered with a black cloth. Jennifer nodded and the officer prompted her to call Renée and Belle together so that they could prepare for their new duties.

"I do not like eet in zis place," Belle admitted quickly. "Zere are too many dead people. It eez an 'orrible sight to see."

Her sister nodded. "Zese men are so young," Renée added mournfully. "Zey are so young and 'ave so much living to do." Everyone was in agreement.

"Well," Jennifer began, taking the girls' hands, "you are not going to like me for this, but I've just been told that we are expecting a large group of superficially injured soldiers. There has been an explosion our end of the field, and we have been asked to deal with the casualties who'll be arriving here shortly."

The twins gulped and looked down at the ground. "Well, I guess zere is nothing we can do about eet," Renée said quietly. "We 'ad better get on with our jobs and 'ope zat ze others are all okay." And with that she turned away and for a moment looked towards the entrance of the makeshift medical tent, just as a group of medical soldiers entered in pairs, carrying their comrades on stretchers between them.

* * *

They reached the height of the conflict by moving nimbly between trees, ducking for cover. The way remained clear, but still they kept their weapons primed. Together they passed through a patch of forest, Chris leading the way and Ewan bringing up the rear. Their priority was to keep Thomas safe, as his wandering mind might lead them into danger. In that state he would make them an obvious target. The thick canopy of trees covered them in darkness, and the closer they came to the location, the louder the sounds of war became.

Each of the soldiers felt a shiver down his spine as they emerged from the forest and crossed down towards an open area of heathland. The opposing end of the battlefield was marked by a thick strip of sharp barbed wire and there were muddy tracks traversing the space between, where soldiers had moved in the hours before. From here they had a clear view down towards the mass of United men, groups who stood spaced out across their end of the battlefield. There were steadfast machine gunners, who stood behind their weapons and always held their position, while others had constructed a series of tarpaulin tents, under which they could seek minimal cover and plan their next offensive move. Each side was holding its ground well, and the sounds they had heard on the descent came from an isolated group who were fighting fiercely at the far right-hand side. Here the Reformed troops were trying to press home their advance, however, their skills in close combat were limited and the United forces were protecting their own in a business-like manner, gunning down anyone who dared to cross the line. Above them in the sky, the fierce battle had not alleviated, the war jets teasing each other with a close bout of gunfire, before moving off towards the horizon.

For a moment Chris wondered if he had made a dangerous decision in leading his friends towards the very heart of the conflict, for it looked to him as if outright combat could begin at any minute. But now there was nothing else to do, and as he watched the soldiers fighting in the distance, he witnessed something which confirmed in his mind that he had chosen the right course of action. The Reformed forces may never have excelled in close combat, but they had always been well known for their use of sudden and dangerous weapons. From their position on the hill, Chris, Ewan and Thomas watched in horror as a small man in Reformed colours broke away from the rest of his group, only to kneel down on the ground. His behaviour seemed strange, but his comrades seemed quite aware of his motives as, no sooner had he hit the ground, than they turned quickly to run in retreat. The small man followed, although he was not quite quick enough, and seconds later a small, yet sophisticated explosion broke through the air, sending his body and those of the many United soldiers who had not escaped, up into the air and then back towards the hard ground.

"My God," Chris shouted, turning to address his friends, a look of shock on each of their faces. It was hard for him to be heard above the noise that followed. "There's no way that any of them could have survived that. We've got to get down there now and help our remaining men!" And with that, he pointed towards an oblong-shaped trench which had been dug several feet into the ground, before proceeding to adjust his headgear and pull down his visor. "There's a sharp incline from here down towards the battlefield, boys," he continued, eager to begin the descent. "We're going to have our weapons primed and then we're going to run straight down towards the nearest trench." Everything happened so quickly that there was barely time to resist.

"Isn't this a bit risky?" Thomas shouted, looking across the expanse of open terrain and the medical soldiers who were now running to aid their injured comrades.

Chris replied quickly and seriously. "We've two chances. I'm hoping we can divert the enemy's attention and that might provide some welcome relief." And before there was time for Ewan or Thomas to resist, they were off down the hill, their camouflage clothing providing little cover between the dark vegetation and the blue of the sky.

As they continued downhill Ewan could see the enemy regrouping, guns raised in earnest. At the front a Reformed private had broken away from the rest and was running towards the corner of the field. From there he fired a round of bullets up towards Ewan and the others, his aim dangerously off target. But it alerted the rest to those three United soldiers, making a desperate dash for safety.

The first round of machine-gun fire passed somewhere to the left, if Chris was to believe the way in which the sound was travelling. It helped them that the artillery in question was some distance away, for it meant that the aim would be impaired, thus giving them more time to escape. Then a second and a third round were fired and Ewan wondered why no United soldier had yet shot and killed the unknown enemy who had started the whole furore. Instead, the United forces were responding to a sudden uproar from enemy lines that led to them regrouping right along the length of their trenches. Chris took a moment to consider where Commandant Babineaux might be at a time like this. He hoped the French officer was somewhere near the front, leading his men into battle.

Just beyond United lines and past the barbed wire, the Reformed soldier who had first run out to take his aim at Chris, Ewan and Thomas remained motionless where he stood, his weapon on the ground as if it were out of ammo. Chris watched with annoyance as at least a hundred Reformed mercenaries climbed slowly over the edge of their bunker and marched out into the main battlefield. They swarmed towards the barbed wire that marked the beginning of no-man's land and then suddenly, as rapidly as they had begun, they stopped. They were waiting for the next move; they had an advantage over the United forces and could bide their time.

But there was still hope. And soon several things were to happen at almost exactly the same time. Ewan and Thomas, following Chris as their leader, had almost reached the very bottom of the hill and were preparing to jump over a small brook and down into the United trench, when that solitary Reformed soldier picked up his gun one final time. Slowly he hoisted it up to his waist and then fired another round of bullets up over the top of the United dugouts. He was not out of ammunition after all; he had merely tricked the better nature of the United men, so that he now had the perfect site from which to aim at the three United soldiers who had been his target in the first place.

"Get down!" Thomas roared from the back of the group, diving forwards the moment he saw the man move and pulling his comrades down with him. Chris was so fixated on achieving their goal and making that final crossing into certain safety that he did not realise what was happening. The moment they hit the damp grass, he heard first the man fire, and then the simple and efficient rattle of a United response. Instinctively they knew that their would-be assassin was no more. Immediately, they sprang up from the ground and dashed down towards the brook, before finally jumping down into the trench, their boots making a great thud as they landed on the wet earth. The conditions here were far worse than they had experienced on the other side of the mountain range and immediately their boots began to sink into thick mud. At the same time, a great roar erupted from the furthest barbed wire as the Reformed mercenaries rushed forwards to seek revenge for their fallen comrade, and, although they didn't know it, to meet their inevitable destiny.

The entire battlefield was alive, as men now began to surge forwards from United lines, with little time to spare. "You idiots," someone shouted to Chris as they passed, not recognising his higher rank. "Now look what you've gone and done." Men were moving everywhere, out into the battlefield in great hordes, standing to face off their rivals. Chris was not going to dignify the soldier with a response. Instead, he gestured to Ewan and Thomas and with some difficulty they pulled their boots from the muddy ground and ran forwards to join the rest of their men. His position didn't matter anymore; instinctive fighting was all that Chris Aston knew.

Along the length of the battlefield were various hideouts, trees that haphazardly grew in the barren land and cover which was provided behind metal sheeting and the huge and bulky machine guns. Both sides fired rapidly towards each other, the Reformed troops believing they still held the advantage. By now Chris had managed to move across to the cover provided on the left flank and from here he fired above the canopy, quashing the enemy as they tried to stake their claim. He was lucky to have a view right across the battlefield and that meant he could keep an eye on Ewan and Thomas. Men were fighting, some were retreating. A great many United and Reformed soldiers were gunned down in that first five minutes. Now they were equal, no side had the advantage. The United men were holding ground well and Chris hoped his comrades were safe.

Thomas was moving towards the front of a group who were intent on holding back the enemy in whichever way they could. Several Reformed soldiers were heading towards them at a fast pace, their guns aimed and primed, and across the space between he heard one of the men scream something in a strange Arabic language which he did not understand.

"They're trying to break through," the United soldier beside him shouted in French, and suddenly he realised that he was fighting alongside armed forces who did not speak his language. Quickly he made up his mind to follow the others, who by now had raised their weapons in response and quickly fired towards their approaching enemy. The Reformed men dived to the ground, one falling in the first round of fire, before the others jumped back onto their feet and continued their approach, leaving their comrade lying lifeless in the mud. The French soldiers primed their weapons ready to fire again, but now there was a problem.

"Je suis à court de munitions," one of the men cried in horror.

"Retraite!" screamed another, as the approaching enemy realised what was happening. They had no choice but to run for it, dropping their weapons and sprinting back towards the trenches. But one of the men was too slow, and he soon dropped down behind his comrades, a series of bullets penetrating his body armour, sending him flailing towards the ground.

The other soldiers dared not even turn to look as more and more Reformed men moved in to push through the gap which had now been created. Quickly they rounded on the United lines, using strength in numbers to push the other men away from their own end of the battlefield.

The United troops had no choice but to retreat, while random shell fire attacked them from every side. Chris was one of the last to move. He didn't understand the commotion; these men who had been led into battle by Commandant Babineaux were falling at the first hurdle, the strongest soldiers were retreating uphill, towards the forest, many of them with little hope of survival.

Begrudgingly, he joined the ranks as they ran. But he was not giving in and as they made their way uphill once again, he turned and fired down towards the enemy, sending several rolling down the hill. If they were going to be forced into retreat by these rebels who had no idea what a civilised society was all about, he was going to take a few out in the process.

Thankfully there came a time when the barrage of bullets receded, as the last of the United soldiers made their way into the safety of the forest, and the Reformed troops felt they had secured their first deserved victory. Quickly these men turned and began to move back down towards the battlefield, where they could make use of United machine guns, supplies and ammunition. There lay the bodies of the many men who had been sacrificed in the first of several dangerous confrontations.

The Reformed troops would not wait long, for although their numbers were greatly depleted when compared to the United Army, they would fight to keep the upper hand. For a little while, each side would regroup and discuss the continuation of their combat plans, but inevitably the Reformed troops would once more seek out their prize, pushing on towards the heart of the Chaîne des Puys.

21

For days the United forces waited under the cover provided by the forest, biding their time and recuperating their losses. The men were no longer worried about their Reformed counterparts, the enemy that still needed to be wiped out, for they would not dare to venture into even the opening of such a forest. Every soldier knew those hiding between the trees had the greatest advantage.

Chris, Thomas and Ewan spent those few long days chatting about their own fortunes, musing whether they would come out of this horrible war alive. The days of waiting were tedious, and the nights were cold and damp, with little warmth apart from that provided by one central fire, on which they cooked meagre meals. The enemy knew where they were hiding, and so there was no fear that the fire might alert them, but even so, their meals were never interesting, as much of their supplies had been left behind.

However, on the fourth day, things began to look up. Chris had strung a makeshift hammock between the trunks of two trees, and he was taking advantage of the darkness, recovering his strength by dozing lightly through the afternoon. Beside him at the base of another tree, a tall soldier who carried the company's radio equipment was trying fruitlessly to contact the barracks and call for reinforcements. He had been repeating this process over and over since they had arrived and yet he was still unable to contact either Du Tale or any of his officials. They were fast running out of options.

"Mon dieu," the soldier exclaimed suddenly in his thick accent, throwing the radio box across the ground. "We are never going to get 'old of them." The noise of the object skidding to a halt several feet away was enough to wake Chris from his daze.

"Not got it working yet, eh?" he asked sleepily. The man shook his head sadly. "Here, let me try it," he continued, believing that another pair of hands might do the trick. "You never know, hitting the ground just then may have knocked some sense into it." It was a simple solution to an ongoing problem.

Swinging himself out of the hammock and picking up the radio from where it lay, Chris secured the battery pack and twiddled the various knobs and dials that adorned the front. All at once they were confronted by the hideous sound of static, a crackling and hissing which sent the birds circling up from the trees. The radio man ran to Chris's side and adjusted the volume before proceeding to type Major General Du Tale's believed location into the small electronic screen. It was a fusion of old and new technologies which made this sort of equipment so effective. Within moments the interference died away and a clear, recognisable voice could be heard over the speakers.

"This is French base Charlie Delta Papa, Major General Sir Adam Du Tale hearing you loud and clear. Over." The radio man stared at Chris as he reached for the headset and prepared to respond. The headset sat awkwardly on his head, with a microphone that reached down beside his mouth.

"Sir," he said loudly. "It's me." There was a slight pause as the message travelled over the distance. "Christopher," Du Tale replied gleefully, before his tone turned a little more grave. "How are you coping?"

"Ok. But I'm not so sure about the others. We've lost a lot of men in the past few days. It's hit our morale rather badly and we're hiding out in an area of forest." Chris spoke quickly, for he had no idea who else might be listening in.

"Yes, I've heard," Du Tale replied after a pause, his voice crackling slightly. "Very bad business all in all mind. I thought you'd have these Reformed rebels running, Chris..."

"My men are still waiting beyond the furthest hills. They are unaware of what is happening."

"Well, that's something." The Major General breathed deeply before continuing. "I must confess, Chris, I have been down to the battleground myself and I've seen the carnage."

By now the radio man was eyeing Chris eagerly, suggesting that it might be time to wind up the conversation.

"We need reinforcements, sir," he said quickly.

There was a sudden crack, the sound of a twig breaking underfoot and both soldiers immediately drew their weapons in response. Between the trees they could see something moving. From his strategic position Chris fired a round into the shrubbery and saw a flash of red. Now he knew his target. This time he moved forward, and fired again. Behind him, Du Tale's voice echoed through the tiny speakers and Chris realised he had pulled the headset out of the machine as he moved away.

"Chris? Can you hear me? I've requested reinforcements by air. Over."

"Message received. Over and out," the radio man replied. He turned off the set and took out the batteries. Whatever was approaching had now escaped and Chris heard it crashing away from danger, back to safety.

"Well, at least reinforcements are on the way." Chris knew now that it was a time for action, and hurriedly he began to gather his belongings. Pulling his backpack up over his shoulder, he said.

"I never thought to ask your name." The man smiled and realised that he too, had forgotten to introduce himself.

"Steadwell, Charles Jean Steadwell." Chris nodded, and the men shook hands, before walking off together.

* * *

Their walk was brisk, and soon they arrived once again at the centre of the remaining operation. Chris wasted no time gathering the men into a group, he knew Du Tale was sending reinforcements by air and, given the direction of the barracks to the north and that there wasn't a strong wind, they should hear the jets long before they actually arrived.

While the men Chris commanded were waiting on the opposite side of the mountain range, he wondered what had happened to Babineaux. Where and how had he disappeared? After deliberating, he realised he really hadn't any choice. He would dispatch Ewan Roberts to meet with his own men and warn them that once the rebels had been destroyed on the front line, the battle would almost immediately transfer to their quarters, meaning that they would be the last line of the defence. As for Babineaux, Chris would take on his role for the present while Thomas attempted to source further information.

It soon became clear that the last man to fight with Babineaux had fled from the battlefield. He was a small man, of Eastern European descent, who had found himself fighting for the United French Army after escaping from his native Russia when Reformed dictatorship took hold. Babineaux had been injured, that much was clear, and if he was alive, he would be weak. He could have made his way back towards the barracks and safety, or he might have died. For the moment Chris was in full command.

* * *

The air strike and reinforcements soon arrived, and a second battle began in earnest. Chris positioned his men on the brow of the hill, for when he heard the great machines approaching, he knew that they could negotiate a two-pronged attack. From their position on the edge of the forest, they could see everything that was happening below and yet were close enough to retreat again if they needed to.

The three United jets appeared like great grey birds on the horizon. As they crossed the river they cast a great shadow on the barren battleground. The largest jet reached the area first, firing a barrage that sent the enemy fleeing in retreat. Days after the previous skirmish, they were still salvaging vital equipment from behind United lines and now the gun battlements lay open in the field, while packs of ammunition were dropped to the ground as the enemy soldiers rushed for the cover of their own trenches. The first round of fire was only strengthened by another, as the second and third planes came in close. Slowly they hovered there above the centre of the field, before one descended towards the ground. This was an Albatross 34, the very latest in military design, and on its soft underbelly it carried a heavily armoured tank which came to rest on the ground as a group of men climbed down from the cockpit. Now was the time to move and Chris was the only one who could issue such a command.

"Men, descend!" he shouted calmly to those who waited behind, "Thomas, with me. And the rest of you, regroup behind the armed reinforcements and keep to the cover as much as possible." Thomas was soon at his friend's side and quickly the swarm of United men began to move down towards the battlefield. They hit the ground running, and Chris saw the soldiers who were unhooking the tank from its supports, and who would undoubtedly be joining them for the fight. These men were prepared, heavily armoured, with grenades and sub-machine guns, and amongst the faces of many innocent people, Chris caught a glimpse of one expression he recognised. It was Alan Waldow, a man in his own command, who had been kept behind waiting for a call that signalled the need for reinforcements. Well, that call had come from Chris's own lips, and silently he wished the man good luck, as the tank was disconnected from its carrier and the young soldier climbed inside.

By now, the aerial bombardment had killed many of the remaining Reformed soldiers, meaning that hand-to-hand combat could finally complete phase one of the operation.

"We have to destroy these rebels completely this time," Chris shouted over the noise from above. It was unclear as to whether or not anyone heard his plea, but the message at least was clear, for quickly they began to move forwards, as a hail of bullets from the sky above halted just for a moment. They were crossing enemy lines, jumping down into Reformed trenches and beating the enemy at their own game, with a great armoured tank rumbling along in their wake.

Chris raised his gun to his waist and shot a man in the chest. He was running towards him and fell like a rag- doll to the ground. The enemy had no idea who they were dealing with, a United commanding officer, perhaps the only one that remained. Beside him, his comrades were locked in a bitter fight with two burly Reformed men. For some, close combat out in the field was their only option. Here the enemy were resolute, shooting down several United soldiers, only to be killed themselves by the waiting tank.

Chris knew they had won, and he was glad that Ewan had parted from them; it was one less person for him to worry about. He kept Thomas close, covering the man when he could not cover himself. He would keep him alive at any cost.

When the Reformed men were almost none, Chris climbed out of the trenches and back onto the battlefield. It was sprinkled with the dead. On the far side, close, in fact, to where they had been fighting days earlier, Chris saw movement. From the dead that lay all around, someone was climbing weakly to their feet. They could not have been injured in the current combat, as they were lying far from the immediate area, so had been on the field for days. Now, a Reformed soldier had seen the man. At the same time, Alan Waldow's head appeared above the parapet of the tank. What was he doing, taking the chance to view the battlefield from such an angle? Did he recognise the man who was moving? Did he realise the danger that he was putting himself in? Chris moved to the left, fearing above all his own safety.

It was unbearable, but as the man who stood up amongst the dead limped towards the mass of United soldiers, Chris recognised his face. It was Babineaux, his uniform covered in blood. The single Reformed soldier moved slowly towards him, and Chris hoped at that moment that he would shoot and that Babineaux would be killed. But instead, something astounding happened. Painfully Babineaux reached down to his belt and pulled a hand pistol from the holster. Then, although his aim seemed nervously off target, he fired two shots towards the top parapet of the tank.

Chris heard the dull thud as Alan's body hit the metal shell of the armoured vehicle and he saw the Reformed soldier stop dead in his tracks. Babineaux was a coward, shooting down his own man to protect himself, pretending that he was in fact one of the enemy. Who would go to such lengths in order to save themselves? Who could be so cruel and heartless? It left Chris with no choice.

The Reformed soldier turned in confusion, as all across the battlefield United men realised they had won the first offensive. Chris ran forwards, waving his gun madly. He shot the soldier and was somehow grateful that he killed the last one. It didn't make up for Babineaux's actions and it wouldn't bring Alan back, but it immediately stemmed his anger.

Minutes later the United soldiers began to regroup, Babineaux had put away his gun and was nearing one of the three fighter planes. He felt physically sick as he saw the officer hauled inside, before the plane took off and began a journey that would lead him to safety.

22

Chris and the others soon took advantage of a break in the fighting. The Reformed troops had retreated back into the mountains, and while the United men recuperated, a stalemate developed between the two sides. For a while every solider rested more easily.

The following morning dawned bright and breezy. The sun rose to cast a welcome glow upon the French hills. Chris knew things were looking up when the weather cleared. For days they had been fighting a losing battle against sheets of rain, a thick fog which engulfed the Chaîne des Puys and made it hard to see anything beyond a metre ahead. But now there was an eerie silence. A hint of desperation dancing on the cool breeze, something that they had not noticed before.

Before long everyone piled into one of the standard army pick-ups, with an open back and faded tarpaulin hanging from the cab, and with Ewan in control of the wheel and Jennifer in the passenger seat beside him, they set off for the French coast. Chris and Thomas thought the cool breeze from the back of the vehicle was similar to sitting on a double-decker bus back in England.

Beyond the tallest hillock of the Chaîne des Puys, a narrow track led down towards the expressway and from there to the coast. They all knew that they were unlikely to make it back to base before sundown that evening, but none of them cared. The fresh air would do them good, give them a chance to forget their troubles and become better acquainted with the twins.

Jennifer was particularly excited. She hadn't been to the beach since she was a child. Miss Marmalade had only performed on the British coast once; on the historic Blackpool Pier. Part of the town had long since been demolished to make way for one of the new United Rocket Landing Ways, with the Blackpool Tower turned into a radio receiver and public hologram hotspot. So many changes.

Reaching the expressway, the views to the west, back towards the mountain range from which they had travelled were outstanding. They could pick out each hilltop and freshwater pool as it shimmered in the sunlight. It was hard to believe that the hills hid a battle so harsh that it was barely imaginable.

Their route was clear, which allowed Ewan to drive faster than usual. Hardly any vehicles travelled the expressway any longer. Instead, its path, which twisted along the very edge of rural France, provided direction for the many hover cars bound for the coast. Only because the men had enlisted, they learned how to drive manually geared, fuel-powered vehicles. With the last of the fossil fuels reserved for the armed forces, they could drive without the fear of a speed limit, anywhere in the world, wherever they were posted.

* * *

The golden sands of the beach stretched out into the distance where at last they met with the shimmering expanse of the ocean. Ewan steered the battered old pick-up around onto the gravel patch which had once been a car park. High above them were stop-locks for the hover cars, already occupied by early arrivals. Piling out into the heat of the day, each of them was filled a need to escape the horrors of conflict, if only for a little while.

The twins couldn't wait. They knew this place, because their father had brought them here when they were children. Now it felt as if they were returning to some long-lost home. Together, they ran over the dunes and down onto the beach, giggling like the happy children they had once been. Jennifer reached out and locked fingers with Ewan, an instinctive reaction, while Thomas marvelled in the beauty of the landscape. For the first time in years he was going swimming! Even Chris had to admit that they had picked a glorious day for their break.

Down on the beach, Grandparents and mothers looked after the little ones, absent of the men who were away fighting. The children built sandcastles, while their mothers tried to relax in the sun. In a while, the grandparents would take them paddling. The scene was a long way from the battle they had so recently left.

When the rest of the little group finally made their way down onto the sand, they looked around for the twins, hearing their voices long before they saw them. They were standing a little further down the beach, with big smiles on their faces.

"Down 'ere," Belle shouted gleefully, waving her hands in the air.

"Isn't eet marvellous?" her sister stated happily.

They laid a blanket down on the sand and secured it with stones. Renée and Belle had changed into the shortest skirts they could find, and had tied their shirts up in the middle, exposing their stomachs to the sun. With Belle's hair tied into pig tails, they headed off towards the sea, their feet padding against the dry sand and their long legs shining in the sun. Thomas couldn't draw his eyes away as he watched them jumping in and out of the waves.

"Why don't you join them?" Chris said, looking over at his friend, trying to use as much tact as possible. "We're here to have a good time." Thomas thought about this for a moment.

"Yeah, you're right, Chris," he smiled, standing up and beginning to unbutton his shirt. He placed it down on the blanket, rolled his trousers up to his knees and then walked off in the direction of the shoreline.

"Thomas," Ewan shouted. His friend stopped suddenly and turned on the spot. "Take that silly cap off; it'll ruin your chances." Thomas muttered some sort of reply, smiled weakly, and skimmed his cap through the air like a Frisbee. The group was dispersing quickly, with only three of them now left at the top of the beach.

"I'm going for a walk," Chris said simply, getting up from his position and looking out towards the horizon. "I need to clear my head." Slowly he headed off further down the beach, his hands in his pockets, leaving Ewan and Jennifer alone.

"Well that's it, they've deserted us," Ewan smiled, happier than he was letting on.

"It'll be nice to have some time alone again," Jennifer replied, pulling her flowery patterned shirt up and lying down on the blanket. "At least this time we are relaxing. You know, I was really looking forward to getting a nice tan, before everything else kicked off." She turned to Ewan and smiled, the look in her eyes said it all. She was right, of course, for today they could forget about everything else and concentrate on themselves. So thinking only about the night he had spent in London in the dressing room, Ewan leaned down and brushed the hair from Jennifer's eyes. Then he lightly kissed her and watched as she smiled mischievously at him.

"You're the Forces' Sweetheart; beautiful, sassy, sexy," he whispered, looking into her eyes and running his hand through her hair. "And I'm the luckiest soldier in the world."

For a while they lay there on the blanket, eyes closed and hands locked together. Ewan had no idea how long they lay like this, but he opened his eyes in surprise when his side of the blanket fell into a sudden shadow. A young woman was standing over him.

Slowly his eyes focused in the sun, and Ewan found she was young, no older than seventeen, slender and with dark hair that fell to her shoulders. He nudged Jennifer, who opened her eyes, just as the girl smiled.

"I'm Lili." She reached out her hand and Ewan took it, before realising that he would need to stand up if she was going to embrace him.

"I'm Ewan Roberts, soldier in the United Army," he replied sheepishly, "and this–"

"Oh, I know who this eez," Lili beamed, walking over to Jennifer, who stood up and smiled shyly. "She eez my idol, Mademoiselle Marmalade. It eez not just ze boys who appreciate your work; I'm a dancer, and I started because of you." Jennifer had never met anyone who appreciated her work in this way. All of the soldiers she had been associated with before had wanted only to boost their status. Yet here was a young lady who really appeared to be star struck. "I couldn't believe eet was you," Lili continued, taking out her purse and handing a card to Jennifer. "They are my details and ze contact number for my dance school. If you ever need dancers, please give me a call." Jennifer smiled and hugged the girl, showing her appreciation.

"I'd really like you to come and meet ze rest of our group. We are playing volleyball. We thought you may want to play with us?"

"Oh we'd–" Jennifer smiled, but Ewan interrupted,

"We've got to stay here for our friends I'm afraid, so we really can't–"

"Yes you can," came a voice from behind, and all three turned to see Chris pacing back towards them. "Go and enjoy yourselves." And dusting sand from her legs, Jennifer again took Ewan's hand and they followed Lili off down the beach.

* * *

On the very edge of the sands, where the waves lapped against the shore, Renée and Belle were frolicking in the surf. They saw Thomas approaching, and knew it wouldn't be long before they were chasing him up and down through the waves. And soon enough they were, jumping this way and that to avoid the surf, before Thomas took a nose dive and fell face first into the shallow water. He came up seconds later with sand on his face.

"Seeing as I'm wet," he shouted, "I'm going for a swim." And he dived again into the surf, taking long strokes to deeper water, leaving the twins back on the shore. Renée and Belle looked at each other. What would it matter if they had a few wet clothes?

"Hold on," Renée called, splashing forwards and nearly falling in herself. "We're coming too."

* * *

Before long, Ewan and Jennifer found they were losing rather badly in their game of volleyball. Ewan had never played and Jennifer couldn't remember the rules. The girls they were playing, with Lili at the helm, were tall and agile compared to them and it was clear from the outset that they were dancers.

There came a point where Ewan gave up completely and continued to play merely for the enjoyment of seeing Jennifer jump up for the ball and topple over in the sand. The ball flew up again, and he missed it, prompting Lili to smile.

"You can do better than zat."

"No, I think it's time I sat out," he said. "You ladies play and I'll watch."

"I'm sure you'll enjoy that," Jennifer giggled. He had not seen her this happy in a long time. Presently he wondered if it would be best for him to return to Chris, and take over manning the blanket.

When Ewan stood and slowly made his way back to where he'd left Chris, he was not the least surprised that Jennifer continued to play, oblivious to the fact that he had left. He had reached the dunes, when he heard footsteps in the sand behind him and turned quickly thinking Jennifer had caught him up. Several feet behind, Renée Lavètte stood with a smile, her face flushed from running up the length of the beach. For a moment he couldn't take his eyes off her. She was beautiful; her wet clothes clung to her shapely body, water droplets ran down her arms and legs, and she was smiling.

Without a word and before Ewan had a chance to resist, Renée pulled him behind the nearest sand dune and pushed him playfully down against the dry sand. Her eyes shone as she reached to kiss him.

Everything about this was wrong, yet as she pulled away, Ewan found himself drawn into her waiting arms, reaching around to cup her head in his hands.

When they parted, the tension was palpable. Ewan tried to speak, but was unable to string any words together. Renée placed a finger against his lips and smiled knowingly.

"Shush, soldier boy," she whispered. "Eet does not matter." The heat of the day was suddenly insufferable.

"But I'm in love with Jennifer," he replied simply. "You must know that."

The French girl breathed deeply. "Oui, of course I do. But I 'ave wanted you all of zis time, and now I 'ave 'ad you." Ewan didn't understand. Finally Renée said. "What 'appened here today, won't 'appen again… If zat is what you want." Again she leaned in and this time kissed his cheek, before getting up to walk back to the main beach.

* * *

The sun was already low in the sky and the tide had drawn in when they decided it was time to leave.

"It's been a long day," Chris said, his mind already returning to the ongoing battle. The others remained silent as he pushed the vehicle into first gear and drove out onto the single-track road which led back to the expressway. Leaving the beach behind, they all knew there would be far worse to come.

23

War has disastrous consequences, and Chris had seen people die right before his eyes. Those, who, moments before, had been comrades fighting for the same unique vision, were shot to the ground and lifeless. Their flame extinguished in the blink of an eye. It's never possible to become blasé about war, nor to prepare yourself for it. It merely hits you square in the chest every time, with a pain of thankfulness that it wasn't you, and guilt that it should have been.

In the days that followed their trip Chris had once again taken to worrying about their futures. He had been thinking about Alan, the thought of that man falling against the metal shell of his protection haunted him. He hadn't stood a chance.

Returning from the expressway, they had parked behind the Major General's private quarters and taken the opportunity to gather much-needed supplies from the barracks. Then they traversed the dangerous path that led back towards the Chaîne des Puys, crossing a makeshift bridge over the river and parting ways when they reached the first open field. The girls headed off towards the hospital tent with medical supplies, while the men continued on towards the very heart of the conflict.

* * *

When the sun rose again, they noticed a chill in the air and fog which hung like a spider's web over the land, causing the mountains to appear more severe and intimidating. The conflict was intensifying and so too was the land in response, highlighting the mystery of such an unknown wilderness.

Chris had decided early on, to move Babineaux's remaining men to the far side of the mountain range. Here they would join the rest of the United soldiers and would have time to prepare battlements and machinery. Stationing men across this area meant they were prepared for any threat, and knowing that the battle to come would be far tougher than anything they had experienced so far, it was an intelligent move. Their Reformed enemy could appear from any direction, hiding across the entire range of the Chaîne des Puys.

Several hours later and Chris was helping to secure barbed wire along the very edge of their area. Soon a small machine would move along this path, to place mines that would provide them with extra security.

"A bit further this way," a burly soldier shouted from the opposite side of the field. He had a deep voice but spoke very good English. His comrade did as he had asked, securing the deterrent tightly at his own end before making sure that it stretched across the entire length. A sub-standard job could mean their lives, and they required all the protection they could muster if they were to ever stand a chance of defeating their enemy once and for all.

"Chris," the other grudged, patting his commanding officer on the back. "A good job well done." He smiled and waited for the response. But, Chris was in no way complacent.

"It will help, but it won't rule out destruction," he answered. "Weapons are the only real tools that can help us to see this through." He paused for a moment, looking around and then drawing in closer. "And I believe the Major General ordered the drop-off of some supplies yesterday?"

The soldier nodded, and for the first time that day Chris smiled. "Then what are we waiting for?" And they headed off to inspect the goods. As they walked, they passed other groups of men, working together to secure the field.

"Don't you find it a bit odd," the soldier continued, "that when we were growing up, we were lead to believe that in the future fighting would be at more of a distance?" "That view was common after the Second World War, when it was said life would never be as expendable again," Chris replied firmly. "You can always count on reality getting in the way."

Behind United lines and as far from the front as possible, they found a stash of machine guns, ammunition and FARs – Fast Action Rifles. The latter, named after a firearm of old, was a new and intelligent design, electronic and specifically designed for difficult targets. Throughout the morning and well into the afternoon they studied the weaponry, with Chris calling his men together to discuss how they could make use of the new hardware. They studied the holographic maps that had also been provided and decided on locations in which the remaining companies of men would position themselves from the moment the conflict recommenced. All in all, by the time they had finished, Chris, Ewan and Thomas felt more prepared for the future than they had ever done before, and their planning and preparation would surely mean fewer soldiers would end up paying that eternal price. But things could never stay as rosy as they seemed.

There was something approaching on the horizon and suddenly their little patch of the world went black. Chris had been watching the clouds that day, noting how dark they had become. Now, far in the distance and framed below by the great mountains, they were an angry and threatening blue-grey. No longer was this a place of safety, and all at once the birds rose from the trees and circled high in the sky, great cackles and caws reverberating all around.

"I think we'd best get everything under cover as quickly as possible," Chris said, looking around at the groups of men who were peppered across the field.

"If we can get everyone under those few areas of tarpaulin or at worst under the cover of trees or shrubbery, we can leave the machinery and hope for the best," Ewan suggested.

"Sounds sensible to me," Chris agreed. Thomas nodded in response. "Then we had better get to work."

And so the men set about their task, drawing groups of soldiers together and alerting them to the danger that could affect their advance. The weather could not distract them now, they fighters against an enemy who must be eradicated if the United forces were going to stand any chance of winning the war.

Slowly at first, the rain began. Within minutes it was pelting down from the sky, the tiniest drops free-falling to land on every surface. Nature was reclaiming the mountain landscape, cleansing it of death and destruction and preparing a clean slate on which to start again.

***

Chris, Ewan and Thomas huddled under a tarpaulin cover. The rain fell and thunder roared above. They had little protection and would soon develop cramp in their backs, caused by crouching down for such a prolonged period.

"Just what we wanted," Chris muttered. "This weather is really going to help the conditions…" He breathed in deeply; the air was saturated with the scent of thunder and rain.

Thomas was fiddling with the holster of his gun, clipping and unclipping the bracket. "It could be worse," he smiled. "It's the same weather for the enemy and will hold them off for a while."

"I wouldn't count on that, Thomas. I doubt these fighters will be deterred by a little rain." Ewan had positioned himself at the very front of their small tent-like square of ground, and it gave him a direct line of sight across the full length of the field.

"The others have formed small groups and are doing the best that they can to find cover," he shivered, as a great flash of lightning hit the ground not far from them, followed by a terrible clap of thunder overhead.

"Sounds like the storm is right above us," Thomas said gravely, as another flash of lightning struck an enormous tree close to the edge of the forest. With a crash that was mixed with the screams of fleeing men, it toppled to the ground. It was Ewan who muttered the first expletive.

"That's all we need," Thomas said simply. "I'm going out there to see if everyone is okay." Quickly, and now not worrying about the rain and the danger they might be putting themselves in from further strikes of lightning, all three crawled out from under the tarpaulin and raced over to the scene of the disaster, their boots squelching in the mud. Luckily no soldiers had been caught in the fall, but the remains of a small tarpaulin tent were pinned beneath the massive trunk, while the very topmost branches were alight.

Chris saw that a group of soldiers were standing together shaking from the cold. He turned to Ewan and closed his eyes for a moment.

"Thank god they escaped," he whispered, hardly heard over the sound of the rain. "It's not as bad as I first thought. The fire will soon be out, and many of our fortifications are a good distance behind where the tree has fallen."

Ewan smiled, his wet hair plastered to his forehead and his uniform soaked through. "The tree might even provide us with a secondary defence, as they are going to have to scale it if they want to reach the very centre of our command."

Chris nodded and looked forwards. There he noticed a huge black mass was moving towards their location with pace and force. For a moment he wondered if his eyes were playing tricks. But, like the others who had turned to notice the movement first, it was only as they looked downwards to the bottom of the hill that they saw men in dark uniforms, moving towards them with malevolent intent.

* * *

The Reformed troops stormed forwards. There were but a few men at first, dressed in heavily armoured uniforms, the rain running from every surface. Some carried guns, others appeared; suicide soldiers, carrying explosives and giving their lives for the cause.

"Get back," a voice shouted from behind, "and hold your positions."

The United men followed the command and took up positions right across the field, grouped behind the various areas of cover. All were prepared for attack. The weather was against them, but they had the strength and the will to win all.

Ewan had been right; the tree trunk was to be a useful second defence, and the men behind it had the perfect position from which to aim at the approaching enemy. But at the far end of the great trunk, where the roots of the tree had been pulled from the ground, there was a small gap through which to pass, and Reformed troops quickly began to filter through, machine guns armed and ready to fire. Those who made it past first were caught out by the mines which lay just before the barbed wire, but the bodies of the front-runners alerted the rest to the obstacle and they tried to avoid it. It didn't take long for the suicide men to be joined by others, creeping through the trees and over the edge of the defences.

Chris saw it all, as the enemy swarmed all around; his mind was set only on one feature. Towards the back of the field, reaching the brow of a hill and still a way off from the fighting, was a single soldier. The figure seemed to be lagging, having fallen away from the rest of his group, and Chris had a sudden urge to do something. He knew it was a foolish idea, but it was a chance to make amends, to equal out the death and pain. All he had to do was leave his own position, high above the fighting. There was a clear path through the trees that lined the side of the field, he knew because they had negotiated its route only that morning. It was feasible that Chris could reach this man, and if it was feasible, then he wanted to do it.

Turning quickly to the soldier standing on his left, Chris motioned for him to drop down below the cover of the tower's metal casing.

"I'm leaving," Chris hissed, never taking his eyes off the distant figure. "There's something I have to do." The other seemed apprehensive, and he had every right to feel that way, given that Chris was suggesting he leave his men without a commanding officer.

"You can't," the other soldier replied quickly, wondering why they were having his conversation at all. "You'll be leaving us without a leader. That's desertion."

"Don't tell me what to do," Chris breathed. It was clear to the other soldier that whatever he intended to do, he had a passion for it. "I'm the one in charge."

"But what if you get killed?" There was a pause in the conversation, reminding them that the battle was continuing all around them.

"I won't," Chris replied indignantly. His youth all too evident that it caused a momentary worry. A vision appeared in his mind that he would be like Babineaux, deserting his men on a whim for his own personal indulgence. But he soon overcame it. His suspicions were too strong not to.

Chris began to move. "Don't tell anyone I'm gone."

He was taking a risk, he knew it. But he was certain it would pay off; he had survived alone many times before, and would certainly not be killed. So it was decided, and silently he slipped towards the ladder and out of sight. He cowered beneath the barbed wire at the bottom, crawling along the ground until he reached the entrance to the forest. His gun, one of the new FARs, hung from his shoulder as he raced along the forest track. Speed was now imperative if he was going to reach this single soldier before he rejoined his fellows, and he breathed deeply the aromas of the forest, a deep pine scent tinged with smoke.

Chris exited the wooded area just below the battlefield and realised that his pace had done him well, the lone figure was only marginally further forward than he had appeared before. Pointing his gun forwards, he saw the man was of Chinese descent and that his right leg had been injured in some previous skirmish. Walking such a distance looked to be causing him a great deal of pain.

"Halt!" Chris shouted clearly, as the Reformed soldier looked up, but did not react. "Halt," he repeated, priming his gun and preparing to fire. This time the man took notice, and stopped where he stood. "Who are you?" Chris asked, "and why are you separated so far from the rest of your company?"

"I do not know," the soldier replied in broken English.

Chris wasn't going to give him the benefit of the doubt. "How did you injure your leg?" he asked next, still holding the gun firm. The soldier thought about this for a moment, considering how to form the words.

"Shot, by plane from United base," he said simply, shrugging his shoulders.

Chris didn't believe him for a moment, for if indeed he had been shot by one of Du Tale's jet planes, this man would not be standing before him now; he would be dead on the field. And besides, something else was beginning to draw his interest, something which made him both angry and annoyed, and which gave him a motive.

The man wore the Reformed uniform and that much made it easy to identify him as a foe. However, his boots looked familiar, as did the weapon on his back. The boots were thick soled, with an inch of rubber underneath that stopped the water seeping in, fixed with a special kind of resin they kept your feet warm. Oh yes, he recognised them.

Chris ordered the man to turn around on the spot, and he did so, not wanting to confront this angry United man. The gun confirmed Chris's greatest fears. It was an M6 Carbine, a substantial weapon developed in America and produced in Britain, based on the M4 Carbine, which had been used to great effect in the second Iraq War and, like the boots, was exclusively available to United forces.

How had these items got into the hands of this Reformed soldier unless he had stolen them, taken them from the dead or the dying? At that moment it was all that Chris could imagine had happened, but it was as he looked the soldier up and down, from his boots to his weapon and back again, that he felt his blood beginning to boil.

"Where did you get those boots and your weapon?" he said loudly, so angry that his gun was shaking in his grasp. The soldier merely stood and stared.

"I not understand," he said finally, shrugging his shoulders. Chris moved forwards a little. He steadied himself and phrased the question differently.

"Who did you steal those items from, which dead soldier was it?" Again the man shrugged and Chris now moved so that they were face to face. For the first time he realised that the man in front of him was quaking with fear.

"I not understand," he stuttered, his eyes glazed over yet still staring. "I only know my gun and my boots, they come from England." And then Chris's anger peaked. Slowly, he lowered his gun and from the holster that hung on his belt he removed a dull-black pistol. He was going to end this once and for all.

"Turn around," he ordered quickly. And again the man turned so that he was facing away from the field. Silently, Chris raised his arm and held his pistol against the man's head. Then he proceeded to look him up and down one final time, searching for something on the weapon that might give him a clue. Suddenly he found it, etched into the barrel of the gun – 6568-9087-994352 – a serial code, and one which matched exactly that etched into the handle of his own pistol. "Oh my God," Chris whispered, his body all of a sudden rigid as a plank of wood. It was as if his mind had opened on a world of new possibilities. "What the hell has Colonel Smith been doing now?"

The words escaped without thinking, in much the same way that his hand acted involuntarily. His rage and anger focused on one point, as he pulled back the trigger and fired the single shot.

* * *

Chris watched the man fall, slowly and painfully to the ground and now he was standing, pistol in his hand, looking down at the lifeless mass at his feet. What had he done? This was not Chris Aston; he was not a murderer, a taker of innocent life. His rage had caused him to kill in cold blood, for even though this man was one of the enemy, he alone had no right to die. What of his family? Wanting to forget, but knowing it would be impossible, Chris reached down to take the man's Fast Action Rifle.

Standing up, the wet grass of the Chaîne des Puys came up to his knees, and the uniform he wore had become hot and stuffy. The weather had turned now and the atmosphere was becoming humid. Before him, marching across the lowest plain of the mountain range was what surely must be the final company of Reformed soldiers. Seeing such a sight brought Chris back to his senses and he realised that he must return to his men, that he was in command and more than anything else, he could not be found standing over the body of a single dead Reformed soldier. So he ran, back the way he had come, back to safety.

24

On the other side of the forest the United soldiers were making slow progress. Several groups had taken strategic locations which would prove far safer than those on the ground, and the United Army's technical developments seemed far and above those of their Reformed counterparts. These soldiers had a plan; they had knowledge, but perhaps lacked power. On the other hand, funding and economic problems meant that in certain parts of the world Reformed soldiers often received sub-standard training. Many soldiers were enlisted from the uneducated lower classes, and relied strongly on raw power in their fighting style.

Ewan Roberts was positioned towards the back of the field, hidden in a trench with Thomas Fisher and behind several tall towers which had been erected in the days before the fighting. There was cover on the edge of their area making it reasonably safe, without compromising their various targets. A Reformed soldier ran towards them and Ewan shot him fiercely to the ground. Another group followed and dived to the ground as gunfire from the bunker ricocheted off the top of their helmets. But before Ewan and Thomas had a chance to react again, the men had jumped the smallest gap and landed in their trench.

There were five of them in all, speaking in a language that was unrecognisable to the United men, who merely stood, staring helplessly.

* * *

Chris was running as fast as his legs would carry him, away from the scene of his crime. The sight that met his eyes on his return to the battlefield worried him greatly. Hundreds of men engaged in hand-to-hand combat across the entire length of the field. Amongst them, he saw several of the Reformed suicide bombers.

From this angle and position, it appeared that the United men held slightly more ground. He couldn't be sure, but he knew it would be far too dangerous to climb back up to the tower he had once vacated. He remembered his friends were hiding in a bunker towards the back of the field and so he primed his weapon once again and ran to join them. Chris took a final look down into the distance and he saw the last Reformed men approaching fast. There was no turning back now, from here until the end it was fighting all the way. This was the end of one of the most strategic battles in the entire Third World War, and Chris was ready to play his part.

***

Ewan looked up from the bunker in which he and Thomas were positioned with three United comrades and a group of five enemy soldiers, talking nervously. He saw Chris approaching from the right flank, running down a clear path, from where he could make it into the safety of their trench. What Chris didn't know, was that he was heading towards the opposite end of their hideout where, unbeknown to him, a group of nervous Reformed soldiers had sought refuge.

Chris's boots landed on the damp ground with a thud and he steadied himself against the earth wall of the trench. He looked up and saw five Reformed soldiers standing in the bunker between him and his friends.

As they turned to face him, one of the Reformed soldiers fiddled with a small device clipped to his belt. The belt was punctured by a series of rivets, several more resting at different positions along its length. Whatever the soldier was trying to do, he appeared to be having great difficulty. Others around him soon moved in to help, shaking nervously as they grouped together, and Chris instinctively raised his weapon in response. It was then that a thought crossed his mind; he could be dealing with some kind of improvised explosive and all of them could be in deadly trouble.

The man with the belt was consciously weighing up the situation, for Chris could see the glazed look in his eyes. If he was carrying improvised devices and they were to be detonated, it would make not only him, but his comrades into glorious martyrs. Within the space of this trench alone, there were many United soldiers and their courageous sacrifice would be remembered.

Chris saw Ewan and Thomas staring at him. They were frozen, well understanding the seriousness of the situation. Around them the battle was going on, the sound of gunfire ringing in their ears, and yet they were oblivious to it all, to everything except this moment as they clung on to life and prayed they might escape death.

The armed soldier moved, a little away from the rest of his group. Chris could fire at any moment, and on the opposite side of the trench Ewan and Thomas were armed too. Chris breathed deeply and tried to clear his mind as the man moved backwards to rest his body against the wall of the trench. He closed his eyes. His head was facing towards the battlefield and the fighting that was going on so close to them. His Reformed comrades were moving back now, the silence lasting seconds, before the solider jerked forwards, suddenly, and a low, monotonous ticking signalled the end.

"Twenty seconds," the Reformed soldier wheezed, opening his eyes momentarily and speaking for the first time in English. He had a hideous little smile and when he closed his eyes once more, it became all the more sinister. "Then… Boom!"

By the time the man was illustrating his idea with a set of blind hand gestures, all the soldiers, United and Reformed were scrambling up and out of the trench. They reached the top and hit the ground running, not knowing where they were heading. One of the Reformed soldiers had fallen behind the rest of the group. There was no hope for him, as the ground behind them exploded in a barrage of mud and dirt. Others died too, thinking perhaps the men were retreating, not running to save their lives. In the panic Chris, Ewan and Thomas were separated and not knowing where the others were, each knew that their only choice would be to rejoin the fighting, until the very bitter end.

* * *

Those last few moments didn't make any sense to Chris, for his mind was working slower than his body and he was still thinking about the blast. How had it happened and how had they managed to escape? The force of the explosion had thrown him to the ground. As he made a conscious decision to look around him, he noticed figures moving in every direction. His ears were full of the continuous dull thump of boots against the wet ground. He had to do something, he had to move. The thought of Commandant Babineaux rushed through his head and he seriously considered playing dead for a while, before realising that he could never live with the shame of being labelled a coward.

Slowly and with effort, Chris Aston pulled himself up from the ground and spat the mud from his mouth. His left arm hurt unbearably and he soon found that he couldn't move it at all. It was perhaps good luck, then, that he was right handed and thus still able to hold his gun at an almost direct angle merely from one side.

The major remnants of the battle appeared behind him, and the Reformed solders looked as though they were falling fast. He wondered now how many of these possessed weapons of United design, and he almost wished he could count them in order to gauge the extent of Colonel Smith's deception. But even this was not enough to save the Reformed enemy now. Chris subdued the initial threat with two shots of his rifle, the electronic aim locking onto the approaching figures. The first, second and then the third fell in quick succession. Chris knew their crude way of fighting would soon die out, if only through the invention of new technology.

Needing cover, Chris's gaze skimmed across the horizon and the length of the field. He spotted what remained of the tarpaulin they had used earlier, stretched over a line of oil drums. If he didn't mind the distraction of the battlefield, he could perhaps reach it.

Jumping from space to space across the full width of the field and, by keeping his head down and his body close to the ground, he managed to pass without harassment or attack. Breathing a sigh of relief, he slipped under the tarpaulin cover and positioned himself alongside several other United soldiers, looking out from the space between the barrels. And he arrived just in time to see Private Thomas Fisher running down from the left flank of the field, pursued by a small group of his own comrades towards the very heart of the conflict.

***

Thomas knew that things were getting serious. He knew this was their only chance. They had been through so much together, all of them, surviving not only the jet crash, but the long and dangerous journey that followed. And they had made friends, great friends, who were thrust into a world which they did not understand. It was not Miss Marmalade's job to look after the injured or the dying, and neither should two innocent French teenagers be caught up in such destruction. But it was his job, and he was here to do his duty.

For a long time Thomas had felt inferior. After signing up, he had realised that he was not cut out for the day-to-day trials of training. Chris was a remarkably fitter soldier than he would ever be and Ewan was showing new promise all the time. But now, as the Reformed Army was giving all it had, Thomas knew that he could not let them win. He would not let it happen. The enemy did not realise what would happen if they won. He, on the other hand, was a proud and patriotic Englishman, and he would fight, and pay well any sacrifice, in order to remain free.

"Thomas," a tall soldier with dark eyes and a stern look had said when he had approached his group of men shortly after the suicide blast. "We need you to lead our final offensive." He had placed a hand on Thomas's shoulder and directed him to a patch of trees where he was joined by several other United men of various nationalities. He was then introduced to the tactics of their final plan. The enemy were weakening and the end was in sight. These men felt that, for their own sanity, they must make their way to the very heart of the battle and kill as many of the enemy as was physically possible, before exiting into the forest canopy on the opposite side. The idea sounded foolish, but the men remained stocked with a decent supply of ammunition and they looked confident. Thomas was humbled to be asked to join the group and immediately accepted their offer.

The men wasted no time in taking up positions, two lines facing towards the battlefield, where at last the fighting appeared to be dying down. From here it was clear that the United forces greatly outnumbered their Reformed rivals, and every now and then there came the crack of a bullet as it hit against a sheet of metal armour or the outer casing of a heavily fortified artillery vehicle.

The order came quickly, and soon they were sprinting head-on towards the Reformed soldiers that remained, destroying all who blocked their path.

"Fix… bayonets," the tall soldier with the dark eyes shouted as the other men secured their blades to the end of their muzzles. It was an age-old tradition, one which had as much relevance now as ever.

"Charge!" Shouted Thomas, advancing forwards. He took just enough time to look back from the corner of his eye at the tall soldier who had given the initial command. He had not moved, and while the others surged forwards he remained a safe distance from the enemy. By the time Thomas realised that he had been deceived, it was too late.

Thomas Fisher watched soldiers as soldiers he barely knew, aligned alongside him, their feet pounding against the ground. Ahead of them a group of five Reformed men turned in the mud, ready to attack. Thomas held his machine gun out before him and fired a round of bullets as the enemy got closer. It made no difference. To the left, two United men were straying dangerously close to the barbed wire which marked the battlefields edge. An explosion rang out as the men hit land mines, and Thomas dare not look as the men were thrown into the air before hitting the ground with a dull thud.

But their sacrifice was useful. It caused a series of small explosions up and down the battlefield, each set off by the other like a row of falling dominoes. It was a signal for help, and what had, moments before, been a sparse and empty battlefield, was soon filled again with soldiers who had been taking refuge in trenches, or under cover. Running to escape the falling shrapnel, many took charge of the armoured artillery vehicles whose drivers had earlier been killed.

As the men rushed forwards, those who had been fighting alongside Thomas disappeared into the crowd, leaving him alone. His keen eye for danger was set on the enemy, and yet he was a single soldier pitted against five who were probably far stronger and faster. Turning his head, he looked around helplessly for Ewan, Chris or anyone that he recognised. Soon, a patch of open ground formed around the small group and, taking a gulp, Thomas Fisher made his final decision.

Running forward, he pushed through the men who had raised their guns on either side. There was a strange bewilderment amongst these soldiers now, for so few Reformed men remained that it was almost safe to stand alone on the field. They could not help it, there was nothing they could do but stare as Thomas headed ever forwards. It was only when the two sides met, that they were drawn from their stupor and rallied on their comrade, firing left and right to try and conceal his attack. A rogue bullet pierced Thomas' boot and he reeled backwards in pain. It was unbearable. Inside his mind he wanted to give up. Nevertheless he had to keep on, with one final task left to complete. Dragging his injured foot behind him, he moved forwards, primed his weapon and fired at the nearest Reformed soldier, sending him flailing to the ground and provoking a barrage of bullets from soldiers on both sides. The gap between them was quickly swallowed up, as the men rounded to fight against each other on two sides, ally and enemy, good and evil. And this was how Thomas found himself at the front of the group, injured and aware of a pain he had never before experienced.

With no path of retreat, or any substantial protection, he primed his gun one more time, but it was just too late.

Everything, from the hail of bullet fire and voice to the shrapnel from those exploding landmines, froze for a split second. Then, in slow motion, Private Thomas Fisher fell forwards and gripped his chest. He had no idea who had fired the bullet, but he felt the thump as he hit the damp ground and he noticed his vision blur. There would be no more pain, no more killing, and no time to say goodbye.

25

It didn't sink in at first. It had not happened and Chris would not listen to all those around him. They were strangers shouting in voices that he could not recognise, lost on the wind. Events had unfolded right before his eyes. He had seen the men turn on each other and that first horrible crack of a gun. In horror he had watched his friend fall, as if part of himself had died there. It appeared few Reformed soldiers remained, but still he couldn't leave Thomas out there, as his body would surely be blown to pieces. His friend deserved to be laid to rest with dignity, at home. Chris would make sure that it happened. So, it was in that split second that he made his decision and at that moment that he knew exactly what to do.

Checking from the left flank that the enemy were not advancing, he lifted his head above the cover of the parapet and moved to the front of their blockade. Behind him, United comrades were calling him back, shouting that it was far too dangerous, but Chris blocked out their cries; nothing was going to stop him. It was no-man's land now and he had only one chance.

Keeping his eyes fixed straight ahead and looking from soldier to soldier, Chris Aston secured his helmet and tightened the zip on his camouflage jacket. This was more important than any other battle, this time success was not only for himself, but for everyone back home who knew or loved Private Thomas Fisher. It was for their sakes that he had to retrieve his friend's body.

To reach the location, he needed to manoeuvre around the very edge of the battlefield and hope that his approach went unnoticed. By now the mud was thick and sticky, for the saturated ground had been pounded by endless boots. It made things that bit harder, slowing him down and causing him to be wary of everything around him.

He watched as three United soldiers passed him to the left and one shouted for them to turn and approach the enemy. For a moment Chris hesitated, wondering if he recognised one of them. But it was only a second glance and thinking about it for too long would hinder his already slow progress. Before him, on the opposite side of the field, were the beautiful mountains of the Chaîne des Puys, their very summits reaching for the sky, and for a moment he wondered how death and destruction could centre itself in such a breathtakingly beautiful landscape as this.

Now he was moving forwards again, racing towards the end of the battlefield. But where Chris had picked up the pace, so had a group of stray Reformed soldiers, the last that remained. They passed him on the inside, running faster than he was and looked back as if he were a target. The others had retreated from the battlefield, to save themselves and submit to the surrender. But these men were in no such state of mind; they were here to fight until the bitter end.

But still Chris continued, prepared to fire with expert precision. He was running straight towards the men now, as his first round of fire cracked through the air like a whip, and was immediately followed by the enemy's retort. Again and again they ducked and dived on the muddy field.

These men were stronger than Chris had first thought, and he saw why they had survived so long. They seemed equally matched, however the struggle couldn't continue forever, and at this point Chris found himself on the ground.

He blinked, looking up at the sky and suddenly Ewan Roberts was at his side, fending off the enemy with a round of machine-gun fire that sent them scattering like a flock of birds.

"Chris," he mouthed, kneeling down beside his friend. "What happened?"

"I don't know," the soldier replied feebly, his face pale and his eyes half closed. "One moment I was running to retrieve Thomas's body, and the next I'm lying on the ground beside him."

Ewan looked the soldier up and down before making a diagnosis. "It looks like you were shot in the leg," he said. Chris sighed. "You're going to need some serious medical attention."

"But, the enemy! The medical team will never be able to reach me…"

Ewan chuckled and watched his friend, so brave when upright, so feeble against the ground. His condition was deteriorating, and it seemed that he might have hit his head on impact with the ground.

"I don't think there's much chance of that, Christopher," he smiled. "The remaining enemy has scarpered, and our lot are just standing here unable to believe it."

Just for a moment a smile fell across Chris's face and he was happy. "Does that mean…" he began.

"Yeah," Ewan replied before he had a chance to continue. "It looks like we might have won. No doubt Reformed air transport will try to break through somewhere between here and Switzerland to recover the men who were lucky enough to survive, but that's only if they avoid capture by our lot in the meantime."

Again Chris breathed in, great lungfuls of mountain air, as a group of medical officers moved in towards the centre of the battlefield in quick succession, carrying stretchers and equipment between them. "Here come the reinforcements," he laughed. "I sent one of the young guys off to alert the medical corps." The group moved closer and closer and only now did Ewan's eyes fall upon the body of his dearest companion.

"I didn't know it was Thomas who had fallen at first," he said quietly. "I still can't believe it." Around them the medical officers took their places and Jennifer, Belle and Renée took their chance to attend to Thomas.

"I can't believe it," the Forces' Sweetheart said. "Can he really be gone?" The twins were in tears.

"Zey did not want us to be 'ere," Renée said suddenly, looking up at Ewan, her face as white as a sheet and splattered with teardrops. "But we were… we were… forceful. We 'ad to be 'ere for 'im." Beside her Belle squeezed her shoulder and drew their hands together. "Dieu le bénisse," she said meekly before turning away, unable to look upon the scene any longer.

At the edge of the tight group, an army doctor was making light work of patching up Chris's injuries. They had already attributed his condition to a bullet wound in the right thigh and although it was not a life-threatening injury, the doctor had called for a helicopter to transport the Chris to hospital. The same means of transport, he said, would stop en route to deliver the body of Private Thomas Fisher back to the barracks, while a further series of aircraft would then land on the field to transport those who remained.

"Sounds like a plan," Ewan smiled after listening to the details. "Jennifer, Renée and Belle with me, we have to mobilise these men in order to give the helicopter somewhere to land." Quickly he drew his arm in, gesturing towards the other soldiers who were standing in groups all across the battlefield and immediately they got to work, splitting up to reassure the men that they were safe.

Fifteen minutes later the first helicopter arrived, sending a wind washing over the battlefield and those who lay there. It landed in the mud and slowly the whirring blades came to a stop as Chris was carried on his stretcher towards the sliding door of the craft. Ewan followed them before heading to the cockpit to speak with the pilots, who assured him that another aircraft would soon be on its way.

And then it was off again. Ewan, Jennifer and the twins watched it go, following its route until it disappeared from sight, a black dot on the horizon. Then they walked together to the edge of the forest and sat on a log, settling down to wait until it was their turn to leave the field and the beautiful mountains of the Chaîne des Puys.

26

Chris didn't know where he was. He woke to bright lights, strange sounds and the cleanliness of everything around him. Then he realised he was in bed, lying between cleanly pressed sheets, and if he tilted his head a little he could see further down the ward. He must be in hospital, but he had no idea how he had got there.

"Ah, Mr Aston," the voice was suddenly there, drowning out all other sound, and yet Chris found he could not pinpoint its exact location. "I'm glad to you've finally come round. We were all a little worried about you last night." Having had no luck in locating the voice on his own, Chris asked for guidance.

"Where are you?" he said feebly, his voice far removed from the one that he knew. There was a giggle, a body filled his vision and the person moved towards him, and then he moved his gaze upwards to take in the name badge and the pretty face. "Amy," he said slowly, "there you are." The nurse smiled and helped the soldier to sit up against the pillows.

"What… what happened?" Again she smiled, now standing at the foot of his bed.

"Well, Mr Aston," she began, looking him up and down, "You were injured late yesterday afternoon out on the battlefield. You've got a rather bad bullet wound to the right thigh, and you hit your head when you fell to the ground."

Silently, Chris strained to think of what had happened, but he appeared unable to draw it from his memory. "I… I… I don't remember," he stuttered.

"Yes, I'd be surprised if you did," the nurse replied in her own soft tone. "Your condition deteriorated on the journey here. The doctor was quite worried when you arrived; you were unconscious. They operated on you, though, and managed to remove the bullet. But you lost a lot of blood, and now that you are awake, we believe your memory will return within hours."

There was a silence while Chris tried hard to compute this information and the nurse busied herself with adjusting the sheets and copying down details from a screen to the left, before attaching this to a clipboard at the bed head. She then paused and looked at her patient, hands on her hips. "Well, I must be going; I have many more soldiers to see this morning. The doctor will be along soon and last night there was mention of some visitors for you. That'll be nice, won't it?"

Chris half smiled. "Amy," he murmured as the nurse started to walk away. She turned and waved to him.

"I'll be back later," she called before disappearing around the corner. Chris breathed a deep sigh of relief and slipped once more into sleep.

* * *

Mere hours after Amy had left his bed; Chris was graced by a visit from Major General Sir Adam Du Tale himself. He did not expect this, so was surprised when the rotund figure appeared through a door at the far end of the ward.

"Christopher," his voice boomed, from three beds down. Getting closer to the bed, he drew up a chair and took a seat.

"What are you doing here?" Chris managed to stutter.

"Well, Chris," Du Tale said in a low voice, deadly serious. "I feel as if I have betrayed you. There are things that I didn't explain, never had time to explain, and now I feel your hospitalisation is partly my responsibility."

In truth, Chris had never expected this from the leader. He had not for one minute thought that he might come here to explain. It was not only intriguing, but gratifying too.

"There are certain things I need to say, loose ends that need to be tied up," the Major General continued. "Firstly, the secret documents that were found on Jennifer's person were indeed meant to be transferred to me via the President of the United Isles of Great Britain. I am sorry that it needed to happen as it did. I feel it is important that I tell you these files were stowed upon her, in secret, without her prior knowledge or consent. At the time there was no other option–"

"I had my suspicions," Chris broke in; he had a strange feeling that Du Tale would now reveal what he had long feared.

"Yes, but that is not all. You remember me mentioning my investigation of Colonel Smith?" "Of course."

"Then you will forgive me for being frank with my assessment of the situation. Now the war is almost over, my own intelligence has proved correct. Colonel Smith was responsible for the crash, as you probably know, his reason being to destroy the files before they reached me here." Chris considered his next move; would it be best to reveal his own prior knowledge?

"We had worked out that much too, sir. You see, as we're now being frank, the others and I discovered the secret documents at the crash site. So we had our own suspicions about Colonel Smith. We kept quiet, but were always unsure as to his motives."

Major General Sir Adam Du Tale laughed, and the sound rang around the ward, causing other soldiers to look up in surprise. "You don't know how relieved it makes me feel that we are both in a position to reveal truths. I, though, happen to know a little more. It would appear that your leader Colonel Smith was working undercover for the enemy, providing United equipment and sometimes even channelling the funds meant for the Thames Regimental Barracks, over to the Reformed government. I am led to believe that he was promised a large sum if and when the Reformed Army were victorious."

This shocked even Chris, for he couldn't believe that one man could have such an evil intent inside him. How could Colonel Smith do this to his country and all those who had died for it?

"He is a traitor," Chris breathed; it was all he could think to say. Du Tale nodded.

"People of that nature have no soul," he said grimly. "I am only glad that Commandant Babineaux was able to aid me in discovering this fact, working as a secret agent for both myself and Colonel Smith."

"Hold on a moment," Chris said suddenly, the constant revelations were now beginning to tire him out. "Babineaux was working undercover for you? I have to say, I don't consider him a very nice person."

"You would not be the first to say that," the Major General smiled. "But he is strong willed and effective in his job, and I am grateful for that." I'm glad you think so, Chris thought, although he knew he couldn't say it out loud. Instead he returned to the matter at hand.

"So what's going to happen to Colonel Smith?" Du Tale smiled and Chris noticed the other soldiers on the ward. Many were sitting up in their beds, their heads turned just enough to be able to overhear the conversation.

"Well," he began again. "Colonel Smith has known for a little while that the net is drawing in. Deep down I believe he knew all along that the Reformed Army would fail. But, as I have said many times, money drives people to make crazy decisions. Shortly I will be dispatching a small group back to London who will attend the court case."

Chris nodded; it was the obvious course of action for someone who had committed such evil crimes. Du Tale, believing he had covered every point, now got up from his chair and moved to stand at the end of Chris's bed. Here he leaned against the metal frame and looked the Capitaine up and down.

"You're a good man, Chris," he said finally. "And I hope I have not tired you out today."

"I admit that I'm weaker than I was," Chris replied bitterly. "But it was good to see you all the same." This time it was Du Tale who nodded, turning away to walk back towards the end of the ward.

"Oh and Chris," he called. "We'll see what we can do about making your new rank permanent." He smiled at the soldier before disappearing around the corner. Chris was pleased. Slowly he lowered himself into a comfortable position and was soon asleep.

* * *

Later that afternoon Chris was surprised by a visit from those whom he loved so dearly. Ewan and Jennifer brought him flowers, while the twins had decided on a large box of chocolates. Chris beamed from the moment he saw them all walking towards him.

"Chris," Ewan called as they neared the soldier's bedside, "it's really great to see you." The Corporal was smiling, and walking hand in hand with Jennifer.

"Yes," she continued, placing the flowers on a table at the end of the bed. "We got a call last night to say that your condition was serious, and we were more than prepared to see you lying in some sort of coma."

Chris grunted and ignored the last remark. "I have always been strong, Jennifer, you know that," he said mildly. "A single bullet wound is not going to get the better of me…" Beside him, Ewan Roberts nodded and placed a hand on the young woman's shoulder.

"We were worried, that's all," he finished. Chris shifted his weight and everyone watched, shocked to see such a strong man reduced, attached to tubes and drips at his hospital bedside.

"We're going to go and get some coffee," Ewan said, after a moment's pause which was filled only with the conversations of other injured soldiers who occupied the beds all around. Chris made the slightest of acknowledgements, pointed and smiled at the flowers. Then he was left alone with the French twins, as Ewan and Jennifer exited through the nearest doorway.

Belle and Renée edged closer to the injured soldier's bedside. Of them all, it was they who knew the least about Chris Aston. Yet at the same time, they were the ones by whom he was most intrigued.

"We 'ave brought you some chocolate, Chris," Renée said in her thick French accent, slowly producing a box from behind her back. She placed it on the bed and waited for a response.

"Thank you," Chris replied slowly, "but you really didn't have to…" For a moment the twins felt rejected, but then they began to understand.

"War is no place for young girls like you and Jennifer," he continued, pausing to sip from a glass of water on the side table. He had not realised until now how dry his throat really was. "You should never have been in that medical tent, any of you, and I thank God that none of you were injured. But Ewan Roberts has a wayward personality, probably from being a professional actor. He got you involved and for a while I was angry with him. But he has since explained every detail of your arrival, and I now feel I have no choice but to approve of his actions, in the circumstances…"

"I am glad zat you can understand," Renée replied, taking a chocolate and handing it to Chris. "You see we 'ad no choice but to get out of our village and away from our papa…" Beside her, her twin shifted awkwardly and unfortunately for her, Chris noted such behaviour.

"Belle," he asked slowly. "It looks like there might be something you are not telling me." It would have seemed to any outsider looking in that he was treating her like a naughty younger sister.

"No, Chris," she replied, suddenly fixed to the spot, "Eet is just zat I 'ave discovered something and only today told ze others about eet. You are ze only one who does not know." Immediately she blushed and looked up towards the dirt-speckled ceiling. Two beds down from Chris, a soldier coughed loudly and repeatedly, causing a diversion of attention for a split second and it was then that he caught another glimpse of Amy moving down the hall towards the man. His heart lifted with thoughts of her nearby presence, before he turned his concentration back to the matter at hand.

"Well then," he said authoritatively. "I think you had better tell me what's going on."

Almost instinctively the twins looked at each other and nodded. Then they moved two chairs which had been placed against the opposite wall, sat down and began to tell their story.

"Well," Belle began tentatively. "Ze best way to explain zis would be to… well… when I was in ze house with Papa, he told me something zat I would never 'ave believed 'ad it come from anyone else…" Tears were forming in the French girl's eyes, and they clung to her eyelashes, catching the light.

"What she is trying to say," Renée continued, placing an arm around her twin sister so as to comfort her, "is zat our papa told us zat our mother iz not dead." She paused for a moment, allowing Chris to compute the information. "I 'ave to say zat I was shocked when Belle finally told me."

"I'm not surprised," Chris interjected, making his verdict on this damning piece of information. "Surely that affects what you want to do now, though?"

"Naturally," the twins sighed together, not breaking eye contact. "We 'ave made plans and we 'ope to soon begin searching for 'er." Their continued explanation and Chris's response were interrupted when Ewan and Jennifer reappeared with a tray of coffee cups. They were grumbling rather loudly.

"Damn coffee machines," Ewan fumed, a little too loudly. "It took forever to even dispense the stupid things." Gingerly he moved forwards and placed the tray in front of the flowers, revealing a somewhat flustered Jennifer behind, who was the first to notice the twins' distress and the expressionless look on Chris's face.

"You've told him then," she said patiently, leaning down to squat between the twins. "That must have been a really hard thing to do." The twins turned to the Forces' Sweetheart, who had been their idol for so long, and smiled. Here was a woman who knew the exact words for any situation. She never failed to comfort the upset and, as had been proved by recent events, care for the injured and the dying. She had a loving nature which instantly soothed the situation.

"Oui," the twins replied in unison.

"I 'ave been dreading telling Chris ze most," Belle continued. "We always thought zat 'e 'ad something against us. With us turning up out of ze blue, we thought keeping zis secret might only make things worse."

At the back of the group, Ewan smiled. "That's just Chris's nature, I'm afraid," he said simply. Chris didn't look pleased. He gave a short and sharp cough, bringing them all back to reality.

"We still haven't accomplished anything," he said simply. "What is it that you are planning to do?"

"Well, we're going back to London, of course." Ewan Roberts' voice grew in volume as his head appeared from behind the bunch of flowers and he began handing cups out to each of the group. "Thank God for Nerobucks," he added before Chris had a chance to reply.

"You're going back to London?" Chris questioned, eyeing them suspiciously. This time it was Jennifer who fielded the question.

"Yes, Chris, we are. The Major General has asked us to undertake some very important business."

"Oh." The soldier's reply left little to the imagination, as he considered the court case that would soon engulf them all. "Du Tale was here earlier. He told me that a group of you were going back to London to oversee Colonel Smith's time in court..." There was an audible sigh of relief. Ewan Roberts had not wished to explain and so was glad that the Major General had done this for him.

"That's right," he answered truthfully; "I felt that we would be more use over there. Hopefully, we won't get too involved, but it will give the twins a nice break before they begin their search." For a moment Chris was still, wondering if perhaps his friends were deserting him.

"I shall miss you," he said quietly.

"We're not deserting you, Chris," Jennifer smiled.

"We'll be in contact with the hospital every day and if your condition deteriorates we'll be straight back here at your bedside."

"That's good to know."

"Well, we did ask if you could be transferred to the Royal Military," Ewan said simply. "But the doctors here said your condition needed to be monitored so soon after the incident. They told me that they would consider the move if your condition improved."

Chris nodded. That explanation seemed to suffice, and yet he still wondered what it was that Du Tale had planned for them when they arrived back in the capital.

Until now both Belle and Renée Lavètte had been sitting in silence, taking in the conversation and straightening it out in their own minds: the idea that, within a week, they would be cast out on their own again and this time they would be seeking a mother who they had always considered dead.

"We 'ope zat we will enjoy our time in London," Renée smiled, breaking the tension almost immediately. "We 'ave 'eard zat it eez a lovely city."

In the bed beside them Chris turned his head towards her and smiled. "Oh, you will love London," he said after a pause, reminiscing on the happy times he, Ewan and Thomas had spent training at the Thames Regimental Barracks. "London is a beautiful city, and my adopted home." Around him everyone's spirits seemed to be lifted.

"We leave in a few days' time, as soon as feasible," Ewan said finally, placing the plastic cup he was holding down on the table. "It will take time to make the arrangements, and the Major General did say that he might call on us once more before we leave."

To Chris everything seemed settled; his friends were heading back home, while these beautiful French twins were off to seek an entirely different future, one which meant that he might never set eyes on them again.

"Well, I wish you good luck," he said almost in parting, adjusting his position so that he was able to lean over and shake his comrades' hands. "And if I don't see you again," he continued, gesturing towards the twins, "then I hope you find your mother, and with that a better future." Suddenly the girls were no longer sitting; they were up and at Chris's side, planting kisses on each cheek.

"We will not forget you, Chris," they said in a chorus of giggles and they joined Jennifer and Ewan at the end of the bed.

"Are you sure you will be alright?" Jennifer cooed as the others began to walk towards a door at the far end of the ward.

"Well," Chris said hoarsely, aware of how much energy he had exerted, "you've worn me out, but I'm in capable hands." He turned to point towards a nurse who was still dealing with a patient two beds down. Jennifer couldn't help but smile when she saw Chris staring. She thought the nurse prim, proper and very pretty, even from this distance.

"Jennifer," Chris called as she was walking away. She turned and looked back. "Look after him, eh?" The girl nodded, knowing she would.

27

It had taken a day or two for Jennifer to embrace real life once again. She was Miss Marmalade before everything had started to go wrong, and indeed her job had been to perform for the United soldiers. Unintentionally she had forgotten her task, allowing herself to be pulled into the real horrors of war for almost a month. She had sided with soldiers who knew far more about combat than she did, a group she had met only by chance, on a night no different from her regular routine, except now she found herself beginning to plan her future with them. For surely, after the fighting was over, there would be no need for a Forces' Sweetheart, and her job would be over.

Several hours earlier, Major General Sir Adam Du Tale had finally got his way and persuaded her that it would be a lovely surprise for the returning soldiers if she could perform for them that evening. Jennifer had accepted after only a little convincing, and now she was sitting in an office at the back of the hall, one which would become a makeshift dressing room, wondering how an earth she could prepare herself to return to the stage.

For a little while she sat there, shifting nervously in the armchair and thinking uncertainly about what she could do without any real sound equipment, dancers or a director. She had not been sitting long when the door clicked open and Ewan Roberts marched in with a suspicious smile across his face.

"Why so glum, sweetheart?" he teased, kissing her slowly and drawing one of the few remaining chairs to sit opposite.

"I don't know," she replied quickly, the hint of a smile beginning to spread across her face. "I guess I might be worried about this evening, just a little bit." The soldier shook his head and Jennifer looked at him confused.

"That doesn't sound like the girl that I met in her dressing room all those weeks ago! A fiery little minx she was, and she knew exactly what she was doing." The Forces' Sweetheart blushed. Things had changed so much.

"Well, I've got no equipment and no dancing chorus," she replied nervously. "I'm all on my own."

Ewan clicked his fingers; he wasn't having any of it. The door opened and a very sheepish young soldier entered carrying a large metal case. He placed it down on the floor in front of Jennifer, who looked on with interest.

"This," Ewan smiled, "is one of the first CD players ever produced. There were a batch of them built a very long time ago, and, surprise, surprise, Major General Du Tale had one in storage here. He hoards all kinds of bits and pieces." The young soldier was smiling, obviously extremely pleased with himself. "It works," Ewan continued simply, reaching down to embrace this beautiful lady. "Oh, and I thought you might want this too." Silently he reached into his pocket and pulled out a small business card.

"Lili," Jennifer grinned.

"Exactly," Ewan replied, already beginning to edge from the room. "Use it, sweetheart. Oh, and when you get a chance, go down to the bunkhouses. A pair of French twins have been singing there all morning, entertaining the soldiers. I think you might be able to make better use of them." She nodded and mouthed a silent thank you, before Ewan disappeared from the room followed closely by his comrade.

For a long time Jennifer sat and looked at the old CD player, wondering if this really was her ticket to performing that very evening, the one thing that she had been longing to do all along, and the only thing that linked to her past. She wondered whether her I-Touch digital music device would work with an old piece of technology like this, and if it didn't, surely that would be the end of it. Or would Ewan be able to fix it, find some way to combine old and new together to form a coherent bond? Jennifer smiled at the thought of her loving soldier being able to do such a thing, and then suddenly she was convinced. If she was ever going to make this work there were three things that she desperately needed. Performers, music and practice; the latter, of course, being impossible without the other two. And so to secure both music and performers the Forces' Sweetheart decided to call the number printed in bold on the little card in her hand.

"'Allo," a voice crackled on the other end of the phone line, a million miles away.

"Lili?" Jennifer asked quickly.

"Oui," the voice replied.

"It's Miss Marmalade…" The tone of the conversation changed instantly.

"Jennifer, my God, 'ow are you?" Lili called excitedly down the phone. Even over this distance her voice made you smile.

"I'm fine. But I need of a favour."

"Qu'est?"

The singer thought about it for a moment. "Well," she began, "when we met you on the beach you offered your services to me at any time, and the Major General has convinced me to do a show for the soldiers to boost their morale. But I haven't got any music or performers and I thought you might be able to help. But it's okay if you're busy. I understand..." Jennifer took a breath and tucked a strand of hair back over her ear, the whole message was rushed and garbled. Lili would never be able to accept and it was too short notice anyway. There was a silence at the other end and only the crackling of the line could be heard across the distance.

"I will do eet," was the simple reply after what seemed like an eternity.

"But..." Jennifer went on to think of a million different reasons why the girl shouldn't accept.

"No buts. I will bring some of ze girls along to ze barracks later this afternoon. We will be able to cross ze border at ze end of ze expressway?"

"Yes, I'll give them your name on the gate. Things are starting to die down here now; almost all of the men have returned to base." There was another slight pause.

"Good, I will bring some music along too and we can mix eet with ze stuff zat you 'ave already got and then rehearse as much as possible."

Jennifer breathed a sigh of relief. "That's great," she said. "Oh, and Lili..."

"Oui?"

"Thanks." Several miles away, at the other end of the expressway, Lili leaned back on her office chair and smiled.

"See you later, Jennifer." And she hung up, leaving the Forces' Sweetheart to breathe a deep sigh of relief.

* * *

Phase two of the plan was to find some music, but before she made her way to her own dorm room, Jennifer knew there was one place that she needed to stop along the way. By the time she arrived at the main bunkhouse, the soldiers had almost completely dispersed, leaving the twins, Belle and Renée, alone at the back of the room. They were singing some catchy French pop tune a cappella when Jennifer pushed opened the door. At first they did not notice her, turning in surprise only when they had finished.

"Jennifer!" they shouted in unison running towards her. "We 'ave been singing for ze soldiers." They were grinning like Cheshire cats as the Forces' Sweetheart flung her arms wide to embrace them.

"Yes, I know," she smiled, glad to see the twins so happy after all they had been through in the days before. "Ewan has suggested…" She paused for a moment, considering if there was any harm in revealing her intentions straight away. "…that I come and see if you were interested in joining me as backing singers. It's for a concert that Du Tale has roped me into doing tonight." The twins looked at each other, shock plastered across their faces.

"Oui, Oui, Jennifer," they replied in chorus.

"Zat eez if you really mean it," Renée added, fluttering her eyelashes. Jennifer laughed.

"Of course I do. I think as Miss Marmalade, I deserve no less than up and coming young stars for backing singers." The twins blushed and again they each embraced each other.

"The only trouble is," Jennifer said finally, "we have no music. But hopefully Lili will bring something suitable with her dancing girls later this afternoon." Slowly the twins drew away and looked at each other; there was something mischievous about their grins.

"Why don't you see if Ewan 'as anything?" Belle giggled, trying to be serious. Jennifer looked confused. "Well," she continued, managing to control the laughter this time. "We 'ave been wondering to ourselves who zis Ewan really is ever since we saw you on zat day back in ze barn. Afterwards we were saying 'ow 'is face was quite familiar. Eet was only today, when we were singing ze songs, zat we realised we 'ad seen 'im on ze television. 'E was in a show where zey wanted to find a new star…" Belle stopped mid flow, for the Forces' Sweetheart was staring right though her, wondering if the story could really be true. It turned everything on its head.

Jennifer had never thought, even for a moment, that Ewan Roberts was a performer. But Belle Lavètte had been right, for when Jennifer, Lili and her chorus of dancing girls were rehearsing in the soldiers' lounge later that day, and he sneaked in at the back of the room, tapping his hand against the bar in time to the music and sometimes singing along, she just had to enquire further. She even went as far as to hand him the water bottle that she had been using as a microphone. With all these girls present, how could he resist? And boy, were they surprised when he sang the first verse of 'A Love Like You', before being forced to reveal the true extent of his West-End stardom.

Jennifer was completely embarrassed. Here was a seasoned performer, his face undoubtedly plastered on billboards all over London, and she hadn't even recognised him. She was forced to ask more of the twins, finding out which show he had been auditioning for on live television and they had told her that they thought it was the story of the British singing sensation Matt Monro. Of course, Jennifer knew it almost immediately. Born Free the musical had been causing waves in London right up until the start of the war. But Ewan hadn't got the part; she knew that much and it was enough to give her an interesting idea.

In the end, things were not so bad, for Lili's arrival instantly brought them under control. Not only had she a wide selection of music in various forms, much of which was to Jennifer's taste and meant that she no longer needed her I-Touch, but the bubbly young dancer had carefully picked out a series of extra costumes from which Jennifer, Belle and Renée could create their own outfits.

By early evening, rehearsals were going well. They had decided on a running order and Lili had quickly drawn together a series of simple moves that would work nicely with the music. But, with such a fast-paced rehearsal, a certain level of the performance would be left down to improvisation, especially on Jennifer's part, who would be required to interact with her audience. This, she had only ever done in London, and with an audience she barely recognised. Here, it was far more personal.

***

Ewan Roberts was pacing backwards and forwards in the little room at the side of the stage. From here he could see the dancing girls were halfway through the opening number, a jazzy routine which he recognised from somewhere, but couldn't pinpoint exactly where.

Lili had pulled out all the stops, gathering together a talented group of girls who knew all the moves. From the tall redhead with the figure to die for who moved elegantly across the stage, to the small brunette with the striking smile, these girls were all truly stunning. And at the back of the group, swaying in time with the music and looking far more beautiful than he had ever seen them before, Ewan could just make out the twins. Belle, with her long legs and Renée, who seemed to know more about dancing than she had ever let on. Both girls wore matching crop tops in a flowery pattern and as they watched the others dancing before them, they shot the occasional smile in the direction of a longing soldier, enjoying themselves enormously.

For a moment Ewan paused, leaning against the doorway, and considered how he too would soon be performing in front of such a large audience. His days on the stage in London seemed so long ago and silently he wished that he didn't have to do it. He had told himself, from the moment they had met, that Jennifer was the one who was destined to perform.

When the last of the dancing girls had excited, Ewan Roberts ascended the steps and stood before the microphone.

"Good evening, ladies and gentlemen," he began, as a hush fell across the audience. "I hope you are all enjoying yourselves and I know you'll join me in thanking all the talented performers here this evening. I would also like to pay thanks to Major General Sir Adam Du Tale who, in the last weeks, has stood strong and united us against our common enemy. We will never forget those who paid the ultimate sacrifice. They wouldn't have missed this for the world and I feel that tonight they are with us here." He paused for a moment and noticed that Du Tale was sitting in the front row, his head bowed in respect. "Well, that's enough of me. We all know why we are here. And I am both pleased and proud to introduce, in her debut French performance, Miss Marmalade, the Forces' Sweetheart."

And even before he'd finished speaking, the crowd erupted, as Jennifer walked out to take her position centre stage, beaming at Ewan and mouthing a thank you.

The evening went without a hitch. Miss Marmalade performed for a full forty minutes to a crowd who were begging for more. The set list featured a variety of the most popular modern tunes, songs from the musicals and pieces that were timeless, such as the classic 'We'll Meet Again' and 'The White Cliffs of Dover', updated to include new lyrics that reflected their current situation.

Ewan sat in his side room at the bottom of the steps for the whole performance and fully enjoyed himself. He had never quite understood what it was like to be a part of the audience, but now he had experienced it, and he liked it very much. So much so that he almost missed his last cue, to introduce the finale. Realising that Miss Marmalade had left the stage, and that that meant only one thing, he bolted up the steps and laughed to himself as he looked out again upon the sea of faces.

"And now," he smiled, speaking into the microphone for the very last time. "I would like to thank you for being such a wonderful audience and introduce, our finale." There was a loud burst of applause, whistles and cheers from the audience, and suddenly Ewan realised that nothing was happening. The stage was empty and Miss Marmalade was nowhere to be seen. And then it happened. He heard the opening bar of a piece of music that he had always loved, the song that he had sung for an audition many years ago, and suddenly Jennifer was walking towards him, two microphones in her hand.

"Ladies and gentlemen," she said sweetly, addressing the audience. "I would like to take this opportunity to introduce to you a star who has performed in the West End of London, and who is standing on this stage tonight." She paused for a moment, looking at Ewan who was frozen to the spot. "This," she continued, "is a song from Born Free, the Matt Monro musical. I picked it because I know that it's one of his favourites and he has never had the chance to perform the part. But more than that, I picked it because I love him." There, she had said it, in front of all these people who loved, not her, but her alter-ego. The difference was, this time she really meant it. "So I would like to introduce you to, and I hope he will take this opportunity to sing with me, Corporal Ewan Roberts." This time the applause roared around the small hall like a tidal wave, and Ewan realised that he simply couldn't resist. After all, it might be his first and last chance to perform with the Forces' Sweetheart, an opportunity that, no matter what his true thoughts were, was too good to miss.

And it was as the introduction began again and Jennifer started to sing, that he retrieved some of his old confidence which had been knocked out of him by the horrors of war. The first verse was shaky, to say the least, and he held on to his lover's hand for all he was worth. But by the time they reached the middle eight and repeated the chorus again, it seemed almost as if he had forgotten that he was still in France at all.

When they had finished, it was so well received that they were made to sing again. The soldiers of the French barracks stationed in this remote location next to the Chaîne des Puys loved the Forces' Sweetheart dearly, and they had been through so much pain and so much trouble, that this was their escape. A little light entertainment on an evening where they could forget the rest of the world, the horrors of war, and remember the good times with family, friends and those who loved them. That was why this on-stage pairing worked so well; because it was built on a foundation of love, respect and friendship.

28

Arthur Bingham walked slowly forwards, careful to avoid the various debris which scattered the floor. This building was deserted; it had been for nearly a month now, the first location to see locally based troops phased out. Colombia in the Americas: the battles here were over and it was one of the United Army's greatest achievements, pushing the Reformed enemy back to the coast and forcing a retreat out into the Caribbean Sea. Yes, the government detective mused, glancing from one end of the room to the other. It is definitely quieter.

His mission here was one of intelligence. A seek and destroy task, or rather a steal and destroy task. He had been dispatched to search the former office of a French Commandant and return to London with anything he deemed to be suspicious.

This was not a dangerous mission. Following the terrorist bomb plot which struck the Strand, and Arthur Bingham's subsequent loss of sight in one eye, the United Government had been wary to post him any farther afield than was necessary. He had been lucky to escape with his life, and had since had a number of skin grafts. Nobody would tell Arthur who was behind the blast, he could rely only on his personal suspicions.

Moving a little quicker now, his footsteps shattering the silence, he headed through a small archway and out into the open. From here he noticed the shell of the aircraft hangar he had just left, the workplace of engineers and mechanics who had long since been redeployed or discharged. It was shaped like a half tin can on its side, with large sheets of corrugated roofing and steel supports that jutted out into the open. To the left, a wall emerged from the side, the start of another one-storey building with a flat roof. Scattered along the exterior were a series of doors, one of which lead to the French Commandant's office.

This place is spooky, Arthur thought as he looked upon the doors moments later. This must be the future, thousands of empty barracks and airfields across the world, abandoned and silent. But things were not going to get any better, for the office he was to enter, had been deserted for much longer than the rest of the complex.

In recent weeks a rumour had been spreading from one United Government to another. The French Commandant that Arthur was investigating had shot and killed a man on his own side, almost blowing an entire operation. Working undercover for Major General Sir Adam Du Tale, the Commandant was to collect information on a corrupt British Colonel who was funding Reformed offensives with money meant for the United front line. Trouble was, shooting down a United soldier to save himself meant that nobody was sure on which side the Commandant's loyalties now lay.

At last he found the door he was looking for. Cast in thick metal and painted red, it was locked. But the detective had been given a key, and as he reached forwards to turn it in the lock, he felt the years pass by. As the door pushed inwards, Arthur focused on a name plaque above the keyhole, covered in the dust of time gone by. He rubbed it with the cuff of his sleeve and read the name with a smile.

J.A. Babineaux. Yes, he thought, I am in the right place. The man was Commandant Jean Andrew Babineaux and had travelled the world during his career. In the Americas he had served for many years in charge of deployment and planning. In Colombia he had befriended a number of high ranking United officers and gained a promotion. Babineaux was widely known as the one to ask if you needed a favour. But when war broke out, he was suddenly transferred back to his native France, leaving everything he had worked for in Columbia behind. Then Adam Du Tale chose him as his undercover agent and work began both in France and across the channel, keeping tabs on Colonel David Smith. But Babineaux got close to the Colonel and they found a likeness in each other.

For a long time the United Government had suspicions that Babineaux was working for both sides, fuelling Smith's Reformed support, but at the same time reporting on these actions to Du Tale. What happened in the battlefield provided the suspicions correct.

It was Arthur Bingham's job to make sure any evidence of corruption from Babineaux's service in Columbia was collected. The United Government wanted to prove the Commandant innocent. They had enough trouble on their hands already.

Inside, the room was surprisingly well preserved, and Arthur realised it remained exactly the way it had been left so many years ago. Before long, the detective was sifting through drawers and opening files. An hour passed and then another, with Arthur unable to find any suggestion of wrongdoing. If anything, the documents suggested Babineaux to have a pleasant and approachable character, intelligent, conscientious and good in a crisis.

This will please the President, Arthur Bingham thought. After many long hours, the only conclusion that could be made was that Commandant Babineaux was indeed trustworthy. It seemed his actions on the battlefield were down to a single lapse of judgement, and in any case the truth would surely out once Smith was arrested. Arthur was a firm believer that a bad deed could be cancelled out by a good one. Commandant Babineaux would surely have to defend his character, but if he could do it under pressure and without cracking, he would be all the better for it.

29

The first document of surrender, which encompassed the largest Reformed nations, was signed some two months after the battles fought amongst the Chaîne des Puys, and it meant that the war in Europe, the Middle East and much of the world was over. As for the other countries, smaller factions of the Reformed Government that still remained in island colonies or in the southern hemisphere, their leaders were preparing to sign the declaration within days. Closer to home, Corporal Ewan Roberts, the Forces' Sweetheart, Miss Marmalade, and the French twins, Belle and Renée Lavètte, had kept their promise. Days after their visit to the hospital in Clermont-Ferrand, they were at the airport, ready to fly back home to the United Isles of Great Britain and to London, where they had agreed to follow the trial of one Colonel David Smith, much to Ewan's delight. The flight itself passed by without incident, even with the added trepidation felt by two of the passengers, for the last time they had been flying together in a United jet it had hurtled towards the ground.

Life in the Capital did not seem so different from when they had left, but then, why should it? There was no welcoming party here, nobody to congratulate the bravest of soldiers and those who had made the gravest of sacrifices. They landed at Heathrow, quickly exiting the aircraft and bundling what remained of their belongings into the back of a squat black hover car, supposedly designed in the same way as a black London cab, before being driven to Central Park Hotel. It was highly recommended by Jennifer, with a staff who were shocked, but excited at the arrival of such an impressive party and the Forces' Sweetheart herself. Here they had been told that the United Army would provide them with a whole wardrobe of new clothes, toiletries and everything that might be needed to gently reintroduce them to reality.

Of course, Renée and Belle Lavètte were in their element and overjoyed to be in the city that they had longed to visit all of their lives.

"Eet iz so beautiful," Renée had commented as they made their way up the hotel staircase, where the balustrade and tops of the walls were lined with a beautiful gold leaf. "We simply 'ave to go and see ze sights." She was bubbling with excitement, while Ewan held Jennifer's hand tightly and grinned back at her.

"Slow down, Renée," he laughed, happy to finally be back in the city where his memories remained. "We have just returned from the front line where our dearest friend fell, while the leader of our little troop is cooped up in some French military hospital recovering from rather severe injuries. I don't know about you, but I could do with a rest."

Quickly they made their way to the rooms, Belle and Renée taking the door on the right, while Ewan and Jennifer used their key card for the one on the left. The fact that the rooms were adjacent to each other meant they would never be separated for long. The twins could giggle and gossip for as long as they pleased, while Ewan and Jennifer enjoyed the chance to relax. And that was exactly what they intended to do, for almost as soon as they had crossed the threshold, Ewan collapsed onto the large double bed.

"Ah, this is my kind of comfort," he smiled, looking up at Jennifer, who was standing over him. "You don't know how much I've missed a comfortable mattress…"

"Yes I do!" she teased back at him, "I've been through the exact same hell that you have." Quickly, she leant down and kissed him once on the cheek, before joining him on the opposite side, sliding her hand in behind his back and cuddling up to her very own soldier. Mere minutes later, they were asleep.

* * *

Standing in the doorway of the tall building, his head concealed by the hood of his jumper, Colonel David Smith looked worried. Normally he would have no need to don such attire, but today the weather was unseasonably cold and there was a chill in the air which caught you the moment you stepped out of the door. But maybe such bland clothing was befitting of the day's events. Even as he stood and waited, thrusting his hands deeper into the pockets of his scuffed and torn denim jeans, the Colonel knew that some low-paid secretary or civil servant would arrive to open the door for him. They would be expecting his arrival, of that he was quite sure.

Suddenly the silver touch-screen panel on the wall behind him lit up and the thick glass doors buzzed as they opened inches to the left and right, just enough to allow the Colonel to pass through.

"Good morning, sir," said a small woman with thick- rimmed spectacles and hair which was drawn tightly into a bun. "If you would follow me." Colonel Smith pulled the hood away from his head and followed the woman down the corridor.

Inside, the layout of Lennons Bank was far classier than the Colonel had ever imagined. Of course, he had known for a long time that the company was no longer admitting the general public, and indeed the bank's commitment to privacy and air of secrecy had been one of the main reasons he had chosen it. Outside, you wouldn't think this was a bank at all. The plain brick exterior had black-tinted windows and a single glass double door secured through an intercom. But here, on the second floor of the building and along a corridor that opened up into a large atrium filled with various desks and computer workstations, were framed photos of the past CEOs and large vaults secured with thick metal doors.

"Wow," David Smith whispered to himself as he followed the small woman towards a row of doors at the very back of the atrium, "this is surreal." They passed through the very heart of the company's operation. It was like one gigantic call centre, with voices talking all at the same time in a number of European languages. The sound was so intense that the Colonel didn't notice the woman stop and direct him towards a door which was slightly ajar.

"The meeting will be in here, sir," she said. Her voice was level and unwavering, as if she had repeated this process a hundred times already that day. "You will find that your associates are already waiting." Slowly, the Colonel reached for the door handle and entered the room, pulling it shut behind him. Suddenly all the noise from outside disappeared.

"Ah, David." rasped a long and low voice in English, with the slightest hint of a Chinese accent.

"We are so glad that you could make it." Slowly the Colonel's eyes moved across the three other faces present in the room. At the head of the table he recognised his personal banker, a large man with thinning hair and a small grey moustache, while beside him sat the Colonel's French counterpart and informant Commandant Babineaux. Finally, and closest to him, the Colonel's gaze fell on the man who had spoken first, with thick black hair tied back into a ponytail and a pair of dark sunglasses perched on his nose. Suddenly David Smith had recollections of the many letters he had received from Major General Sir Adam Du Tale in the intervening weeks. There had been one every seven days, like clockwork, and even through letters the Major General had made it quite clear that a United win in the Chaîne des Puys was a certainty and it was this, along with successive missed payments, that made the Colonel very nervous indeed.

"Sit down, David." This time it was the familiar voice of his banker that spoke, and obediently he drew the nearest chair towards the table and sat down. "Now, before you say anything, I guarantee that you will receive your missed payments…"

The sigh of relief was almost audible. "That is good news," David Smith said thankfully.

His personal banker smiled. "Well, you have been a great help to us, David–"

"Yes," the man with the ponytail continued, cutting the banker off mid-sentence. "I mean, how were you to know that the soldiers you deployed to the Chaîne des Puys would survive such a horrific crash and then walk many miles through fields and woodland to the nearest military base without any kind of direction." The man's tone was horribly sarcastic.

"They are still alive?" Colonel Smith felt sick just asking the question, even though he was already sure of the answer. The man's smile faded as he reached forwards to place a small scrap of paper in front of the Colonel. On it was the bottom half of a photo which showed a large tank and several dead bodies scattered all around.

"Yes, they are," he replied seriously. "Well, all but one survived the harshest of battles this war has seen. The private, he was killed in action on the final day of fighting, but the corporal and the staff sergeant are alive, as are the females who were with them."

Colonel Smith was about to ask for more details, but something convinced him that this would be a bad mistake and so he remained silent, choosing instead to focus on Commandant Babineaux, who until now had contributed nothing to the conversation. For a minute there was silence, each of the other men focusing in upon the Colonel as if they wished him to respond.

"So when will I receive my money?" he asked, having run through every other available topic in his head, while at the same time trying to draw the conversation away from his own mistakes. All at once the room was filled with harsh laughter and when it died down, not only did David Smith realise that the banker was pointing directly at him, but he could swear somewhere in the distance he could hear the faint drone of a siren, a sound almost unheard of in London these days.

"David, David, David," his banker replied, breaking out into fits of laughter. "I have promised you that you will receive the money, but whether you will be able to spend it, that is another question."

"The war in Europe is over," the man with the ponytail continued, turning to face the Colonel directly.

"The Reformed troops were forced into a harsh retreat. They have lost all hope." This time the laughter stopped as Colonel David Smith tried to hide from the eyes that were looking right through him. He was unable to do so, and again he heard the siren, louder this time and mixed with the faint ringing of a telephone. Soon the second sound was so loud that it drowned out the siren altogether and for the first time, David Smith heard Commandant Babineaux speak, as he lifted the receiver, nodded and placed it back in the holder.

"Very good," he smiled, nodding to his counterparts, "It seems there is someone outside for you, David. They're saying that they are ready to take you away."

Silently the man with the ponytail stood up from the table and took the Colonel by the arm, pulling him to the door. As they passed through the atrium everyone fell silent, the atmosphere was almost eerie. And through a large clear glass window which he had not noticed before, David Smith saw a series of police cars draw up to the front of the building, blue lights flashing and sirens wailing. He began to sweat profusely.

***

"Why do zese things always 'appen when you are out shopping?" Renée Lavètte cried as she watched her friends disappearing around the nearest corner. They had been in the middle of some well-deserved therapeutic relaxation, as Jennifer called it, when Ewan had spotted the police cars speeding past them at the end of Oxford Street. Suddenly, he had run to get a better view and had been just in time to catch a glimpse of the cars disappearing down Regent Street.

"We've got to follow them!" he shouted back to a rather flustered Jennifer.

"But why, Ewan?" she cooed, struggling to catch up with the soldier, various bags hanging off each arm.

"Because," this time he turned to face the Forces' Sweetheart and placed his hands on either side of her face, smiling, "you never hear sirens like that in London anymore; think about it. Something serious must be going on…" For a moment Jennifer froze and did think about it, even in the many years she had spent living in the city, she could never recall having heard sirens like she had done when she was a child.

"You're right." She flushed suddenly, turning to face Belle who was slowly walking towards them. Renée made no effort to move at all, turning away to look in another shop window.

"Belle," Jennifer whispered as the young girl arrived at her side. "We have got to trust Ewan and follow those police cars; he thinks something serious is happening…"

The French girl looked a little confused, as if she too wondered what was going on, one moment shopping and the next chasing after a procession of police cars. But she was as willing as ever to go with whatever was suggested.

"Come on, Jennifer," Ewan called from in front. "That road leads down to the Thames and if we head to the Tube we should be able to reach the action before anything else kicks off…"

Jennifer and Belle nodded in bewilderment, and then, with one last look and a wave in the direction of the remaining twin, they disappeared around the corner, leaving Renée with no choice but to follow them in disarray, hurling her bags all around her as she struggled to keep up.

* * *

On Victoria Embankment, traffic was beginning to back up as the road was closed off. The cordon was patrolled by a series of burly policemen, while two of their colleagues entered the headquarters of Lennons Bank Plc. and headed towards the second floor.

Ewan, Jennifer, Renée and Belle had joined the London Underground via Oxford Circus, and came up just inside the cordon at Embankment station. Upon reaching ground level once again, they were immediately confronted by a tall policeman with a very large personality.

"Excuse me," he boomed, blocking Ewan's path forwards. "Where do you think you're going?"

"Well," the soldier began, assessing the options. "We were hoping to get to the Millennium Bridge." Even as he spoke, Ewan Roberts was already reaching into his back pocket to remove his army ID card, while the policeman looked on disapprovingly. Quickly, he flashed the card before the officer's eyes, just as Jennifer cleared the top few steps and excited out onto the embankment.

"MISS MARMALADE!" The policeman's voice rose several octaves as he shouted and pointed in Jennifer's general direction. She was surprised, having purposely dressed down in the hope that people would not recognise her. This man must be a real fan.

"Hello," she said sheepishly, looking him up and down. The man didn't even wait for her to breathe.

"Are you back then, from France?"

"I guess so, yes," was her response, and it gave just enough time for Ewan and the twins to duck past them and get closer to the action. From here they had a perfect view of the doorway and were just able to see two other policemen heading out towards the street; the convict handcuffed between them.

But it was only then that things got really interesting. Renée and Belle Lavètte felt the excitement and danger running through their blood, as Corporal Ewan Roberts moved just a few steps forwards and the policeman who had until now been distracted by Jennifer, suddenly turned around and lunged towards them.

"What do you think you're doing?" he shouted, knocking Ewan to the ground, as the other policemen and the figure under arrest passed through the doorway and out into the street.

"Jennifer," the soldier shouted as loud as he could, his voice muffled by the body of the policeman. "That's… That's… Colonel Smith!" There was so much surprise in his voice, that even the policeman who was pinning him down dropped his guard for a moment.

"Hold on," he said gruffly, standing up, dusting himself down and pulling Ewan up to stand beside him. "Do you know this man?"

"Yeah…" the soldier replied nervously, "he's my commanding officer and he deployed us all to France."

"Whoa," the policeman said again, taking a step back, and then slowly he reached down to his belt and removed his radio. "I'm afraid you're going to have to come with me to the station," he continued, pointing to each of them individually. "Even if you can't give us any further evidence, it will be safer for you in the long run, especially if you know anything about this man." He took one further step back, but this time pointed towards a parked police car. "Man," he added quickly, "you lot shouldn't even be here."

Slowly Ewan looked around again for Colonel Smith, and was not surprised to find him seated in the back of the closest car.

"Come on, guys," he said with regret, "we had better do as the officer says."

And that was how Ewan, Jennifer and the twins found themselves spending the night at the headquarters of the Metropolitan Police. They answered questions, detailed their side of the story and generally played ball until the early hours of the morning. Not once were they told any further information about the case, not once was the fate of Colonel Smith revealed. In fact, the only piece of solid information that could be drawn from the night's adventures, was that within days Colonel David Smith would be standing in one of the biggest war trials ever to be carried out in the city. Corporal Ewan Roberts couldn't help wondering if Major General Sir Adam Du Tale had planned it all along.

30

At the very edge of London are the suburbs, those far more green and leafy areas of the great city. And if you were to leave completely, you would soon find that the sprawl of modern suburbia gave way to the fertile farmlands of the Home Counties and East Anglia. These are the flat lands, a million miles away from the winding, claustrophobic streets of the capital. Here the ground is open, with fields flanked by old roads, running long into the distance. The farmland in this region and the crops that grow in what were once the wetlands feed each and every person in the United Isles of Great Britain, in one way or another. Here, the cities of Norwich and Ely, and the towns and villages that lie in between, are far enough away from London not to be greatly affected by the war. Of course, they are still included in countrywide propaganda. Troops from United America were stationed at various small airbases, and the residents were adversely affected by worldwide rationing and the occasional bombing raids which summed up so much of the first long months of war.

But the vast majority of hardship was unknown by those in the east. It was one of the joys of living in an island nation. Life was stronger here, and that made it the perfect location for a very important meeting.

Hidden away on the edge of a patch of forest is a small village where many of the old traditions still remain. There are farmers here and fishermen, who take their boats out to sea like their forefathers did. However, these men are very lucky. With the introduction of Final Fishing Laws across the world, laws which nobody dared to break, these fishermen were given the right to trawl in the North Sea, one of the world's more prosperous locations. They had a mountain of paperwork, but it was worth it to keep their traditional livelihoods going.

Every year in the month of September, the village held a fête; a day of singing and dancing in the memorial hall, craft stalls and a market, alongside tea, coffee and cakes which were on sale in the church. It was a tradition, and the one event of the year that everyone looked forward to. It had always been that way, like clockwork.

But as September came around once again, this time some strange kind of trepidation hung in the air. No one in the village could have guessed they would be greeted on the very morning of the fête by a representative of the government of the United Isles of Great Britain. The man said he was visiting on official business from the President himself, and would be assessing the village and the surrounding area for its suitability to hold a highly important meeting. He had then asked for directions to an abandoned country house that was situated on the outskirts of the village, before taking a swift walk around the various stalls and entertainments on offer, only to leave in his modern sports car as quickly as he had arrived.

The building in question had been the greatest of country houses, hidden away in a secluded location just outside the village. At the front there stretched a wide, open driveway of white gravel and at the back, a path which led down to the sea from the furthest reaches of the garden. The windows each had a pair of wooden shutters and the doorway loomed vast, flanked on both sides by tall marble pillars of a style which originated in the temples of ancient Greece.

But if the outside was grand, the inside put it to shame. Great corridors stretched the entire length of the house, passageways to rooms and banqueting halls which had long since been deserted. No one walked the floors any longer, and the gold leaf which made up much of the paintwork had grown dull, with time coating every surface in a thick layer of dust.

So many hidden treasures waited here in the darkness. They lay waiting to be found, and it was only when a meeting of world leaders was suggested, and the President's personal representative returned with pleasing reports of a friendly community far enough away from the troubles of modern suburbia to provide a safe and quiet location, that everything changed.

The double doors were forced open; years of solitude crackling away into nothing. And then the builders arrived, and an army of people who set about cleaning, polishing and restoring every dull and decrepit surface.

For months they worked tirelessly to bring the building up to scratch. It started with the builders who fixed the holes in the roof, the painters who restored the fading colours both inside and out, and it ended with the gardeners in the late summer, who arrived to replant the flower beds. In fact, by the time all the jobs had been completed and the old country house was finally ready, it was nearing the end of autumn. The government was eager to move things forwards quickly, but even with the best officials working together, it took several weeks before a date for the meeting was finally set and it wasn't until two weeks before Christmas that the leaders of the world finally descended on the countryside of East Anglia.

***

With grand formality, a procession of black vehicles appeared at the far end of the winding lane. Everyone anticipated the President's arrival, the most influential of all the leaders who had agreed, without being asked twice, to both organise and chair the meeting in his own country. Indeed, he was one of the few people who still arrived in such a way, having never adopted the powerful new hover car. There was a sudden intake of breath as the cars turned into the driveway and snow crunched under the wheels. On such a crisp winter's day, the black of these security-clad official vehicles clashed with the pure white of nature, telling of the danger that had been and gone.

The President opened the passenger door with ease and waited for his second in command to join him at his side. He looked skyward and paused a single moment for the cameras. There at the front of the pack was an eager young lady who snapped at every available opportunity. She was much smaller than the others and wore a dark duffle coat and a thick blue scarf. She seemed determined to get that perfect shot, and if the President had noticed her, or known anything about the world of entertainment, he would have recognised her as Ella B, the new London Press photographer who was taking the world by storm. But how had the press even discovered such an event? Long enough ago, he remembered signing Article 72, a blanket ban on media publication which saw that state and military business remained hidden.

Shifting slightly, the President buried his hands deep into his coat pockets to protect them from the chill. And then, with his deputy at his side, he took the first steps towards the entrance of the building, noting the applause which erupted from the small but select crowd.

"These men," he whispered gruffly, nodding towards a gaggle of photographers who had now been joined by a single lone reporter who was scribbling furiously on an old notepad, a brown scarf wound tightly around his neck, "get everywhere. They can't seem to leave you the hell alone." Beside him, his deputy grinned, understanding the point perfectly as they moved slowly towards the open door, shaking hands and passing comment, before finally disappearing inside.

For the President of the United Isles of Great Britain, he did not have an exuberant personality. Standing at only five-and-a-half feet tall he would be barely recognisable in a crowd and his mundane clothing, consisting of a pair of black or grey trousers, a white shirt and a plain waistcoat, did nothing to lighten the image. But it was his oratory skills and the way in which he handled a crisis that made him so revered; at the time of the dissolution he was the only man for the job, nobody doubted that.

The meeting was due to take place in the grand ballroom. At one time it would have played host to all manner of society, influential men and their glamorous women, dancing waltzes and foxtrots while swapping stories of life in the far-off cities of London and Edinburgh. It had taken many months of painstaking work to restore this room to its former glory, and now the beautifully veneered parquet flooring had been covered by a plush cream carpet and a long rectangular table, around which were seated representatives from all the most important countries of the world.

The meeting began with the handing out of agendas and documents. The United leaders perused these items with interest, knowing full well that there was only one real topic up for discussion. Before long, though, the shuffling of papers and muffled noises of disapproval died down and the President stood at the head of the table and introduced himself.

"Good morning, ladies and gentlemen. You are all aware of why we are here," he began, raising his hands in gesture and smiling at the many faces that looked back at him. "As you know, I am Sir James Barker and I am President of the United Isles of Great Britain. I am delighted to be joined today by the leaders from various European nations, France, Germany and Italy, as well as honorary dignitaries from the United Lands of America and the United States of Australia and New Zealand." There was a short burst of applause and acknowledgement, before the President continued, clicking a button on the table before him so that a large, paper-thin display screen descended from above. "May I remind you," he added, "that although this is a very auspicious occasion, as we sit together as leaders of the world's foremost powers, the winning side of what we hope was the very last full-scale global war, we still have some very tough decisions to make."

It was at this point that a small man in a bright blue suit and wearing large-rimmed spectacles coughed quite loudly and interjected. He was Alexander Treetstad, a delegate from the United Federation of Russia. "You mean decisions about the future of the Reformed nations of this world, and the way in which we ought to punish them?" His accent had a Middle Eastern tinge to it and his speech was slow and precise.

The President smiled, perhaps anticipating the comment. "Not so much punish as trust to learn from their mistakes, Treetstad. But yes, with the utmost respect to both you and the people of the far Eastern European countries, we will today be deciding on how to move forwards together in a calm and peaceful world collaboration."

The small man nodded and returned to perusing the various documents laid out before him, as the President pressed another button on the table and some flashing images appeared on the screen above his head, followed by an official video.

The video not only detailed the governmental views of the United Isles of Great Britain, but outlined the Reformed countries of the world and detailed in hard statistics the numbers of soldiers they had lost, coupled with their current economic prosperity. Such details were supposed to help these leaders come to an informed decision, and as the video presentation ended the details of these Reformed countries were mixed with those of the rest of the world's powers and ranked in descending order depending on their current prosperity. At the top of the list were the United States of Australia and New Zealand, simply because they were so far away from any of the most important war zones. No wonder President Erving was grinning! At the other end of the scale were the Reformed lands of the Middle East, comprising a variety of countries all bundled together, with an unbelievably high level of loss. Great Britain and America were placed somewhere in the middle, while the highest charting Reformed country was Russia, who had greatly restricted the numbers of soldiers released into any of the European war zones. These were certainly interesting statistics.

"As you can see," the President began again, turning to address his audience as the video came to an end. "These are the harsh statistics that accompany a war of this scale. The Reformed Army have sustained some serious losses over a period of three years, but so have we. And I feel that now, above all else, we need to plan for the future and decide on a peaceful way to move forwards…"

"I'd threaten them with crippling reparations," a deep voice shouted, cutting the President off. There were mutters of approval.

"I'd shorten their borders, take some land away and reduce the power of their armed forces," another said, a female voice this time. The mutters grew to a whisper.

"Now, now, ladies and gentlemen," the President said loudly, waving his hands in the air and looking somewhat flustered. The leaders were soon silenced, before the President's attention was drawn towards a lady sitting at the very front of the table with her hand in the air. He read her name badge, *Chancellor of Germany*, and he nodded, allowing her to speak.

"Sir James," she began, wary of what she was about to say, "facts and figures mean nothing if we are to sit here and debate how not to punish those who led the recent atrocity. You know as well as I, or anyone else in this room, that the UN was not the only problem all those years ago. Many of the countries that became known as the Reformed nations were preparing for an arms race long before that decision was reached." The Chancellor paused for breath, realising everyone in the room was looking at her intently. "I agree that we need to find some form of peaceful replacement for the UN, one which encompasses every country of the world, but I also advocate a quick and appropriate punishment for the perpetrators. And I would go as far as to ask for a show of hands in support of these views."

At first only the odd hand was raised, but by the time the German Chancellor looked back at her counterparts, there was a forest of hands in the air. The President considered his options.

"Very well," he said finally, although he was still nervous about such an extreme idea, "we'll do it."

And over the next three hours the leaders of the United countries of the world did just that. In heated debate they thrashed out a plan for the future that included punishment for the Reformed perpetrators and a gathering, in peace and harmony, of all the countries of the world. Along the way they discussed the issues that had led up to the declaration of war, Russia's mobilisation of troops along its borders, the arms race between the countries of the Middle East, who had eventually merged into one and, most importantly, the one single event that had led to both the United Isles of Great Britain and the United Lands of America joining the war, and the aerial bombardment of the Southern European territories. But more than that, they discussed their own failings, the deployment of troops, provisions and reinforcements, and they praised the work of Major General Sir Adam Du Tale. In fact, by the time the debate started to die down, they had identified the main clauses to their agreement.

The Reformed countries would be punished with a mixture of long-term redemptive payments and land division, together with laws that would disband their armed forces and so prevent them from interfering in any type of future conflict. In order to keep peace a priority, the leaders of every country in the world would meet together on a series of dates within a period of ten years, to discuss the future and prevent conflicts from spreading out of control again. The President stood to his feet.

"It has been a successful and rewarding day," he said, glad to be bringing the long day to a close. "We shall reconvene in a month's time to finalise these plans. In the interim, please consider the decisions we have made here today and to convey the views of the United leaders to your own governments and the people of the world. Thank you."

The room erupted with applause as the President returned to his seat. Now they were all agreed on a way to move forward and things felt easier, following a path together. Before long, the room began to empty, the various leaders making their way back towards their waiting vehicles, and it was only then that the President breathed a deep sigh of relief.

"You know," he muttered, turning to his deputy, who was gathering papers from the table, "I used to think these discussion were a complete waste of time."

His deputy paused for a moment. "Yes, but sir," he pointed out, "we came to a decision this time, and it will do wonders for your European reputation."

"Let's hope so," the President replied, taking a step towards the door. "Come on, Watson. No doubt we'll have another mountain to climb tomorrow."

"Yes, sir," the deputy replied, following his leader out of the room. "If I may, sir, tomorrow we have been asked to consider the evidence that will be used at the military trial. I've heard back from Detective Bingham, who reports that no evidence could be found in Columbia to doubt the Commandant's story."

The President didn't reply, choosing only to nod as they passed along the hallway and out through the gaggle of photographers who remained, the young woman with the duffle coat and blue scarf snapping frantically at the back of his head.

Seated safely in the back of the car, driving away from the impressive country house, the President sighed.

"Sometimes they push us Watson, and I feel that the days to come will perhaps be worse than those we have already witnessed. For then we will be dealing with the errors of our friends." Watson nodded, watching the leader, the stress of the job visible in the lines on his face. They passed along country lanes and through picturesque villages before joining the expressway. Through the changing landscape, the President and his deputy sat silently all the way back to London.

31

For Chris, his days in the ward were lonely and fragmented with the mundane happenings and the day-to-day comings and goings of the hospital staff, which reduced him to improving the dragging hours with only the occasional memory of happier times. In short, he missed his friends and he longed for his family.

Amy, the nurse who had treated him upon first arrival, was visiting so infrequently now, her attention perhaps focused on some other poor soul in need, that Chris watched himself slowly grow green with envy. The last time he had spoken to her was three days previously, when she had been burdened with the task of revealing the true extent of his illness. Chris had been in the hospital for weeks now and so far there had been little or no improvement in his condition, which was a cause of great concern to the senior doctors. Streams of new tests and samples had been taken, with shocking results. The patient had contracted a debilitating illness of the blood, one which, although not life threatening, required immediate treatment via blood transfusion and antibiotics. The first stages of transfusion had gone well, for Chris had a relatively common blood group, and now he was slowly starting the road to recovery. But with the good came the bad, as the soldier was immediately moved to an isolated room and in the days that followed was fed horrible nutrient-rich broths and sugary drinks that were, he was told, supposed to bring around new health and a stable condition.

Being in solitary confinement did not suit Chris Aston and in many ways it seemed to make his condition worse. There were times when he felt depressed at the thought of being laid up in a hospital bed, when only days earlier he had been fighting on the front line of the United offensive, and periods when he just sat and stared at the paintings on the walls or, more often than not, the blank wall itself. He was an independent man who knew better than to trust others with his own safety; it was part and parcel of being a soldier. And yet, within the space of seventy-two hours he had done just that, left the future of his very life in the hands of doctors, surgeons and one very beautiful nurse.

Alone in his room, Chris blushed at the thought. Something had clicked with Amy from the moment he had laid eyes on her, but it was a strange feeling and one that he did not profess to understand.

Love was nothing like the game of war, even if they say that all's fair in both. But Chris knew that war was never fair and, with the departure of his saviour, the one who had made him smile on the darkest of days, he was beginning to think love was unfair too.

But for all he had been through, things were not so bad. Chris had his life, where so many did not, and on his third day in solitary confinement he was deemed well enough to be graced with a very surprising visit. The first he knew about it was when Amy quietly pushed the door open to see if he was sleeping. It was still rather early, just past 10.00am, and the late autumn sunshine was yet to reach the surface of the window; the domain of the fog where spider's webs clung to the frosted panes. But Chris did not need a wake-up call, for he was dozing following a troubled night's sleep and even the slightest of movements in the shadows of his room was enough to rouse him from slumber.

"Chris," the nurse whispered as she watched the soldier turn under the covers. For a moment there was no response. "Chris," she repeated, louder this time. Again the nurse waited, noting the undistinguishable sound, something like a low groan, followed by a strained voice.

"Amy…" Knowing that the coast was clear, she entered the room and made her way towards the bed.

"It's time to get you dressed, Mr Aston," she soothed, tugging back the covers. "You've got a visitor."

Slowly Chris opened his eyes and took in the dullness of his surroundings. By now he should have been used to it, yet it was obvious from the confusion in his eyes that he was not. Perhaps it was the change to the daily routine that baffled him, seeing Amy standing at the side of the bed and hearing her soft voice in his ear. For days he had been greeted by the stern, lined face of the deputy hospital matron. She was a woman lost in the ways of the past, who believed in strict discipline above all else, and that all ailments could be alleviated with a continued dose of harsh medication. Such treatments had been proven over the years, handed down across the generations and the deputy matron swore by them, much to Chris's disgust.

For a time, Amy helped the weak soldier to dress, a cleanly pressed uniform provided by the United Army. Not a word passed between them. Presently though, he began to realise what was really happening. He was to be visited by someone he knew, a comrade perhaps, a friend, and suddenly it made him all the happier.

"Who is it?" he asked slowly and precisely, already a collage of faces was passing through his mind.

"Well, they will be here soon," Amy said sweetly, drawing back his hair and planting a kiss on the soldier's forehead. Chris blushed. This was immediately followed by a knock on the door. "There you go," the nurse smiled, already pacing towards the sound. By now the first chinks of light were passing over the floor of the dull room. "I'll show him in then, and I'll be back to check on you later, Mr Aston." With that, she waved politely and left through the wide double doors. Her presence was instantly replaced by a man of stature and intrigue, and one about whom Chris had almost forgotten.

"Bonjour, stranger," the man said slowly, savouring every word. "'Ow are you?" Suddenly Chris was sitting bolt upright in the bed with no recollection of how he got there. This was a surprise to say the least, and someone he had never expected to see again.

The man wore the clothes of a civilian, but Chris knew he had the air of a soldier. His attire was simple, a dark jacket over a pair of striped trousers, wearing at the seams, and on his chest he wore one single pin badge depicting the French flag. But to Chris, the most obvious change was that this man was cleanly shaven, while his long hair was drawn back and tied in a tight ponytail.

"It is good to see you again, Lieutenant Beauchamp," he said in awe, stumbling over the prospect of why the man was actually here.

"Oui, eet iz," the Lieutenant smiled, drawing a chair from the corner of the room so as to sit closer to the bedside. "I 'ave to say zat eet took a lot to find you."

"I can imagine. This is no way to end up for a soldier like me." His voice was strengthening all the time, and slowly he lifted his hand and motioned around the dull room. "I could have been considered a hero. Instead, I fell at the final hurdle." The Lieutenant considered this for a moment, moving a hand across his wide forehead.

"Zat iz no bad thing, Capitaine Aston." Chris was surprised that this man even remembered his name. "I myself 'ave been in zis very hospital at one time. Zat was many years ago, and things 'ave changed a great deal since."

Sitting in the bed, Chris was hanging on this man's every word. He wondered if it was because they had met before, in a time so long ago that it seemed like the distant past, or if it was simply because he was a soldier and his first proper companionship since being placed in solitary confinement.

"I can't help wondering why you are here," he said suddenly, airing his thoughts aloud. Beside him Lieutenant Beauchamp smiled.

"Well, I offered you my 'cuse, and you left ze next morning without a word of goodbye. I 'ave to say it got me thinking…"

"Yes, I am sorry about that. Looking back, I regret it now, for we were all alone in an unknown country and you offered us shelter, having no idea who we really were. Sometimes I can be a little over-suspicious." This time it was Chris who wiped his brow, glad that this one trait of his personality was finally out in the open. For the slightest time there was a silence between the two men, as they thought upon what had been said.

"Well, sir," the Lieutenant began slowly and with as much authority as he could muster, "I 'ave to say zat I do not blame you. I was not a very nice person to know zen. But now I 'ave changed… Your visit made me think upon the way zat I was living."

"And I can see the change has been positive." Chris smiled, the first for a very long time and Lieutenant Beauchamp nodded in agreement.

"Oui," he said. "Zat is why I wanted to 'unt you out, so zat I could apologise and thank you at ze same time." "There is no need to thank me, or apologise." The soldier moved to push a red button at the side of his bed.

Before long, a nurse appeared in the doorway, one that Chris had not seen before, and he asked her to bring tea and biscuits.

For the next hour and a half the two men discussed and debated any issues they could think of. They talked about battles and the war, with Chris detailing as much of his story as possible and revealing the sad demise of their comrade, Private Thomas Fisher. The Lieutenant, in return, promised to pay his respects to the fallen soldier as soon as possible, and told of how he had contacted the deputy of Major General Sir Adam Du Tale in order to find out the whereabouts of one Chris Aston.

"War eez a very dangerous game," the Lieutenant said when their discussion was through, "and eet iz just so unimaginable when you lose one of you own."

"Mmm..." Chris replied distractedly, his mind seemingly elsewhere. "You say you spoke to the Major General's deputy?"

"Oui, zat eez correct."

"Well, if that is the case, and you mentioned my name, why did you not speak to him in person." For a moment Lieutenant Beauchamp just looked at the soldier: did he not know?

"Well Chris," he began slowly, "all zey told me was zat 'e was on special business in London. A military matter..." The old Lieutenant stopped suddenly and watched as the soldier jerked forwards in the bed.

"He never said that he was going personally," he garbled quickly, taking deep gulps of air, his eyes glazing over. Finally he understood what had been making him so depressed; everyone was in London but him. Everyone would be represented in court and yet he would remain here in bed. Somehow he had to make sure that their side of the argument was effectively channelled.

"Going personally?" Beauchamp replied in confusion.

"Du Tale visited me in hospital," Chris continued, beginning on a story which it seemed like he had told a thousand times before. Already he was reaching towards the drawers at the side of the bed for a pencil and paper. "He told me that a small group was travelling back to London, as that is where Colonel Smith's trial is taking place. I later found out that Ewan, Jennifer and the others were part of this group. That means everyone is represented but me…"

The Lieutenant just sat there in amazement, trying to fit together all the pieces, the man he had come to visit was frail and ailing, and yet now he held a folded sheet of paper against his knees and was hurriedly scribbling upon it. Not only was he confused, he was astounded.

"I've got to get a message to Ewan. I need him to be sure of our argument."

"But what eez with ze message," Beauchamp queried, not understanding in the slightest. "Oo is Colonel Smith and what 'as he done zat is so bad?"

"Well," Chris breathed, his pencil moving across the page and his mind suddenly as sharp as it had always been. "He was our commanding officer back in London. In short, we have since discovered that he had been transferring money to the enemy prior to their defeat, in return for some hypothetical reward if they were to win. If that wasn't enough, Du Tale then confirmed my worst fears, that the Colonel was the one who orchestrated the jet crash." For those few moments the Chris's eyes were ablaze with intent, no longer frail as his mind recounted the events of the past weeks and formed them on paper.

As for the Lieutenant, he was so surprised that he almost fell off his chair. "I don't believe eet. Zat eez atrocious. But what eez it zat you plan to do?" he managed to interject before Chris started to speak again. To him the whole situation was quite unnerving, almost as if the tables had turned from the day when he shooed this man away from his door.

Slowly, Chris placed his pencil down on the covers and looked up, meeting Lieutenant Beauchamp's gaze. "I want you to ring this number," he said slowly, drawing his finger across the digits written at the top of the page. "This will put you through to Ewan and I need you to explain to him everything else that I have written." Immediately a horrible silence fell upon the room, for both men seemed to have a mutual understanding that the scraps of paper which now lay at the bottom of the bed were of great importance to whatever was going on overseas.

"I will do my best," Lieutenant Beauchamp said, standing up and saluting to Chris. "But 'ow will 'e know it eez me?"

For a moment Chris was lost in thought. "Read him my regimental code," he replied, fishing around in the drawer again until he found a small identity card with his picture printed on it. Slowly Lieutenant Beauchamp nodded, placing the papers and card into the inside pocket of his jacket. Then he turned and promptly left the room through the double doors. All was quiet again, the mundane atmosphere returned and Chris withdrew his mind to a period of rest, secure in the fact that the Lieutenant would complete the task for which he himself was no longer fit.

32

First mentioned in 1585, and designed as the medieval session house for the Lord Mayor and Sheriffs of London and Middlesex, the Central Criminal Court of the Old Bailey sits on the line of the ancient city's fortified wall between Holborn Circus and St Paul's Cathedral.

Throughout its long history, the court has seen many changes, being destroyed by the Great Fire of London, and then rebuilt, open to the elements in a push to stem the spread of disease. A second courtroom was added in the seventeenth century and various new façades were built into the original design across the decades.

In its first two hundred years, over nine thousand trials were carried out in court, but even this was exceeded in the modern era. Various conflicts, foreign disputes and terror threats led to a multitude of accused defendants passing through the dock, both convicted criminals and the innocent damned to hell. But in recent times this steady flow of trials had stalled, with the war taking precedence and those prisoners who had not committed any serious crime being sent to the front, to alleviate the desperate need for more soldiers. These men, it was perceived, had no real future and were therefore a useful solution to a constant problem. The prisoners would fight, and die, while those who were truly committed proceeded on a mission to spread good in foreign fields.

All of this, then, perhaps explains the hubbub that surrounded those few days in early December, when the doors of the Old Bailey were flung open once again and the crowds gathered on the streets to watch the procession of police cars and vans, one holding the accused, all in preparation for a war trial the like of which had not been seen in London for decades.

* * *

Slowly the squat black van pulled up against the kerb and a man with a slightly bent posture exited on the driver's side. His hair was dark and thick, and he wore a black tailored suit, finished with a pair of sunglasses over his eyes. His clothes matched perfectly with his job description, for this was the man in charge of the investigation. He had been working on the case and gathering evidence throughout the war, before handing it over to officials at Scotland Yard. The man cast a sweeping glance over the crowds, before pulling a small briefcase from the inside of the vehicle and walking off towards the entrance of the courthouse, leaving the black van to pull away from the kerb and head back towards headquarters.

The process was repeated over and over. As one van pulled away, another arrived, and slowly the witnesses, defence, jury and judge from both sides of the Channel, all took their places. The last to arrive, was the prisoner himself, transported in a black armoured police van without any windows and escorted by a single car, blue lights flashing, as it made its way down the narrow street. The crowd hushed as the man was brought in, each individual straining to get a glance of his face.

***

The Recorder of London, the most senior judge that now remained in the city, had taken his position on the bench. The jury were all seated and the last of the public and press had entered the gallery. Finally, the accused, one Colonel David Smith, was accompanied to the dock and proceeded to swear against the bible, the truth, the whole truth and nothing but the truth.

"Good morning," the Recorder began, his face stern and emotionless. "I trust we are all well and ready to hear the case of the State vs. Smith." Several of the jury nodded, but the judge didn't take any notice. "Now I must take this opportunity," he continued in a dull monotone, "to remind you that the accused must be considered innocent until proven guilty. You will deliberate over this amongst yourselves when we have heard the evidence." He ended with a cough, before taking a seat and nodding to a nearby lawyer, a man with very bushy eyebrows, who should now present his opening statement.

"Ladies and gentlemen of the jury and My Lord Recorder of London," he wheezed, before trying to speak more clearly. "I am here to represent my client, the United Army of Great Britain in the case against one Colonel David Smith, accused of treason in the first degree by way of money laundering and the financing of large budget offensives by Reformed Governments. Furthermore, the accused has been found to have intentionally endangered innocent lives on more than one occasion."

In the dock Colonel Smith squirmed, unable to turn away or ignore what was being said. "My Lord, Colonel David Smith has been discovered, through a secret investigation carried out by a British general now working in France, to have been financing the Reformed Army of the world for a period of three years prior to today's date. He did this by intentionally transferring money meant for his own troops into the bank accounts of Reformed leaders across the world. Furthermore, there is evidence to show that not only money, but ammunition, boots and other equipment were also transferred between the parties…" Both the jury and the judge were enveloped, but it didn't stop the second lawyer, a man wearing a threadbare corduroy suit, from speaking up.

"And how can you prove that my client was deliberately transferring the said items and that they did not arrive from some or other source, or, more to the point, were not merely picked from the dead and the dying?" The first man smiled, realising that he might have some kind of fight on his hands.

"We have the word of a leading United solider," he replied strongly. "He has told us that he shot and killed a man matching exactly this description, who was wearing United boots and had a United gun over his shoulder. That soldier will give his evidence in due course." The man in the corduroy suit sat down, defeated for the first time. "Continuing with my case against the defendant, it has become clear in recent weeks that he also orchestrated a jet crash which involved three of his own United soldiers, placing them in a compromising position, and, more interestingly, helped to organise a suicide bomb attack on a café right here in the centre of London, an attack which heralded the beginning of the end of the war."

There was a great intake of breath from those present. Could this man really have been behind the blast? They had all witnessed it, in person, on the television and in the newspapers. Up in the public gallery, Jennifer felt ill as everything finally connected and her previous life came back to her in one sudden rush.

"I would like to know why you think the Colonel would have any motive to do such a thing," the other lawyer shouted in a rage, now standing up so that he gained a little more prominence.

"That is simple. On the morning of the attack a government detective was waiting inside for a woman by the name of Jennifer Wells." Belle and Renee Lavètte sat bolt upright. "She, known by the government to lead a double life as a waitress and the Forces' Sweetheart, was to carry secret intelligence on the inner workings of the Reformed Army into the heart of France and transfer them to one Major General Sir Adam Du Tale. The detective was waiting at her place of work, in order to try and convince her that she should accept the offer, having denied it in the past. As for the jet crash, well the situation following the terrorist blast became so severe that the government had no choice other than to place the documents in the Forces' Sweetheart's belongings without her prior knowledge, given that she was now travelling to France to perform. In both cases Colonel David Smith wished to destroy the said documents."

Everyone loved the revelations, and the public gallery was alive with whispers. For Jennifer though, it was all too much and she remained hunched against Ewan's shoulder, having fainted during the previous speech.

"I would now like," the lawyer with the large bushy eyebrows began again, "to call the first witness for the prosecution, one Major General Sir Adam Du Tale."

Suddenly Colonel Smith, who had kept his head down throughout, looked up to see his French counterpart walking slowly towards the podium. He watched the man swear against the bible as he had done, and presently he thought how much older her looked. The war had really taken its toll on both his body and soul.

"Could you please tell us, sir, of your relationship to the accused and provide evidence of any wrongdoing."

"Certainly. My name is Major General Sir Adam Du Tale, Commander in Chief of the Chaîne des Puys French Military Base and I have been following the work of Colonel David Smith for many years. Prior to the outbreak of war, I was lucky enough to be working in the same department as the Colonel and I found him to be an amicable fellow, although perhaps a little too indecisive when it came to matters of money–"

"Are you saying that military finance confused this man?" the lawyer interjected.

"In a word, no, sir," Du Tale continued. "I am saying that if there was a monetary reward on offer for his department, or the chance of promotion or wage increase then the Colonel would, more often than not, take it." Sitting in his chair, Colonel David Smith smiled. It had already started, the ball of string was unwinding and there was no way he could escape.

The man with the bushy eyebrows continued to question Du Tale, cementing the fact that the Major General had been using his own undercover agents to find large gaps in the Colonel's own finances and those of the Thames Regimental Barracks, gaps of subsequent amounts of money that tallied directly with the purchase of new weapons and machinery on the other side of the world. The jury listened to intercepted phone calls between Colonel Smith and various Reformed leaders discussing financial incentives, evidence which had been shouted down by the other lawyer, his bald head almost turning crimson as he strained to prove his client innocent. His only direct question was to ask Du Tale:

"If you had known about the jet crash before it was going to happen, then why didn't you make any effort to stop it?"

"Well," the Major General said calmly, "if I had intercepted the Colonel's plans, it would have blown the whole operation." The bushy eye-browed lawyer was on the offensive again.

"I would like to ask the defendant how he discovered the said documents were on board the jet plane and indeed on the Forces' Sweetheart's person. Until that point the widely held belief, was that the documents would stay in the United Isles of Great Britain, given the Forces' Sweetheart had already declined several offers to transport them." Colonel David Smith stood in the dock and paused for a moment. Why should he answer the question?

"I overheard a phone call," he said quickly. His voice was deep and shaky.

"And who was taking this phone call?"

"No comment."

"Oh, come on, Colonel, was it not the singer's manager, on the evening prior to the deployment? Any fool could work that much out." There was silence for a moment. Colonel Smith had been beaten again and he turned to sit down defeated. But if he had thought the Major General's evidence quite damning, then there was worse to come.

"Babineaux," he breathed, making sure that nobody else could hear. "I don't believe it." The jury looked on as the lawyer introduced this second witness and asked him for evidence that might corroborate Major General Du Tale's story.

"I must tell you," Commandant Babineaux began slowly, "that in the three years I have worked for Major General Sir Adam Du Tale, I have never once been asked to do anything that is beyond my duty." Colonel Smith faltered. Was he hearing this right, working for Du Tale? Surely his mind was playing tricks on him?

"Yes, that is right," Babineaux continued, as if taunting the Colonel. "I have been working for both sides, undercover and privy to the most personal of Colonel Smith's financial records. In turn, I have been relaying information to the Major General in France. Moreover, I recently secured the arrest of the accused outside the headquarters of Lennons Bank Plc. I can categorically quantify that the Colonel has directed many hundreds of thousands, if not millions of pounds of British money into the hands of the Reformed Governments."

Quickly, the whispers of the public gallery grew to murmurs of surprise and they echoed all around the benches of court. "However, I would like to take this opportunity to tell the court that I am not completely pleased with my own actions. In recent weeks I have been the subject of a United investigation, the aim of which was to uncover any personal support for Smith's actions and a wider Reformed victory. I'm glad this investigation returned a negative verdict, and I will not deny that I have regular nightmares in which my actions on the battlefield are replayed. However, if I had died in battle it would have put the whole operation in jeopardy, and my intelligence on Smith would be lost forever. But that doesn't mean I don't regret, every kill that I made." Ewan Roberts was listening intently, surprised and humbled that this man had admitted his mistakes and was sorry for them. All around him voices were getting louder, as the public gallery traded rumours about what the current witness had done.

"Order!" the Recorder shouted, banging his gavel against the desk. "We still have to hear from two further witnesses for the prosecution, I believe."

Next up was the most controversial piece of evidence, presented on behalf of one Chris Aston.

"I would like the court to understand," the lawyer with the bushy eyebrows began, "that this account is presented on behalf of a soldier who is too unfit to take the stand. Currently he is recovering from injuries received on the battlefield."

In the public gallery, Ewan Roberts, Jennifer and the twins looked on in anticipation.

"I speak as both a passenger on board the jet plane when it crashed and a soldier who witnessed the Reformed use of United resources. At the height of the recent battle I stood opposite a Reformed soldier who wore United boots and carried a United gun." The bushy eyebrowed lawyer looked up from his paper and smiled as his counterpart stood up to interject.

"How did the Reformed soldier say he came across the items?"

"My witness writes that the Reformed soldier appeared to have no recollection of being given any stolen items and that he did not even seem to realise that the items were of United origin. But he goes on to say that the serial number on the gun was similar to his own."

"Similar, eh?" the other lawyer replied. "It sounds to me as if your witness is unsure, perhaps his injuries have affected his memory. This account can surely not be deemed plausible, considering that the Reformed soldier in question has no memory of receiving such goods. Perhaps he took them off one of the many United corpses." Ewan Roberts was angry, unable to control himself any longer.

"Chris would not lie!" he shouted. Everyone was looking in his direction. He shouldn't have said it and was returning to his seat, embarrassed and forlorn at his outburst.

"I think that is quite enough," the Recorder shouted before anyone else could speak.

"Yes, My Lord," the lawyer with the bushy eyebrows replied. "In that case, I will call my final witness."

The dock was soon graced by a short, stocky man with thin greying hair. His only defining feature being a black eye-patch which he wore over his right eye.

"Can you state your name and occupation?" the lawyer asked.

"Yes." The man's voice was slow, as if he had been affected by some great trauma. "My name is Arthur Bingham and until a few weeks ago, I was a full time government detective."

"And how, may I ask, did you develop the loss of sight in one eye?" The man paused, his good eye looking all around the courtroom until it finally set upon Colonel Smith. He grimaced.

"I received the injury after fleeing from Strand Sandwiches prior to the bomb blast. I watched a man walk into the café and was waiting for his return. I deemed him highly suspicious. When he didn't return, I crossed the street to have a cigar. It was then that the blast struck–"

"How do you know–" the defendant's lawyer piped up again, but he was cut off almost immediately.

"Is that all you can say," his counterpart replied in a snide manner, followed by a short and hollow laugh.

"Order," the Recorder called.

"I would like to ask the defendant personally," the bushy eye-browed lawyer began again, "to suggest to the court his feelings at the time and to ask what compelled him to support such an atrocity." Colonel David Smith thought this a chance to repent.

"I fear I went too far," he began. Nobody believed him. "At the time I considered the support merely another facet to my current work. I didn't believe that anyone would discover my link to the attack and it was in my interest to destroy the secret documents, at that point in time."

"Well, now the enemy has surrendered, certain Reformed officials are more willing to talk," the lawyer smiled. If anything, this haphazard confession went against the Colonel. "Thank you, My Lord. That will be all." Colonel Smith's fate appeared sealed. He would be found guilty for his sins, but not before the defence had taken the stand.

"My client, the accused, rebuts all indictments against him," the lawyer in the corduroy suit began in earnest. "He hopes to prove his honour and strong moral conduct both as a colonel and a well-known advisor to the government."

There were whispers in the public gallery once again. Having heard all the evidence against him, would this man really be able to uphold his own reputation? In the dock, Colonel Smith spoke against everything that had been said; he damned Du Tale's morals, and put forward a strong argument. But even he had to admit the future looked bleak.

"We will now hear from the witnesses for the defence." The Recorder's voice boomed around the court and for a moment everyone looked around. The lawyer in the strange corduroy suit was waving his hand in the air.

"Yes?" the Recorder inquired.

"Well, My Lord," the lawyer replied, feeling almost under duress. "Seeing as many of my client's colleagues work for various Reformed Governments, I felt it might be counterproductive to ask them to give evidence today–"

"Are you suggesting that your client fraternises with such people? For if you are, I would consider that good grounds for a conviction."

"Well no, sir, I mean to say…" The lawyer was lost for words as he realised what a grave mistake he had made. Again the Recorder banged his gavel down and looked towards the jury. "Taking what you have just said into consideration, I would call upon the defendant to make one final plea before we break and wait upon the jury's decision."

In the dock, Colonel David Smith squirmed in discomfort. This was the final stand. He had been working on both sides, always hoping that his actions remained secret. First, he had been asked to transfer just a little more money, and then to fax through top secret United documents to his Reformed counterparts. The deception had continued in this way for months. He had been a puppet of a corrupt government doomed to failure. And now he too was corrupt, broken by the very task that had been set upon him.

"Colonel David Smith of the United Army of Great Britain and the Thames Regimental Barracks, London," the Recorder was speaking again, "you are charged with fraud and deception of the highest degree and contempt in openly supporting a successful enemy plot to attack this city and knowingly endanger the lives of three United soldiers and one civilian. How do you plead?"

The Colonel turned his head away.

"Not guilty," he murmured slowly.

The Recorder of London shook his head in disgust and the lawyer with the bushy eyebrows raised them just a little more than should have been possible.

"Right, thank you, ladies and gentlemen. We will now adjourn for a period of one hour to allow the jury time to consider their verdict."

***

That single hour was the worst of Colonel David Smith's life. He had stood in the dock and waited until the very last people had exited, before he paced slowly towards the opposite side. Here he had spoken for a moment with his lawyer, considering the man's professional opinion, continuously trying to come to terms with his fate, a leading colonel stripped of his rank and thrown inside. There was no escape now, no time to repent or even say goodbye. He should have done that on the day they left London.

***

Slowly, the Recorder of London raised the gavel high and brought it down.

"Order!" he called, immediately silencing those who were still jostling for a place in the gallery. "We will now consider the remarks of the jury and their verdict." The courtroom was silent as the judge took his seat again, and an old lady with big round spectacles stood up amongst her judiciary colleagues. She had a sharp pointed nose and small pert lips; it gave her a look of intelligence and she'd obviously been very well educated.

"Having considered all the evidence," she squeaked, "and the strong testimonies from both sides, we found it natural to come to this decision."

"And your verdict is?" the Recorder questioned from behind his desk.

"We conclude upon a guilty verdict for the accused, on all counts."

The crowd were shouting before the lady had even finished speaking, for a verdict like this had always carried such a response. Again and again the Recorder brought his gavel down, calling for order. Colonel David Smith fell to his knees at the edge of the dock.

"I find the defendant guilty on all counts," the Recorder was saying now, "with a prison sentence of no less than twenty years." Immediately, two burly policemen entered court to escort the Colonel away. Then the usher stood up, a man who nobody had noticed before, and gave those final words:

"The court shall stand."

Everyone was on their feet, the Recorder already heading towards a single wooden door, his own exit, while on the opposite side the policemen dragged a dumbfounded Colonel out towards a waiting prison van.

33

In the days that followed Lieutenant Beauchamp's visit, Chris's condition improved greatly. Both the conversation and the mental stimulation of putting pen to paper had given substance and meaning to the dark days spent alone in the ward. Amy was visiting more frequently too, even when she had no reason to check on the ailing soldier. Often she would spend her breaks and lunchtimes at her patient's bedside. Always deep in conversation about the present and future; they were on very good terms.

It was a shock to Chris, when less than a fortnight after the Lieutenant's visit, his condition was considered stable enough to be transferred to a hospital in London. But he didn't leave without saying goodbye.

One lunchtime, while Amy was perched on the end of his bed and they were discussing something entirely unimportant, a clerk entered the room carrying a bunch of red roses.

"I will never leave you Amy," he said simply, watching her stunned expression fade into a smile.

"And I won't let you," she replied, suddenly jumping up from the bed and leaning over to take the soldier's hand in hers. "I'll keep in contact with my colleagues in London, and when it's time for the summer break, I'll be coming to hunt you out." Chris smiled, happy in the fact that he had made an impression. Her visit the following summer would give him something to look forward to.

***

When he finally arrived back in London, Chris was tired. He knew now how weary travellers felt when they finally touched down in the ancient metropolis. It was like coming home after a long time away.

The city was busy, far busier than Chris remembered it when they had left several months ago. Now there were hover cars on the streets again, with Londoners safe in the knowledge that the war in Europe was over. And even the hospital felt more like home, although not as clean and pristine as its French equivalent, there was a real willingness here to do good by those who had been injured in the conflict. The doctors and nurses greeted him as they passed by, and many stopped to talk.

But now that his condition was improving, Chris Aston didn't need to spend all day in bed. From the ward of the London hospital, a world of possibilities existed.

Most mornings, he was bundled into a wheelchair and joined by one or other of his friends. Together they had visited the Houses of Parliament and Hyde Park, places Chris knew well and which reminded him of happier times. Ewan, being the personality that he was, even managed to escort the ailing soldier on a tour of the nearby Menier Chocolate Factory, once the most prominent theatre and arts venues in the city, but now disused. On occasion Jennifer would meet them in the city too, taking a break from negotiating the end of her contract and completing her final performances. It was a lengthy process, but it meant she could start a fresh and shelve her life as Miss Marmalade once and for all.

* * *

It was a Friday, a week after Chris had transferred, and with the others at his bedside, he felt strangely reflective.

"So they sent him down for at least twenty years, eh?" he asked Ewan, who was sitting beside him on a three seater sofa, cuddled up next to Jennifer. Each had a large mug of hot chocolate, an enjoyable way to keep warm on such a winter's day.

"Yeah," his friend replied. "It was as simple as that. He didn't seem to have that good a lawyer, didn't present any witnesses."

"Well, I guess that would be a little hard for him," Chris continued with a smile, "considering most of them would be on a government blacklist for crimes against the nation." Even as he said this, he chuckled to himself, amazed at how they had struggled through the situation. "I guess they've taken him to where he belongs now."

"That's just what we said afterwards," Jennifer interjected, yawning. "It's just a shame that I fainted halfway through." Ewan laughed.

"Well it was a bit of a revelation."

"It's strange to think about everything we've been through," Chris continued, reminiscing somewhat. "It's been quite an adventure and it's changed us. I mean, we would never have met Belle and Renée Lavètte." He smiled at the twins who were sat crossed legged on the end of the bed.

"Yeah, and we would never have ruined their lives forever," Ewan joked. "Taking them away from that brilliant village, where they had so much potential…" Beside him Belle made a face.

"Thanks, Ewan," she said, nudging her sister.

"Yes," Renée agreed. "We would 'ave loved to stay with our papa. You know zere are so many beautiful men in ze village, it would 'ave been perfect." Even as they spoke, giggles were spilling from their lips.

"Well, let's just hope you find your mother, then," Jennifer cut through their laughter, "if your father was that bad!"

Silently, Chris looked around the little group and thought to himself; this is how things are meant to be.

"So, Ewan," he turned to address the soldier directly, a mischievous smile on his face, "when are you going to make an honest women of this one, eh?" The question had been on everyone's lips for weeks.

Ewan blushed, and Jennifer pulled a cushion from the sofa to cover her face.

"We'll see." It was the only reply that came after moments of awkward waiting, but as he said it, Ewan Roberts had a mysterious twinkle in his eye. Jennifer dropped the cushion and moved the conversation on to a more approachable subject.

"It's getting late and we really should be heading back to the hotel. The twins are leaving in the morning and they could do with a good night's sleep." Instinctively she had taken on the role of mother.

"Oh, do we 'ave to?" the twins cried in chorus. "We are not zat tired really and eet iz ze last time zat we will all be together." To look at them painted an interesting picture, each resting their head on the other's shoulder as if they were children again. Ewan had just opened his mouth to agree, when Chris beat him to it.

"No, girls, Jennifer is right," he said slowly. "You should go and get some rest. Ewan's booked a taxi, so I know I'll be there to see you off tomorrow. I wouldn't miss it for the world." It was all that needed to be said.

As the friends embraced each other and wished Chris a good night, the soldier couldn't help but shed a tear. Come this time tomorrow the twins would be back in France, searching for their mother. As he watched them walking down the corridor, he was certain they would find her and that sometime, somewhere in the future, fate would bring them all together again.

* * *

Later that evening, when the sun began to fade at the end of another long day, Chris lay awake knowing that he finally understood. He was loved and in the company of friends. It was them and them alone who had united to fight an evil far greater than any other, the evil of war. The path they had trodden was well worn, for many had followed its way in the past, and countless others would do so in the future. Together they had played just a small part in the history of this ever-expanding world, yet at that moment it was this bravery and personal sacrifice that meant the most.

Slowly, he rose from the bed where he lay and looked out of the window. Even in the dusk of the evening, and the bareness of winter, nature seemed so alive. He could not remember the last time he had felt like this, calm and at peace with the world. All of the wrongs had been righted, and the world was set on a steady axis once more.

Momentarily, a shaft of light reflected from somewhere further down the ward and hit the window, splashing a rainbow of colours across the glass, and for the second time that day Chris Aston realised something. The light was a sign, the rainbow its messenger. All was well with the world, and their dear departed friend Private Thomas Fisher was looking down on them from above, making sure that it stayed that way.

EPILOGUE
FIFTEEN YEARS LATER

They say there is a corner of some foreign field that is forever England. It was in the fields of Flanders, where so many thousands fought and died during the First World War, that the poppies grew. And between the hills of the Chaîne des Puys, God laid his hand upon one man from the United forces. Weak in body, but strong in mind, he carried the weight of his country heavy upon his shoulders.

If you were to walk through the streets of a rural village in the very heart of these historic isles, many things would go unremarked. There is a market there, only on Tuesdays, and the villagers hold meetings, dances and band concerts in the village hall. At the top of the hill, Regimental Road, stands a house, proud and aloof in the midday sun. It is a white house, with dark shutters over the windows. The garden behind stretches far into the distance and the flowers grow tall in the warm spring sunshine. There are berry bushes and a vegetable patch behind the conservatory, where carrots and potatoes grow in neat rows.

As summer arrived, the grass was cut neat and the children began to play outside. There was a girl and a boy living in the house and they ran, with their tiny feet pattering around the great oak tree which marked the centre of the garden. They continued around and around, like the proverbial rings of roses, until they fell down dizzy upon the soft earth. And then came the call of their parents, starting way off in the distance, but growing closer all the time.

"Annabelle! Annabelle Jane!" came the soft female tones that were immediately mixed with a deep male voice shouting.

"Jack!"

"Coming, Mummy and Daddy," the children called in chorus, springing up from their sky-watching. These children had all the youthfulness and exuberance they needed and their parents were happy to let them explore, what was to them the wilderness of the garden.

"Now you must remember, sweetie," came the female voice once again as the young girl bounded up into her mother's arms, "that we are going somewhere very important today. It is a special kind of birthday for one of Mummy and Daddy's old friends."

The child smiled as her mother tried to keep from her daughter the real truth of the day. She wore her hair long, gold upon her shoulders, and she was a little shorter than her husband, with big blue eyes that had faded, but remained piercing. The young boy held tightly to his father's hand as they made their way up past the side of the house and out into the street.

"Oh, Jennifer," the father whispered, keeping his voice from drifting towards the child's ears. "It all seems so very real still, can it really be fifteen years? It's been so hard not to think about it."

"I know, Ewan, dear." This time the mother spoke, quietly reassuring him. "But we have to honour the memory. It's up to those of us who made it out alive to remember his sacrifice."

For a little while the couple walked with their children in silence, remembering the fondest of times they had spent together in the years since, before together they turned the corner at the end of the street and headed on their way towards the community Hover Park which the whole estate shared.

* * *

The transport network of the Historic Isles had never been great. Hover power was easy for those who could afford it, while public transport had always been seen as somewhat second rate. But for those who wished to use it, there were trams and great stretches of network lines that ran all over the country. However much they were feared, and however often they broke down, the trams were always there. And today was special. The People's Council knew that the anniversary of independence was of great importance. And so they had laid on the official People's Tram, free of charge for the occasion.

Chris and Amy Aston boarded the tram in Little Coventry, a green and prosperous suburb of the city itself and they found that they were the only ones seated in the First Class carriage.

"Very nice," Chris muttered, leaning on his walking stick and peering out of the far windows. He was holding hands firmly with his wife and they both knew this journey would be an enjoyable one. For the children, now aged nine, twelve and almost fourteen years, a children's carriage had been laid on further down the track, with all the latest holographic movies and interactive software. There was even a PlayStation 3, something Michael referred to as vintage. And so Dylan, Michael and Emma were happy, as were Chris and Amy, sharing a cuddle in First Class.

Chris had been through a lot in the fifteen years previous. The battle and his subsequent hospital stay had left him with a variety of problems and in the year that followed his return home, he had endured both major and lengthy surgery which had resulted in a reduced sense of feeling in his right leg and meant that he would never again be able to walk without the support of a stick. He had always suffered from the return of haunting memories of his time amongst the Chaîne des Puys, and he often heard voices and saw the faces of those who had not been so lucky.

Chris had support, though. Jennifer Roberts had studied hard in the years since the war ended, attending university to tackle a new challenge, the study of medicine. Soon it had paid off, and she was now the leading surgeon at the Historic Veterans' Hospital in the Midlands, which had been set up in her husband's name, and she had been an immense source of guidance for Chris. She no longer performed, at least not professionally, and it was because she remembered and knew how it felt that she and Ewan were the only ones who could possibly have become Emma's godparents

But, Amy was all that Chris needed. She and the children offered a chance to start life afresh, and now that he had acquired a part-time charity post with the Royal Military Legion, things were starting to look up.

* * *

The gathering which took place at the memorial site was a sombre affair, for where friends, family and old comrades gathered, sadness would surely follow. The monument in question, which detailed the names of those who had been killed during that fateful month in the Chaîne des Puys, was draped in flowers. It was a heart-wrenching sight. They were here to celebrate the life of Private Thomas Fisher, fifteen years after everything had happened, fifteen years after they had fought for so much, and lost so much more.

They had done this before. In the intervening years, they had attended both the funeral of the late Major General Sir Adam Du Tale, laid to rest with full military honours befitting the part he had played in the Third World War, and the lesser-known David Smith, stripped of military rank, and released early from prison due to health complications.

Ewan, Jennifer and the children arrived first, climbing out of the hover car to look upon the scattering of barely recognisable faces. The others were not here yet; Ewan hoped they would arrive soon.

A lot had changed in the fifteen years following the end of the third World War. It had in fact taken a further two years after fighting had ended in the mountains of France for all war zones across the world to fall silent. There was a new period of peace, declared by the UN some two months later, and soon the Earth was in a more prosperous position. Things had turned almost full circle, with each country now controlling its own borders and voting on a government that would rule from home.

Redemption payments were indeed brought in against those countries which had once been part of the Reformed regime, and a great deal of their land was divided between those on the United front. Things were better and the Historic Isles were a far more peaceful place. However, it would take the arrival of the fifteenth anniversary for an enquiry into the start of the war, and indeed the UN's involvement in the conflict, to officially begin.

For a moment Ewan was silent. Together with his wife and children he had walked up the path that led past the church and towards the memorial, but now he stood alone before the names of his comrades while Jennifer held tightly to the hands of their children.

There it was in simple lettering:

Private Thomas Fisher. United Army of Great Britain. Killed in action: Chaîne des Puys, France

The soldier felt a tear well in his eye, for he wore the same uniform that they had been issued with on the day, and slowly he raised his hand in salute to his departed friend. It was as he did so that he felt a clammy grip on his shoulder, and turned around to see the face of a dear friend.

"Chris," Ewan smiled, looking his friend up and down. "How are you?" They shook hands and Ewan realised how much his friend had aged since the last time he had seen him. He looked a little weak, for although they were all growing towards their late forties, the stick that Chris used to support his weight made him seem older than he really was.

"It's good to see you," Chris replied, looking beyond his friend and towards the monument. "It really doesn't seem like fifteen years since it all happened, does it?" For a moment they stood there in silence, and looked at their friend's name, and then at the flowers which lay below. Behind them, Jennifer and Amy were deep in conversation, while the children ran around them in circles, playing tag around the churchyard.

"I've got some flowers," Chris mused again. "They won't do him much good now, still it's nice to show your respect." Ewan nodded and together they walked back towards the group, as their wives produced two beautiful bouquets.

"The service will begin soon," Jennifer called when the men had placed their flowers at the foot of the monument and nodded respectfully. "We had better be going inside."

* * *

Inside the small church, the pews were already beginning to fill up. Here were many more faces that neither Ewan nor Chris recognised. Perhaps they were distant family members, old colleagues or staff employed by Thomas, or even villagers who merely wished to pay their respects.

For those who had fought with Private Fisher, there was reserved seating at the front of the church. Chris, Ewan and the others took their places on the left. The children were surprisingly understanding, quiet and sombre; they did not say a word. Opposite them, on the other side of the church, was a group of three ladies who were quietly chatting to each other, unaware of anything that was going on around them. They were dressed in dark colours, and for a moment Chris stared. Eagerly he nudged the others, those sitting opposite seem strangely familiar.

"Ewan," Chris whispered, looking from his friend to the women and back again. "Are they?" Ewan concentrated hard and wondered why on earth they seemed so familiar. The one in the middle seemed very old indeed, rather frail, and she was flanked on each side by younger women, who looked no older than thirty-five. And it was then that they turned around and Ewan froze.

"Chris, it's Renée and Belle!" he said, amazed at how the girls had grown. They suited their features now, and over time their hair had darkened, so that it highlighted their faces. One thing was still certain, though, they remained unmistakably identical.

"But it's been such a long time," Chris replied, amazed as their respective wives began to wonder what all of the commotion was about. "But who is that lady sitting with them?" He paused for a moment, thinking about everything that had happened since and in particular their final conversation. "No, it can't be…"

"Oh, yes it can," Ewan smiled, already beginning to move from where he sat. "It looks like they managed to find their mother after all." Quickly he beckoned for the others to follow him towards the opposite side of the church before the service began, and soon they were reunited with long-lost friends.

"Ewan, Chris, Jennifer!" they cooed, delighted. "We were beginning to think zat you were not coming." They smiled together, that same expression that took the others back so many years.

"How could we miss an occasion like this?" Ewan replied, quickly embracing both girls in turn before looking down upon their ageing companion. Even in her old age, she showed signs of a fading beauty.

"So," Chris asked, before anyone else could protest, "how are things?" Sometimes the question sounds so silly, but it was all he could think of to say in the circumstances, and it opened up a world of possibilities.

"Well," Renée began, flicking her hair back behind her ears. "As you can see, we found our mother." Her response was matter of fact, but everyone knew she was pleased beyond words. "But it took a lot of searching."

Jennifer seemed not the least bit surprised, for all along she had been telling both Ewan and Chris that the girls would succeed, if their hearts were really in the task. And now the ageing lady was smiling and looking around the happy faces that made up the rest of the pew. She began to speak in her native language, her lips moving slowly over every word.

"She says that she 'as 'eard so much about all of you," Renée translated. "She wants you to know zat what you did all zat time ago, it was a miracle. She says she moved a long way away from ze village, and it took over a year for her beautiful daughters to track her down."

"Chris has told me so much about you two," Amy interjected, looking from Renée to Belle and then their mother. "He was not wrong when he said you were beautiful, but he never forgot to mention how troublesome you were to him." She smiled happily and the twins knew it should all be taken in jest.

"We 'ad to be 'ere," Belle continued, "to 'onour the memory of our friend. And Mama, she wanted to meet you all. Especially after she found out zat Papa 'ad passed away."

Chris's face dropped, but the girls' smiles didn't even falter. "Don't worry about it. Eet iz like things 'ave come right. Belle 'as been married for nearly a year now, and in a few months' time I will be doing ze same. We can return to our old 'ome and finally be 'appy."

It felt as though this was all they needed and it tied up any loose ends in their story. Ewan's and Chris's spirits were lifted by the reunion, and the thought that they were all invited to the wedding and that they now vowed to keep in regular contact, was enough to see them through the whole day. Their emotions lifted, and then they fell. But it had to be so, if they wanted to honour the memory of their friend.

The service was remarkable; to be a part of it became a real privilege. The vicar honoured not only the memory of Thomas, but the memory of all the men who had perished that fateful month fifteen years ago. Together they sang hymns and bowed their heads for the Lord's Prayer, and when it was all over they gathered silently around the monument and paid their respects to those who had given so much. And then, as with so many things in life, they parted.

The small crowd dwindled as each left to resume their lives. Perhaps they would meet again, through children or grandchildren, and talk of history and family stories. One thing was certain, when that same group of friends who had fought together in the Chaîne des Puys all those years ago said their goodbyes and headed home, somewhere in the back of their minds they knew that the story would not be confined to the history books. For now they had families of their own, and they would be sure to educate their children, and pass on their memories. Thomas would not be forgotten and neither would their sacrifice. It was all such a long time ago, but there remained many years of happiness still to enjoy, and peace and freedom in which the friends would live them.

LONDON

London is one of the greatest cities in the world. The capital of England, the United Kingdom and a major settlement for two millennia, Greater London is home to some 9 million people. The city is one of the most diverse in the world, with 300 languages spoken and a wide range of cultures and faiths. Such diversity produces the widest selection of restaurants and eating houses anywhere. With traditional and modern attractions, London draws millions of visitors every year to Buckingham Palace, the Tower of London, St Paul's Cathedral, Big Ben and the Houses of Parliament. The city's world-class museums and galleries are some of the most modern, from the British Museum to the Royal Opera House and the London Eye, the world's largest observation wheel. Retail therapy is also world class, from Oxford Street's department stores to the exclusive shops of Bond Street and Mayfair and the markets of Portobello Road, Camden and Borough. In the West End, home of London's Theatreland, the city hosts the highest level of commercial theatre in the English-speaking world. There have been playhouses in London since 1576 and in the West End since 1663, when Sadler's Wells Theatre opened as a 'Musick House,' to perform opera. Nowadays many millions of tourists see plays and musicals in London's West End every year. In 2012 London hosted the Olympic and Paralympic Games.

www.visitlondon.com

CHAÎNE DES PUYS

The Chaîne des Puys is an area of outstanding natural beauty. Running north-south through the Auvergne region of the Massif Central in France, the Chaîne is a line of mountainous extinct volcanoes. Formed 10,000 years ago, the Chaîne is 40 km long and made up of cinder cones, lava domes and volcanic maars or craters. A puy is a volcanic mountain with a rounded profile, and the Puy de Dome is the highest lava dome in the region. The local administrative department, Puy-de-Dome, takes its name from the mountain, from the top of which are views across the Auvergne to Clermont-Ferrand 10 km away. Long popular with tourists, the area is a well-known centre for walking, paragliding and cycling and the Puy de Dome is an occasional stage finish for the Tour de France. The Chaîne des Puys is now largely covered in forest and because of its natural beauty is often used as a location for film and television. In pre-Christian Europe, Puy de Dome was also a spiritual place and the ruins of the Gallo-Roman Mercury Temple can still be found near the mountain's peak. The romance language, Occitan, was once spoken here.

www.francethisway.com

Printed in Great Britain
by Amazon

38174684R00246